The Somme Legacy

Martin Lee is the author of four previous histori-
cal crime novels. This book is the second one
featuring the genealogical investigator, Jayne
Sinclair. Her third adventure, The American
Presidency, will be published in July 2017.

The Somme Legacy

A Jayne Sinclair Genealogical Mystery

M J Lee

This book is dedicated to my grandfather, Joseph Sheehan, who fought in World War One and was wounded twice. He was one of the many brave men and women who sacrificed so much in that desperate struggle. One of the many who suffered from the wounds received on the fields of Flanders for the rest of their lives.

Also by M J Lee

Death in Shanghai
City of Shadows
Samuel Pepys and the Stolen Diary
The Irish Inheritance

Table of Contents

Chapter 1

Hawthorn Ridge, the Somme. July 1, 1916.

Three hours from now, he might be dead.

Captain David Russell checked the luminous dials of his Mappin wristlet watch for the seventh time. Above him, white cotton candy clouds drifted across the sky lazily towards the German trenches.

The artillery had finally stopped firing in their sector after seven days of pounding the line opposite. A deathly quiet had descended on the trench. None of the men spoke, each one just staring at his neighbour.

Beside him, Crawford, normally so chirpy, pressed himself into the uneven duckboards, his head resting against a painted sign for Lux soap.

What had happened? Had something gone wrong? To his left he could see Malins, the Canadian cinematographer, standing above the fire step slowly cranking the handle of his camera.

He looked down at his watch again. 7.19 a.m. The second hand ticked on, silently tolling his life away. The watch was a present from his wife on their wedding day, inscribed on the back with the words, To David, 25 April, 1916.

He peered over towards the German front line, just 400 yards away on the chalk ridge. As he did so, the ground beneath his feet began to tremble. The tremors increased in power and a massive cloud of dust, dirt and earth thrust violently into the air, spuming forth like a vast, black volcano.

The sound followed a second later; a thunderous boom from the bowels of hell. He immediately clapped his hands over his head and ducked down beneath the rim of the trench. Clods of earth rained down on his men, rattling their new steel helmets.

'Bloody hell, what the feck was that?' one of them shouted above the noise of the falling debris.

'That was a lot of dead Germans,' replied Sergeant Flaherty.

Captain Russell raised his head above the rim of the trench. To his left, a plume of dust had risen high into the sky, reaching fingers of dirt into the white clouds. Beneath it, Hawthorn Ridge had vanished, replaced by a vast depression where the German trench had once been. The dust began to drift down across no man's land and an eerie silence settled down with it.

Why weren't the first line moving forward? Why didn't they attack now?

On his right, a fox bolted from cover and ran towards their own line, disturbed and frightened by the blast. Somehow it had survived all the shelling for the last seven days, but the mine had finally driven it out of its burrow.

Russell listened. A few birds had started to sing. Chaffinches, he thought. Even amongst all of this, they still proclaimed all the dirt, wire, shell-holes, and broken ground as their territory.

'Why don't the first wave go forward now before the Germans recover?' he asked Crawford.

'They're waiting for 7.30. It's General Hunter-Weston's orders. Advance exactly at that time, not a moment earlier,' answered Crawford, staring out from beneath the rim of his helmet.

'But the Germans will be shattered by the explosion; they should advance now.'

Still the first wave of troops waited.

The silence was broken by a loud explosion on the right, followed by two others. The German guns had finally woken up and were shelling the reserve trenches. David heard the plaintive cries of 'stretcher bearer' echoing across the lines.

He checked his men. They all had their heads down, keeping well below the trench.

Sergeant Flaherty edged towards him.

In front, the sound of a whistle followed by others along the line. He heard a faint cheer before it was blown away by the breeze towards the German trenches.

'Move the men forward, Sergeant,' Russell ordered.

'Yes, sir.'

Lt. Crawford pointed to the left. 'I'll chivvy along my platoon.'

'Good luck.' Russell stuck out his hand.

'It'll be a walk in the park, sir.'

'I hope so, Johnny, I hope so.'

Russell stood up and strode forward along the communication trench, keeping his body erect and his shoulders pushed back. Have to set the right example for the men.

He pulled back the sleeve of his officer's jacket and checked his watch once more. 7.32. The men were extending out along the length of the communication trench. In several places it had collapsed and the line was marked out by lengths of white tape held in place by metal stanchions.

He jumped onto a fire step as his men pushed past him to gather next to the ladders.

Ahead, across no man's land, a line of men were walking slowly up the slope, rifles held across their chests, burdened with packs, ladders, wire, shovels and all the other accoutrements for holding a position. A few shells exploded above their heads, creating gaps in the line which were quickly closed up as the men walked forward.

Four hundred yards away, the German lines were quiet, coils of barbed wire nestling proudly in front of their trenches, metal points standing out sharply against the blue sky.

Wasn't the artillery supposed to cut the wire?

Then the sound of the first machine gun. A staccato pop pop pop, like the sound of a sewing machine through canvas. Now joined by others on the right and the left.

The smell of cordite drifted across to his trench. An acrid, pungent smell, tinged with the aroma of death. He checked the men once more. They were pressing themselves into the side of their trench. A few were beginning to look nervous, the bravado of the last few days evaporating like rain on hot stone.

He stared out again across No Man's Land, looking for the line of the first wave, but couldn't see it anywhere. Where had they gone? Had they already reached the German front line?

7.34.

'Order the men to fix bayonets, Sergeant.'

'Yes, sir. FIX BAYONETS.' Sergeant Flaherty's voice cut through the sound of falling shells and the rat-a-tat-tat of the machine guns. It was followed by the sound of a hundred bayonets being pulled out from scabbards and the metallic clunk click as they were attached to the end of Lee Enfields.

'Remember men, walk don't run. We don't want you

girls blown to smithereens by our own gunners.'

Captain Russell glanced at his watch one more. Just ten seconds to go. He peered over the parapet. Was that a man moving forward, waving his arm, encouraging his men to advance? He blinked his eyes and when he opened them again, the ghost in the mist had vanished.

Five seconds to go.

The whistle shone brightly against his muddied hands. He remembered another whistle not so long ago, blown by a policeman lying on the ground. How they had run that day, he and Rose.

He could feel the letter to her nestling in his jacket pocket next to his notebook. Too late now to post it, always too late.

The second hand reached the top of its circle. 7.35 on the morning of July 1, 1916.

He put the whistle to his lips, paused for a moment to draw breath, and blew.

Chapter Two

Buxton, near Manchester. March 28, 2016.

Jayne Sinclair rushed into the nursing home. 'Is he okay?'

The receptionist was as calm as ever. 'Robert is fine, Mrs Sinclair. He's had his breakfast and an extra cup of tea.'

Jayne had received a phone call that morning from the Matron of the home saying her father had suffered a relapse in the middle of the night. Without thinking she had driven from her home to Buxton, ignoring the speed limit despite the traffic. 'What happened?'

'He was found at three in the morning standing in front of the fir tree in the garden. You'd better speak to Matron.'

As if on cue, the Matron bustled through the fire doors guarding the entrance to the reception area. 'Ah, you're here, Mrs Sinclair, would you like to come through to my office?'

The Matron was short and round with grey, white and black hair giving her the appearance of a perpetually surprised badger. She wasn't in uniform, instead she wore a tweed skirt and a lavender cardigan over a white chemise. The voice was Scottish, or at least had been Scottish a long time ago.

Jayne followed her into a compact office with files ranging across one wall and a tall aspidistra in the corner. The leaves were a deep, shiny green with not a hint of dust. As neat and tidy as the woman facing her.

'Do sit down.'

She gestured to one of those institutional chairs designed by a team of Swedes with the personality of an amoeba. Jayne sat down and immediately felt uncomfortable.

'We had an incident with your father, Robert Cartwright, last night.'

'So I was told, Mrs Guthrie.'

'He was found in the garden by one of our security men, standing next to the fir tree,' said the Matron, interrupting her thoughts.

'What was he doing?'

'Nothing much it seems. Just standing there talking to the tree.' The matron gave one of those fleeting smiles that passed for empathy. 'As you know we specialise in the care of Alzheimer's here...'

'It's the reason why Father chose your... facility.' Jayne avoided the word 'home'. She hated its falseness and sense of security. Her father's home was with her, nowhere else.

Another fleeting smile from the matron. 'As you are aware he was diagnosed with the early stages of Alzheimer's a year ago. Since his arrival here, we have been pleased with his adaptation to living in a new environment.'

The woman paused for a moment.

Jayne waited for the 'but' she was sure was about to come.

'But recently, he seems to have deteriorated. Last night was just one example.'

'There have been others? More midnight escapades?'

The matron frowned at Jayne's words. The tone of her voice changed and the Scots accent became more pronounced. 'He has become more aggressive lately to the staff and other patients.'

Jayne sighed. 'Not like my father.'

The matron held out her arms. 'I'm sure it isn't. But it is a sign the disease is becoming more pronounced.' She took a deep breath. 'I'm afraid if it continues we may have to consider transferring your father to our secure facility.'

In her previous life as a detective, Jayne had seen too many people in jail, seen what it had done to them, how quickly they lost hope and conformed to the rules depriving them of their own sense of worth. 'You mean locking him up?'

The matron opened her arms once again. 'You have to understand, we don't want to do it, but it would be for his own good. And for the safety of the other patients, of course.'

It's for your own good. How often had Jayne heard that in the police interview rooms? How often had she used those same words when she wanted a man to confess to a crime? But one thing she knew, she wasn't going to condemn her father until she had spoken to him. 'Where is my father now?'

'I believe he's in the recreation room. He does keep himself to himself. We wish he would socialise more with the other guests, it would help I'm sure.'

'I'll go and see him. Please let me know if and when you want to move my father to the other facility.'

'We will try our best. We will be monitoring his behaviour closely over the next couple of weeks. I'm sure you will understand, the safety of the other patients must be paramount in our minds.'

There it was again. The royal 'we', loved by bureaucrats and all those absolving themselves of responsibility. God, how Jayne hated it.

Chapter Three

Buxton, near Manchester. March 28, 2016.

Her father was sitting in the far corner of the recreation room, in front of the large picture window, away from all the other people. They had chosen this place because of its reputation and the large gardens surrounding the main building. Her father had been an avid gardener all his life and, even if he couldn't grow anything any more, at least he would be surrounded by the beauty of the changing seasons.

Jayne walked over to see him, weaving through two tables of card players and three old ladies perched in front of a large television set with the sound barely audible. On TV, a large fat man sitting on a couch was extolling the benefits of his latest diet to a miraculously tanned man and even more tanned woman. Neither seemed to be able to move the muscles of their faces as they spoke.

Her father was reading the Daily Mail and didn't hear her as she approached behind him. She watched him for a minute, seeing him turning the pages and muttering to himself, shaking his white-haired head and grunting as he did so. He wasn't her biological father; the man who had given her his surname had vanished just a few days after she was born, never to return. Her mother had married Robert Cartwright a few years afterwards. Jayne had never taken his surname. Her mother would never tell her who her real father was: even when she lay dying, her body ravished with cancer, she had remained silent.

One day, Jayne would find out, but not today. Today

was a day to spend with the only man she had ever known as a father.

He looked up and caught her standing there. 'Have they been complaining about me, lass?'

She nodded her head and pulled up a chair next to him. 'Said they found you wandering the grounds in the middle of the night.'

'Couldn't sleep, that's all. Needed some fresh air. With all these old biddies here, it gets a bit smelly in the evening.' He gestured to the women still staring at the TV set.

'They said you were talking to the trees.'

'Aye, I was lass, make more sense than most of the people here. And didn't Prince Charles talk to plants? Didn't complain about him, did they?'

Jayne smiled. Her father was as sharp as ever. 'They also said you had been aggressive to the staff.'

'Aye, told one of them to bugger off.'

'Why did you do that, Dad?'

'She wouldn't order the Guardian for me. I have to read this bloody rag.' He held up the Daily Mail. 'Makes my blood boil this stuff does.'

'You shouldn't get annoyed over nothing, Dad. Have you been doing anything else?'

'What is this, the bloody Spanish Inquisition? You may have been a copper, Jayne, but you're not one any more so I don't have to answer any of your questions.' He held out his hands as if waiting for them to be handcuffed. 'Take me down to the bloody station if you want to ask me more stupid questions.'

Jayne held her hands up in mock surrender. 'Dad. I'm just worried about you, and so are they.' She indicated the matron and one of the staff looking at them from the far side of the room.

Her father's shoulders drooped and his voice softened. 'I know, lass. Maybe this home wasn't such a good idea. Sometimes I feel so…' His voice trailed off.

Jayne put her hand on his shoulder. 'I know Dad, but you have to listen to them. They just want to help you. Promise you will listen?'

Her father smiled and held up his fingers in the salute of a boy scout. 'I swear lass.'

'And I'll see if I can get your Guardian delivered.'

'Aye, 'cos if I have to read this any more, I'll turn out to be as brain dead as those old biddies.' He threw the paper onto the table in front of him. 'Any new cases? I need something to stimulate my mind.'

'Funny you should say, I'm meeting a new client this afternoon.'

'What's the problem?'

'I'm not sure yet, but it seems to be about a lost inheritance.'

'Sounds right up your street. You've been a bit quiet since the American case.'

Jayne remembered the old billionaire Mr Hughes and his nephew, her digging through the records of the Easter Rising, and a fight in a wrecked car.

'Whatever happened to him?'

'Well, after I told him who his real father was, he decided to set up a foundation to unite adopted children with their birth mothers. It's given him a new lease of life at 93, even his leukaemia seems to have gone into remission.'

'There's hope for us all. You'll let me know about the case, won't you? If I can be of help in any way…'

Jayne leant forward and put her arms around him. 'All I learnt about genealogy came from you, Dad.'

Her father pushed her away. 'Don't go all soppy on me, lass. It's time you were off.'

Jayne stood up. 'You will be good, Dad, won't you?'

'I'll be as good as a stick of rhubarb. As long as you get me my Guardian in the morning. I miss doing the crossword.'

Jayne saluted him. 'Orders received and understood. Guardian to be delivered tomorrow morning, sah.'

'That's better. At least they taught you how to salute in the bloody police.'

Chapter Four

Didsbury, Manchester. March 28, 2016.

Jayne waited in Rest for her client to arrive. It was a cutely named cafe, carved out of the side of a church that was still in use. The furniture was eclectic; a mixture of what looked like old school chairs and tables, with a variety of comfortable armchairs salvaged from Oxfam. Toddlers in pink tutus wandered in and out accompanied by harassed-looking mummies desperate for a caffeine and cake fix. Luckily, Rest supplied both in quantity and quality.

Jayne often used the place to meet her clients; the Wi-Fi was excellent, plus it was far enough away from the main dining drag of Didsbury to allow quiet conversation.

A man carrying a battered brown briefcase stepped through the door of the conservatory-like entrance. He was tall, handsome in an understated way and younger than Jayne. He looked around the cafe with the air of a lost schoolboy searching for a missing classroom. She checked out his shoes, something she often did as a detective. They were comfortable loafers that had obviously seen better days.

He saw her looking at him from her corner and walked over slowly. 'Jayne Sinclair?' he asked tentatively.

She stood up and held out her hand. 'Mark Russell, I presume.'

'It would have been better if my surname was Livingstone.'

She laughed. A sense of humour too. Perhaps this client

would be more pleasant to work for than usual. 'Would you like a coffee?'

'No thanks, I've drunk enough this morning to float the Titanic.' He pulled out a chair and sat opposite her.

'You didn't give me many details over the phone...' Jayne hoped this would be enough to get him talking. It was another interview trick she had been taught in the police. Begin with an open question allowing the interviewee to relate their experience without prejudice.

'I'm sorry,' he said pulling out an acetate file from the briefcase at his feet, 'but it's difficult to explain without a few props.' He looked over his shoulder at the entrance. 'My father is supposed to be here as well. I'm afraid he insisted on coming, and it's the only way I could get him to release these.'

He tapped the acetate file in front of him. Jayne could see a couple of envelopes and a few photocopies through the clear plastic. 'Do you want to wait for him to arrive?'

'He's heard it all before. We shouldn't waste your time.' Mark Russell interlaced his fingers in front of him and breathed out, as if beginning a prayer.

Jayne waited for him to begin.

'I want you to recover my inheritance.' He looked up at her and smiled.

'That's it?'

'Well, that's the essence. But I'm sure you'll want me to explain further.'

'It would help.'

'On April 25, 1916, my great grandmother, Rose Clarke, married Captain David Russell, the eldest son of Lord Lappiter. On the 28 June, his Lordship died, with my great grandfather David inheriting the title, the estate and a fortune of 700,000 pounds.'

'A lot of money today.'

'About 28 million pounds by my reckoning.'

Jayne whistled. 'A small fortune. But it all sounds fairly straightforward, Mr Russell. I can't see what the problem is.'

'Unfortunately, my great grandfather, Captain Russell, died three days later on the first day of the Battle of the Somme, July 1, 1916, without leaving a will.'

'It still should not be a problem. The wife would be recognised as the beneficiary in the absence of a will.'

'And therein lies the problem.'

'Where and what problem?'

'There is no record of my great grandmother and my great grandfather ever marrying.'

Jayne leant forward. 'Let me understand this. You say there is no record of them marrying, but you seem to have an exact date. Where did they marry?'

'In Gretna Green, on April 25, 1916.'

The words Gretna Green immediately set off alarm bells in Jayne's head. Couples often eloped to the town when the bride was too young to marry without her parents' permission because Scotland had less stringent marriage laws than England. 'How old was your great grandmother when she married?'

'She was nearly 24.'

'So there was no problem with her age.'

'None as far as we know.'

Jayne frowned once again. 'The only other reason for marrying in Scotland was speed. Couples did not have to go through the usual process of a church wedding or the posting of banns.'

'We think this is what probably happened.'

'We?'

'My family.'

'There's a quick method to check.' Jayne pulled out her laptop and logged on to the Wi-Fi, speaking as she did so. 'Marriages of that period in Scotland are all online. What did you say your great grandmother's name was?'

'Rose Alexandria Clarke, but she never used the name Alexandria.'

Jayne quickly typed Rose Clarke in the BMD section of the Find Your Past website. 'And you said the year was 1916, in Gretna Green?'

Mark Russell nodded.

She added the year and the place name in the filters. The screen responded in seconds. No results.

She typed in Rose Alexandria Clarke.

Again, no results.

She removed the Gretna Green filter and pressed search again. No results.

'Are you sure the year was 1916?'

'My great grandmother was certain. According to my father, she remembered the date and place in vivid detail.'

Jayne opened up another site, The Genealogist, and typed the same search. She turned her computer screen around to face her client. 'As you can see, there are no records of any marriage.'

'I know. I want you to find out why.'

'But how can you be so sure they were married, Mr Russell?'

'Because I'm here, Mrs Sinclair. I'm living proof of the marriage. Rose Clarke had a son with David Russell, also called David, born in 1917. I am his direct descendent. Here's the birth certificate proving it.'

He reached into his acetate file and pulled out a sheet of paper. Jayne glanced at it quickly. A birth certificate for

David Russell, junior, born on February 17, 1917. The mother's name was given as a Rose Russell and the father as David Russell, but beneath this name one word was underlined, deceased.

Jayne looked at them both as she spoke. 'It seems David Russell passed away before his son was born. Unfortunately, a common occurrence in wartime. The registrar will have accepted the father's name as Russell but without some acknowledgement of paternity, or a marriage certificate, it has no standing in law. At this time, illegitimate children were not recognised as being able to inherit.'

'That's what the last genealogist said.'

Before Jayne could follow up on this last remark, an elderly man bustled through the door of the cafe, looked in their direction and limped towards them. A small, squat man, the father was the complete opposite of his son. Even the facial features were different: a sharp nose and thin mouth were crowned by an extravagant wave of grey hair swept back off the forehead. It was as if Elvis had walked into the cafe. But an Elvis who was over 70 years old and no longer able to shake his hips.

'I see you're wasting your time again, Mark.'

Mark Russell looked down at his hands, sighed, and then cast his eyes back up at Jayne. 'Mrs Sinclair, meet my father, Richard Russell.'

Jayne was about to extend her hand when the father stopped her with a welcoming sentence. 'Don't get involved in my son's madness, Mrs Sinclair. Waste of bloody time.'

The accent was a deep London growl, as sharp as the city where it had been formed.

Jayne breathed in. 'Good morning, Mr Russell, your son was just explaining his family history problem.'

'The lost bloody inheritance. Waste of bloody time.'

She could see Mark Russell clench and unclench his fist. 'Perhaps you'd like to sit down.' She indicated the seat opposite her.

'And you shouldn't have taken my grandmother's things without permission. They're mine, not yours. You'll get them when I die and not a second before.'

'How about a cup of tea?' Jayne tried desperately to save the situation. Tea was the usual salve for any British problem.

Richard Russell seemed to relax for a moment. 'I could do with a cup of Rosie Lee. Came rushing over here as soon as I saw your note, Mark.'

Jayne stood up and ordered a pot of tea from the counter. She glanced back at the father and son, both now sitting at the table. They were arguing, but at least having the sense to keep their voices low. Why had Mark Russell lied to her?

'I'll bring the tea over,' said the server. 'Would you like some cake?'

Jayne nodded, it might sweeten the old man.

'The Lemon Drizzle is fresh in this morning.'

'Three slices.' She was supposed to be on a diet, but what the hell, she needed the sugar too. She paid and returned to the table. The father and son were silent now, not looking at each other.

Jayne sat down opposite them; it was time to lay down the law. 'Listen, I have no desire to step into the middle of a family argument. If you want me to go, I'll finish my coffee and my cake and leave you two to finish your discussion.'

Mark Russell immediately leant forward, touching her arm, 'Please don't, Mrs Sinclair.'

Jayne looked down at his hand on her arm. He removed it quickly. 'You'd better tell me the story from the beginning, Mr Russell.'

They both began speaking at the same time.

Jayne held her hands up and pointed at Mark. 'Let's begin with you, Mr Russell.'

One again, Mark Russell folded his hands together and laid them on the table as if in prayer. The elder Mr Russell grunted and turned his head away.

'It all began two months ago. I was, am,' he corrected himself, 'a teacher. I assigned my pupils a genealogy project as part of the General Studies curriculum. You know, ask your parents about your family history and construct a family tree. As I was doing it, I realised I knew nothing about my own family, so I asked my father...'

'Worst thing I ever did, telling you the stories. You've become as mad as she was...'

Jayne held her hand up again. The elder Mr Russell turned his head away once more.

'My father told me the story of my great grandmother and the lost inheritance.'

'Should've kept my bloody mouth shut. It's all a fantasy...' the father interrupted.

The waitress approached and placed a pot of tea in front of the elder Mr Russell and three plates of the Lemon Drizzle cake on their table. Both men said thank you to the waitress in a peculiar English way, as if apologising for the trouble they had caused her by having to serve them. The old man poured the milk into the bottom of his cup, followed by the mahogany-coloured tea.

Mark Russell stared at his cake before picking up his fork and attacking it as if he hadn't eaten for the last 15 years.

'Why do you say it was a fantasy, Mr Russell?'

The father drank a long gulp of tea. 'Tell her the truth,

Mark.'

His son put down his fork. 'In 1923, my great grand-mother was put into an asylum.'

'For how long?'

Mark Russell stared down at the table and said quietly, 'For the rest of her life. She died in the same asylum in 1976.'

'But that's over 50 years. She spent all that time locked away?'

Richard Russell nodded, the quiff of his hair falling forward to be brushed back with his hand. He spoke quietly. 'My dad used to take me to see her when I was young. An old woman she was. All I remember was her smell as she held me close. The smell old women have. Even after all the time in the asylum, she still believed she had married David Russell, still believed she had been cheated.'

'Your father? What happened to him after his mother was put into the hospital?'

'He went to live with a great aunt in Worthing. She ran a tobacconist's in the town. When she died, my father moved to London to work, met my mother and married. Twice a year we used to make the pilgrimage to see my grandmother. I used to hate it but my father insisted.' Richard Russell drank more of his tea. 'I stopped going when I was 13, but my dad still carried on visiting her twice a year. She passed away in 1976. I think my father was glad he didn't have to go any more. My mother was delighted, she hated the old witch.'

'Dad, you shouldn't talk like that.'

'But it's the truth, Mark. She was just a mad old woman with delusions of grandeur. The sooner you accept it the better.'

Mark Russell shook his head vigorously. 'Dad, I know

she was telling the truth. I know it.'

'How? Tell me.'

Jayne interrupted before another row developed. 'So, if I understand you correctly, Mark, you want me to investigate if your great grandmother was married to Captain David Russell, and her son, your grandfather, should have inherited the estate and the title?'

Mark nodded. 'Exactly, Mrs Sinclair.'

'But, there will be other relatives in the Russell line, the second son who inherited in 1916…'

'But that's just it, Mrs Sinclair, there are none. The line became extinct in 1986, no living relations.'

'Then all property and money will pass to the crown.'

'But I checked the Bona Vacantia list.' He took out another print from the acetate file. 'See, it's still there.'

'You know about the list, Mark? Not many laymen do.'

Mark looked up to the skies and began to recite like a schoolteacher explaining quadratic equations to an errant pupil. 'Every day, the crown publishes the unclaimed estates list in the Bona Vacantia Division of the Government Legal Department. Generally, the list comprises people who have died intestate or with no recognisable heirs. Their property and fortune will pass to the crown unless an heir comes forward with a recognised claim.'

'You have read up on the subject.'

Mark smiled. 'Told you I was a schoolteacher. I know a little about a lot.'

Jayne looked at the closely packed list of names and addresses on the photocopy he had given her. Highlighted in green was one name, John Russell, Lord Lappiter. 'You know people have to leave some money behind to make this list?'

Mark nodded.

'If nobody makes a claim against the deceased person's estate then everything is passed to the Treasury.'

'As if we didn't pay enough in tax already,' said the old man, 'they even take your money when you're dead.'

'Only if people die without a will, Mr Russell,' answered Jayne.

'The government will get your money however you look at it, bleedin' leeches.' The old man snorted and turned to his son. 'You're wasting your time. Go on tell her.'

'Tell me what?'

Mark Russell stared down at the table, so his father continued.

'You're the second genealogist who's looked into the old woman's claims.'

'Mark, is it true?'

Mark nodded. 'I found out about the Bona Vacantia list after I was contacted by a genealogist.'

'Was anything discovered?'

The father interrupted again. 'He found nothing. A big fat zero.'

'But he didn't have your reputation or your experience as a detective, Mrs Sinclair.'

'You've checked up on me?'

'I know you were a detective in the Manchester Police. And I heard about your investigation of the Hughes case.' He looked down at his hands. 'You're my last hope, Mrs Sinclair.'

The old man snorted, then he looked across at his son's face and reached out to touch his shoulder. The voice was strangely gentle when he spoke. 'Not again, Mark, give it up. There's no point becoming so obsessed. It's not good for you, look what happened to my grandmother. It just can't be proven. We'll never know.'

Jayne stared at Mark Russell. Was it all a fantasy? Did the grandmother really have delusions of grandeur? And why was Mark Russell so interested in finding the truth? She had to know. 'What's in it for you, Mark? Why do you want to know? Is it the money?'

'I think it probably vanished years ago...'

'Not if the name is still on the Bona Vacantia list. It means the estate is worth at least 500 pounds.'

'A fortune,' the old man sneered.

Jayne held up her hand and Richard Russell stopped speaking. 'Why do you want to find out?'

Mark Russell clasped his hands in prayer once more. 'I want to find out for her,' he said quietly. 'When I think she was locked up in that asylum for over 50 years, but still kept on telling everyone about her marriage. Well, it just makes me wonder, was she telling the truth? Or was it all a delusion? I have to know.'

Jayne knew what he meant and thought of her own father in his place in Buxton. What if people no longer believed what he said any more? What if nobody protected him? She made a quick decision. 'My daily rate is 50 pounds plus expenses...'

'See, she's another one of those researchers who just want your bloody money...'

Jayne held up her hand for the final time to stop the old man speaking and turned to him. '...But in your case, Mr Russell, I will waive my fee and just bill you for any expenses. You can pay me what you want once I have finished my research. Does that sound fair to you?'

The old man grunted.

Mark Russell stuck out his hand and Jayne shook it. 'There's just one thing, Mrs Sinclair, we need you to complete your investigations by April 4.'

'But that's only seven days from now. What's the rush, Mark?'

'It's when the time limit on the Bona Vacantia unclaimed estates list expires. The last Lord Lappiter died on April 4, 1986. If we don't prove a relationship in the next week, the estate automatically passes to the Treasury.'

Jayne thought for a moment. 'We'd better get cracking, Mark, please show me what else you have in your folder.'

The old man grunted and turned his body away. 'Waste of bloody time, if you ask me.'

Chapter Five

Didsbury, Manchester. March 28, 2016.

Jayne reached home 15 minutes after saying goodbye to Mark Russell and his father. She had left them still arguing on the road in front of the cafe. Both bickering like unhappy lovers rather than father and son.

She entered the warmth and security of her kitchen. The cat, affectionately known as Mr Smith, immediately began to wrap itself around her legs in a figure of eight.

'I know, I know, you're hungry, right?'

She was answered by a long miaow. She opened the fridge and took out a small metal box of Lily's Kitchen Organic Lamb Casserole, a bottle of good Rioja Riserva from Cune and a bar of Amano chocolate. While the wine warmed up and the chocolate softened, she opened the casserole. It smelt good, but it wasn't for her.

In her life, the cat always came first. She was certain it could probably go to the fridge and choose its own food, but there was more pleasure in getting the human to do it for him. After all, there was enjoyment in being served.

She squeezed the small metal box of lamb casserole into the bowl and checked the water. The cat approached the food slowly and knelt down to enjoy his dinner.

Jayne glanced at the large Ikea clock on the wall - 4.45. Perhaps a bit early to start drinking and eating chocolate, but what the hell. After travelling to see her father and then dealing with the internal politics of the Family Russell, she deserved a bit of R&R.

She switched on the laptop and while it booted up, she

opened the wine. Since her husband had left to work in Europe, she spent more and more of her time in the kitchen. It had been their joint present to each other rather than going on an expensive honeymoon when they married 12 years ago. She knew it was the best investment they ever made; expanding her small, poky kitchen out onto the former patio, adding floor to ceiling windows, buying Poggenpohl cabinets and giving her the luxury of an island console in the cooking area.

When she was on medical leave from the police, after the killing of her partner, she would often sit here with a cup of coffee or glass of wine, watching the seasons change and the birds flitter from tree to tree in the back garden.

Now this extended kitchen was her workplace, where she could research her clients while perched on a bar stool in front of the island console, her files within reach. It was her place, far from the problems of her marriage, the worries about her father and from the madding crowds. Just her, a glass of wine, a square of the best chocolate she could afford, and the cat. Mustn't forget the cat.

She poured out a glass of the Rioja. Not the best wine, but she needed something earthy and tannic now, not the jammy fruit of Australia. She snapped open a section of the Amano Dos Rios Palet D'Or and placed a small square on her tongue, letting it melt with the warmth of her mouth. The luxuriously comforting sweetness of the chocolate spread across her palate, followed by a hint of minty bitterness. She drank a mouthful of Rioja, mixing the two, strengthening and reinforcing both flavours.

Red wine and good chocolate. A match made in heaven. For a second, the cares of the world were lifted from her shoulders and she luxuriated in the warm comfort of the taste.

A beep from her laptop brought her back to earth with a bang. A message in Outlook from Mark, thanking her for the meeting and suggesting they review progress in two days.

'He's keen isn't he, Mr Smith?'

The cat didn't answer, he never did. Just kept on purring as he ate his lamb casserole, his own private cat heaven.

'Well, it's time to work.' She spoke out loud to herself. It often worried her, this talking to herself, but she recognised it was a way of ordering her thoughts. Even when her husband, Paul, was here, she had spoken to herself. But, in his absence, she was doing it even more.

She pulled out everything from the acetate folder Mark Russell had given her. Inside were two envelopes, copies of the birth certificates of Rose Clarke and David Russell Junior, and the photocopy of the Bona Vacantia list.

Where to begin?

The two envelopes intrigued her. On the uppermost, a name and address appeared in vermilion ink, written in the perfect copperplate script of a bygone era:

Miss Rose Alexandria Clarke
126, Curtain Road,
Shoreditch,
London

The letter was postmarked with a date of 1910. She supposed this was Mark's great grandmother's address. She opened Find My Past on the computer and typed the name Clarke and the location as London.

A little over 235,000 results. Not terribly helpful.

'Let's narrow it down,' she said out loud. The cat ignored her and carried on eating.

She clicked on the 1911 Census and typed in the name and the district of London as Shoreditch. Up popped five results for the surname, one of which was the correct address.

Much better.

A square of chocolate somehow found its way into her mouth, followed by a large gulp of the Rioja. Success always deserved some sort of reward.

She clicked to open an image of the original census return. The Head of the Family was listed as a Hans Clarke, but there were only two other people mentioned, both of whom were male shop assistants and not family members.

What had happened to Rose? Had she missed the census for some reason, or was she listed elsewhere?

Jayne took another sip of wine. She opened up the 1901 census and typed in the name and address. And there was Rose, along with her father and her mother, Hans Clarke and Marion Clarke. Rose was just nine years at the time of this census and listed as a scholar.

So what had happened to her in 1911 and why was she not with her father?

Jayne decided to save the search for the missing Rose till later. But what had happened to the mother from 1901 to 1910?

Jayne poured herself another glass of Rioja. This family was becoming more and more intriguing.

A quick search for the mother's name in the Births, Marriages and Deaths section revealed a Marion Clarke had died in London in 1905. The listing was given as Volume 1c, page 119. If she wanted to know what had happened she would have to apply for a death certificate. Perhaps later, it wasn't necessary at this moment. The mother had died leaving a 13-year-old girl and her father to run the shop. Not the easiest life for a young girl.

She sat back on her seat, the glass of wine in her hand. So Mark's information checked out. At least his great grandmother existed and had lived at the address on the envelope.

But she still had two more searches to perform before she could call it a day. The first was to check out the Russell family and the Lords Lappiter. The second was to find out if there were any records of marriage anywhere, at any time, for a David Russell or a Rose Clarke.

After a sip of Rioja, she decided to work on the Russell family first as it was probably the easiest.

She typed Lord Lappiter into Google. Over four million results. She clicked the first one and was immediately confronted by a lurid headline from the Sun of 1986.

LORD LAP-IT-UPS STICKY END.

She ignored the double entendre of the headline and read the racy copy. Apparently, the last Lord Lappiter had collapsed on top of a prostitute in Manila after a particularly robust session of lovemaking. 'He was insatiable,' said Thelma Gonzalez, his paramour for the evening.

Jayne was always amazed how the scandal-ridden pages of the English rags could be both blunt and coy all in the same sentence. Was it a peculiarly English attitude to sex?

She returned to the article. The late Lord Lappiter had died instantly from a heart attack, leaving no will and no known heirs. The Sun gleefully stated the estate, with a mansion in Derbyshire, would pass to the crown unless it was claimed by a relative.

She checked the date of death in the article. April 4, 1986. Mark was correct, they needed to move quickly. By the laws of inheritance, a claimant had 30 years to make a claim to an intestate estate. If they didn't, the estate was declared forfeit. Mark had just six days left to find the marriage certificate.

The cat suddenly stopped licking its paws and pricked up its ears. The front door bell rang noisily, followed by two impatient knocks on the door.

Chapter Six

Didsbury, Manchester. March 28, 2016.

Another sharp rap at the door.

'Coming, coming,' Jayne shouted walking down the hallway. She opened the door before whoever it was could knock a hole in the wood.

Standing in front of her was a small, dapper man wearing an Aquascutum mac with matching trilby and carrying a briefcase. He doffed his hat to reveal strands of hair combed over his head in the style of Bobby Charlton.

'Good evening, Madam. It's Mrs Sinclair, isn't it?'

Jayne nodded without thinking.

'I wonder if I might come in for a moment. I have something I would like to discuss with you.' The voice was high and nasal, the smile revealed National Health teeth discoloured to a murky shade of yellow.

'And you are?'

'Oh yes, how remiss of me not to introduce myself immediately.' He fumbled in the inside of the mac, finally producing a white card and handing it to Jayne.

Herbert Small, Genealogist was written on the white card in simple block letters. There was a website and phone number but no address.

'It's concerning your clients, Richard and Mark Russell.' Again the yellow-toothed smile.

Jayne stared at him for a moment. All her training said don't let any man who comes to the door into your house, but she stood back anyway. What harm could a man like this do?

'Thank you, you're so kind.'

Jayne showed him to the kitchen and pulled out one of the stools. 'I'm having a glass of wine, would you like some?'

Herbert Small held up two tiny hands like the paws of a hamster. 'Not for me, Mrs Sinclair. I find alcohol doesn't agree with my stomach.'

'Tea then?'

'Not for me.' He patted his stomach, 'it doesn't agree.'

Jayne sat down on the stool, noticing her computer screen was still showing the results of her search. Herbert Small had seen it too. Quickly, she pressed the Alt and 4 keys to close the program window. Luckily, the acetate folder was covered by her notebook.

The small man in front of her sat down on the stool, still wearing his gaberdine. He tried to make himself comfortable but gave up after a few seconds and ended up perching on the edge, his briefcase held to his chest.

'What's this about, Mr Small?'

'Very direct, Mrs Sinclair. I must admit I like that in a woman.'

This man and his patronising tone were beginning to irritate Jayne.

He placed the briefcase on the table and fished out a manila file. 'Mrs Sinclair, I do believe you have just been retained by the Russell family. Is that correct?'

'How did you hear, Mr Small?'

'I have my sources, Mrs Sinclair. Sources I'm afraid I cannot divulge.'

Jayne stood up. Time to put this little man in his place. 'Then I must ask you to leave, Mr Small. Who my clients are is none of your business.'

The man's tiny hands fluttered. 'I didn't mean to offend

you, Mrs Sinclair, please let me explain why I asked the question.'

Jayne hesitated for a moment.

'Please let me explain.' Herbert Small held up the manila folder.

Jayne sat back down on her stool.

'Three weeks ago, I contacted the Russell family. In my genealogical investigations I came across an interesting…,' he thought for a moment before the right word came to him, '…situation that could have been of interest to them.'

'You checked the Bona Vacantia list and found that Richard and Mark Russell might have a claim against the Lappiter estate?'

Herbert Small looked surprised. 'I see you are ahead of me, Mrs Sinclair.'

'I've heard about people like you, Mr Small, but you are the first I've ever met. "Heir Hunters" I believe you call yourselves.'

A look of horror crossed Herbert Small's face. 'I beg your pardon, Mrs Sinclair, I provide a valuable service for society, reuniting relatives with money that would normally vanish into the maw of the Treasury.' His voice had risen one register. 'I have many satisfied and happy customers, who receive money they would not normally know about.'

'You are paid handsomely for your services, aren't you, Mr Small?'

'My fee is standard for the service I provide. Plus I only get paid when my clients receive their money. I have substantial costs to cover.'

'So what has this to do with me?'

The little man placed the manila file on the table in front of him and tried to get comfortable on the stool, giving up once again. 'As I was saying, Mrs Sinclair, I specialise in researching names close to the end of their time on the list.'

'Inheritances near to the 30-year time limit?'

'That is correct. The big firms such as Fraser and Fraser, Celtic Research or Finders International jump on the list as soon as it is published, competing with each other to get to the heirs first. If none are found quickly, most give up after a short time. For them, it is not worth the effort and cost to continue researching.'

Jayne took a sip of her wine. 'So, even though the inheritance could be substantial, in 1986 no heirs could be found?'

'Correct again, Mrs Sinclair. It's so pleasing talking to a professional.'

Jayne ignored the compliment.

'I brought the possibility of a large inheritance to the notice of the Russells, father and son. They hired me on the basis of my standard contract and then, a week later, fired me. Or at least the elder Mr Russell fired me.' He leant in conspiratorially to Jayne. 'I think he wanted to keep all the money himself.'

Jayne pulled away from the man's breath. 'As genealogists, we are hired and fired by our clients all the time, Mr Small. It's par for the course. Did you manage to prove Rose Alexander married David Russell?'

The man shrugged his small shoulders. 'Unfortunately, I cannot divulge that information.'

'I presume you had a written contract with the Russells?'

The little man shrugged his shoulders. 'Alas, I did not.'

'So why have you come to see me, Mr Small? What do you want from me?'

'I would like you to refuse the assignment, Mrs Sinclair. The Russells are cheats and liars. They should not be supported by the skills we bring to our profession.'

Jayne disliked this pompous little man intensely. 'Listen, Mr Small, as far as I'm concerned I have been retained by the Russells to conduct an investigation into their family. Unlike you, I have no financial interest in the outcome. For me, it is a professional challenge and that is all. If I can speak frankly, Mr Small?'

The man nodded.

'I believe men like you are the ambulance chasers of our profession, feeding on people's greed to enrich themselves, and I want nothing more to do with you.' Jayne stood up. 'I have given you enough of my time. I'll escort you to the door.'

'But, Mrs Sinclair, you don't understand…'

'I understand perfectly, Mr Small. And it's because I do that you will be leaving my house.' She took him by the elbow. 'Now, are you going to go quietly or am I going to have the pleasure of throwing you out?'

Herbert Small gathered up his manila folder from the table. 'You haven't heard the last of this, Mrs Sinclair, mark my words.'

'Are you threatening me, Mr Small? Because if you are, as an ex-police officer, I have to caution you such threats are an offence under Section Four of the Public Order Act of 1986.'

Jayne opened the door. The man adjusted his gaberdine coat, straightened his tie, put his trilby back on his head and stepped outside. 'I'm not going to forget this, Mrs Sinclair.'

Chapter Seven

Didsbury, Manchester. March 28, 2016.

'You should have told me the truth.'

'I'm sorry, Mrs Sinclair, I just thought you would…'

'I would not take the job if I knew?'

The other end of the phone was quiet for a few seconds before Mark replied. 'He was an obnoxious little man. Father hated him. He kept asking for money to go here and there checking up on sources, or so he said. In the end, it all became too much, so Father asked him to go away.'

'Was there a contract between you two?'

'Not in so many words. He told me about the Bona Vacantia list but I had already begun to research my family, you have to believe me. The list just makes the research more urgent, that's why we turned to you, Mrs Sinclair. You're our only hope.'

'How much do you owe him?'

'Well, he had put in a bill for 1,220 pounds in expenses. But we were on an agreement where there was only payment if he was successful.'

'If you want me to continue to research your case, Mr Russell, you must pay him what you owe, is that clear?'

The other end of the phone remained silent.

'Otherwise, I will forget I ever met you or your father.'

'But, Mrs Sinclair, we only have seven days left…'

'Those are my terms, Mr Russell, take them or leave them.' Jayne didn't like Herbert Small but his treatment by the Russells had been shoddy.

'I agree, Mrs Sinclair. I'll sign a cheque and send it to

him right away. Will you continue with the search?'

Jayne thought for a moment. Am I getting myself into a well of trouble? Are these people worth the hassle? But the case intrigued her. Why would a woman insist she was married unless she was? And why was there no record of the marriage?

'Hello, Mrs Sinclair?'

'I will continue with the search for seven days, Mr Russell. If at the end of that time we haven't found the answer, then we will stop.'

'Agreed, Mrs Sinclair.'

'And one more thing, Mr Russell, I've changed my mind. There will be no bill from me for expenses, or anything else. Clear?'

'As rainwater, Mrs Sinclair. Thank you.'

Jayne put the phone down. She wondered if she were making a big mistake. But the image of that poor woman locked up in an asylum for 50 years came back to her. What if the same thing ever happened to her father?

Chapter Eight

Didsbury, Manchester. March 28, 2016.

She wasn't going to treat him in such a shabby manner. Nobody talked to Herbert Small in that way and got away with it. He slammed his hand down on top of the steering wheel of his Toyota.

Who does she think she is? He had been doing this job for over 20 years. His clients always paid him what he asked. No client ever sacked him, he was the best in the business. What was she but some jumped-up ex-copper with a couple of years' experience? She wasn't going to take his clients from him.

Not her. Not anyone.

An 'ambulance chaser', him. She had a cheek. Well, he knew what he was going to do with her. He hadn't been in this profession without learning a trick or three.

If the Russells thought he could be discarded like a used tissue, well they had a surprise coming to them too.

A smile spread across his face. He could kill two birds with one stone. Or in this case three old birds.

He picked up his phone and dialled the number. 'Hello, Mr Dunphy? Mr Eamon Dunphy?'

A deep, resonant voice came from the other end of the phone. 'Speaking.'

'Hello, Mr Dunphy, you don't know me, my name is Herbert Small. I have information which may be extremely useful regarding your proposed development in Derbyshire. I suggest we meet at your office tomorrow morning. Shall we say 10 a.m.?'

'I'm sorry, Mr…?'

'Small, Herbert Small.'

'Yes, Mr Small, I'm a busy man and…'

'You have invested four million pounds in this development already, Mr Dunphy, you wouldn't like it to go to waste, would you?'

'Well…'

'It is in your own interest, Mr Dunphy. I am able to save you a fortune.'

'Well, I can give you 15 minutes at 2 p.m. Don't be late.'

'I won't, Mr Dunphy. And just for the record this information is free. But I'm sure once you have heard it, you may believe a small finder's fee is the correct way of rewarding the bearer of such important news.'

'2 p.m., tomorrow, Mr…?'

'Small, Herbert Small.'

The end of the line went dead and Herbert Small smiled like a cat who had just had the cream.

Double cream.

Chapter Nine

Didsbury, Manchester. March 28, 2016.

After deciding to stick with the case, Jayne returned to her research with a new-found determination. She wasn't going to let one of those heir hunters spoil her relationship with her new client, or her mood.

A glass of wine and the rest of the Amano chocolate helped her find out everything she needed about the Russell family and the Lappiter title.

The whole lot of them were a strange mixture of madness and duty, alternating from generation to generation. The first Lord Lappiter had come from nowhere, manufacturing ball bearings and becoming a confidante of Prince Albert. He was ennobled after the Great Exhibition of 1851, having been one of its leading lights. The second Lord had been a wastrel, spending his time gallivanting around the fleshpots of Paris in the company of Edward, Prince of Wales. He had died of an overdose of absinthe in one of the sleaziest bars of Montmartre. Toulouse-Lautrec had even portrayed his likeness in a famous poster.

After him, the family returned to duty again with the third Lord Lappiter, David's father, becoming an academic and a member of both the Royal Society and the Royal Geographical Society and having three species of Asian butterfly named after him.

According to Burke's Peerage, David Russell had only been Lord Lappiter for three days before dying on the Somme. She made a note to herself to check his death notice in the London Gazette later.

After his premature death, the family had gone down-hill. Toby, the fourth Lord, David's brother, had been one of the fast set in the 1920s, discovering an insatiable taste for wine, women and song, and wasting the rest of his money. He had died in 1935 in a car crash. The fifth Lord, James, was more sober, carving out a career in the army and per-ishing at Dunkirk. The madness in the family skipped a generation as his son, Thomas, spent his whole life in the Colonial Office, specialising in the legal ramifications of Independence. He died in 1978, leaving the last scion, Ronald, the freedom to enjoy life to the fullest, dying in the arms of a Filipino prostitute.

What a strange family, she thought as she sipped anoth-er glass of wine. She had done the usual checks, working backwards through the Russell line, researching both the matriarchal and patrimonial sides of the family. There seemed to be no surviving relatives anywhere. 'The Rus-sells weren't a productive lot at all,' she said to Mr Smith. The cat just ignored her, intent on licking his paws, pre-paring himself for his nightly prowl. 'Too much inbreeding, I think.'

She poured the last dregs of the bottle of Rioja into her glass. Was she drinking too much since Paul had left?

Probably.

She glanced across at the acetate folder lying next to her computer. The two envelopes lay inside. Why had Mark given her these envelopes? And why was his father so pro-tective of them? Herbert Small had not mentioned them at all. Did he know they existed?

She picked up the envelope with its beautiful copper-plate writing and opened the flap at the back. Sandwiched between an old blank sheet of writing paper folded in half was a medallion with a woman's face on it, topped with

51

three small hand-tied bows in purple, white and green silk.

The picture was of on older woman, in her forties at least, with a silk scarf wrapped around her neck and her hair tied back and parted in the centre. The face was strong and forthright, with an aquiline nose, sharp, piercing eyes and a determined clench of the mouth and jaw. This was a woman not to be tangled with.

Jayne examined the silver frame. At least, she thought it was silver. It was no more than one inch in diameter with a well-worn message engraved on the back.

To Rose from E.

The silver seemed too thin and shiny, as if it had been touched or rubbed many times during its life.

Who was E? If the engraving said 'To Rose' then this couldn't be a picture of Mark's great grandmother, could it?

Jayne looked again at the picture of the woman. The clothes and the hairstyle were Victorian not Edwardian. If Rose was born in 1892, then this woman was far too old to be Rose. Was it her mother? But her mother's Christian name was Marion. Why didn't it read, 'To Rose from M.?'

She put down the medallion and picked up the other envelope. This was more modern, with the word Conqueror etched into the weave. Inside was a yellowing sheet of paper folded into four. She opened it carefully to reveal a head and shoulders drawing in pencil of a young woman. The face wasn't beautiful, but the fine nose and jawline gave the image an inner strength. She was wearing a starched white collar over what looked like a pinafore. But it was the eyes that Jayne was forced to look at. Somehow the artist had drawn them to show they sparkled with happiness. A wonderful, deep-felt joy radiated from these eyes like rays from the sun.

Jayne instantly liked this woman, was drawn to her as if she were a close friend. Could she be Rose Clarke? There was nothing written on the drawing to indicate who it was. But, if it were Rose, who had drawn the picture of her?

She picked up the locket again. Mark had said these were the only effects his great grandmother had kept with her during her long years in the asylum. A life in two objects. Is that all that remained of Rose Clarke?

Jayne took another sip of wine. As she did so, a thought struck her. One person might be able to help. Jayne picked up her phone and checked her contacts. There she was. It had been over a year since they had last talked, but Maeve might be able to help. Or at least she would know somebody who could. There were some advantages to being part of a woman's network.

She called the number and they arranged to meet at 11 a.m. tomorrow morning.

'Another meeting in a coffee shop, Mr Smith. I'm going to have to go on a caffeine detox when this investigation is finished.' The cat carried on licking its fur, still ignoring her.

The phone rang. She picked it up immediately without looking at the screen. 'You're not going to cancel on me, are you Maeve?'

'I don't think so,' a male voice answered. 'It's Paul.'

She hadn't seen her husband for two months since he had gone to Brussels to work. He still rang her a couple of times a week. They chatted politely about the house, or the weather, or the cat. Occasionally, he asked her about her work, but even those questions had become fewer and fewer recently.

'Hello, hello...'

'Hi Paul.' Jayne tried to put as much enthusiasm in her voice as she could.

'I'm coming back to Manchester at 5.00 tomorrow. Can you pick me up from the airport?'

Jayne thought for a moment. 'Sure,' she finally answered.

'You don't seem too enthusiastic.'

'It's short notice, that's all.'

'I thought you'd be pleased to see me.'

There it was. The little-boy-lost whine in his voice. A sound that irritated the hell out of Jayne.

'I am, it's just…'

'It's just you have an appointment with Maeve…'

It was so like Paul. The whine followed by aggression. The man could play passive aggressive with the best of them. 'Actually, the meeting is in the morning. So, yes I can pick you up from the airport.'

'Oh good.' The sarcasm was clear in his tone. Then there was a beat and he seemed to recover himself. His voice dropped a register. 'I've some news.'

'Can't you tell me now?'

'Let's keep it until I see you. I prefer to tell you in person.'

She wanted to scream. Why did he always do this? Just bloody tell her, don't tease or tempt or hint or bloody suggest. Just say it.

But she said nothing.

The line went quiet at the other end. 'We need to talk, Jayne.'

'We are talking.' Jayne knew the words were wrong even as they came out of her mouth.

'No, we need to talk about us.'

'Right. Let's talk about us.'

The time had come, Jayne knew it would one day. She had hoped it would be a while before they had this conversation. In her life, her job with the police, and now her genealogical work, she had never been afraid of confrontation, physical or verbal. As they taught her in police college so many years ago: get your retaliation in first, Cadet Sinclair, don't ever let the bastards get the upper hand.

But, in her personal life, she found it very difficult. It was as if this was another her. A different person. She found it hard to talk about personal things. Her mother had been the same, hiding her cancer until it was far too late, only letting Robert and her know about it when the end was unstoppable.

'Hello, hello...'

'Paul, let's talk when you get back.'

'About us, Jayne, what we're doing and where we're going.'

'About us.'

'I'm on Brussels Airlines, SN 2177. Check to see if it's delayed, you know what they're like.'

'I will. See you tomorrow.'

The line went dead in her hand. Tomorrow it is. She didn't know what he was going to say to her. But worse, she had even less idea what she was going to say to him. Would she realise how much she missed him when she saw him again? Or would she know it was all over?

She picked up her wine glass and stared through the deep ruby red of the Rioja swirling in the bottom. At the moment, she didn't know what she wanted and it annoyed the hell out of her.

Jayne looked at the picture of the stern woman, encased in her silver frame. 'I bet you wouldn't put up with this shit, would you?'

Chapter Ten

London. April 25, 1913.

The paisley bag felt strangely heavy on her shoulder. It wasn't hers of course, she'd borrowed it from one of the other women in the group. She had checked the label inside as she was filling it.

Liberty of London.

She had been inside the store only once. Such a beautiful place with wonderful fabrics from all over the world. So different from her father's shop. Such choice and all so modern. She had once tried to persuade her father to stock more fashionable items, but his answer had been firm and unwavering.

'We stock what our customers want, Rose. Nothing more and nothing less. And this…,' he pointed to the old-fashioned clothes displayed on the mannequins, 'this is what our customers want.'

She knew it was useless to try to change his mind. Like all men, once it was made up, he was as unmovable as Stonehenge.

She glanced across at Amy Rhodes on the other side of the street. Her head held high, her shoulders back, like the good actress she was, not looking to the left or right. Just another middle-class woman window shopping.

The bag was digging into her shoulder; she moved it so the strap lay closer to her neck. Up ahead, two policemen, wearing their capes buttoned up against the soft drizzle, were walking towards her, the badges on their helmets glistening in the rain. She pulled her coat tighter around her body, making sure her suffragette medallion was covered.

She moved the bag again, holding it tightly against her body. As the police drew level, one of them touched his index finger to the point of his helmet. 'You shouldn't be out in weather like this, miss.'

'I've not far to go, forgot my umbrella,' she answered, adding what she hoped was a winsome smile. Another fragile female.

'You should 'urry up,' the older, gruffer policeman said, 'this 'ere rain is going to get 'eavier or my name isn't Charles Beckett.'

'Thank you, Constable Beckett, I'll hurry home.'

The younger one touched his finger to his helmet again. 'Good evening, miss.'

She hurried past them, picking up her pace. Amy was crossing the road to join her.

'What did they want?'

'Worried about my health.'

'They couldn't care less a year ago.'

Rose thought back to the time in Holloway. The smell of stale urine hanging over the place like a shroud, the rancid kiss of the rough clothes against her skin. And, all the time, the threat of force-feeding looming over her if she had the temerity to go on hunger strike. The others told her what they did. Forcing the tube down a girl's nose as they held her, sometimes needing six men to keep the prisoner subdued. None of the women who suffered force-feeding were ever the same again. It was as if something was taken from them, never to be returned.

And now they were protesting the latest move in their war against a stubborn Parliament full of stubborn men: The Cat and Mouse Act read into law that very day in the House of Commons. It was funny, the British often gave the quaintest names to their most draconian laws. It was as if they could lessen severity with banality.

Amy leant closer to her and whispered, 'The target is just around the corner. No.36.'

'Let's get it over and done.' Rose felt a shiver tremble down her spine. She wasn't sure she could face prison again, not ever again.

The two women picked up the pace and rounded the corner. Number 36, the house of the Home Secretary, Reginald McKenna, was just across the street, the number in black letters against the dark blue of the door and the painted white stone surround. It was a modern building created by Lutyens in 1911 to match the neighbouring elegant Georgian townhouses.

Rose admired the lines and symmetry of the windows and composition. The artist in her wanted to sit down and sketch it there and then. The woman in her revolted at all it represented; a bastion of male privilege and power.

They crossed over to stand in front of the house. Amy glanced up and down the street.

Empty.

'Let's do it,' Amy said.

Rose reached into the Paisley bag and grabbed one of the half-bricks wrapped in a poster from the movement. She had wrapped them herself last night, making sure the words VOTES FOR WOMEN in big black letters could be seen clearly.

Amy was ready to throw, her arm reaching back just as they had practised. Rose copied her.

'One...two...three.'

They both shouted 'Votes for Women!' as loudly as they could and launched the bricks. Amy's flew high into the first-storey window above the door, smashing a hole in one of the panes of glass. Rose drew back her own arm and let fly. The stone wrapped in the suffragette poster flew in a perfect arc to the front window and hit it, bouncing back and dropping down to the pavement.

The glass shivered but stood firm.

'You have to throw harder, like this.'

Another brick was already being launched by Amy. It smashed through the window on the right of the door. All round, they could see people looking out through their windows, trying to see what was going on.

'Hurry up, throw some more.'

Rose reached into her bag, grabbed another brick and threw again. This time, the missile smashed through the window bringing the glass down with a loud crash.

The neighbouring doors began to open. More people came to their windows to look out. And, in the distance, the high-pitched trill of a police whistle pierced the air.

'Let's get out of here,' said Amy, starting to run away from the sound.

Rose reached into her bag. 'Just one more.' She pulled out her brick and, taking careful aim, threw it at the only remaining unbroken window on the first floor of the house. She watched as it smashed through the glass, landing with a heavy thud in the front parlour.

The sound of the police whistles was getting closer. Amy was already 20 yards down Dean Trench Street, shouting 'Come on, come on.'

Rose glanced back at the broken windows. The Home Secretary would get the message this time.

A policeman appeared across the square. He spotted them and shouted something Rose couldn't hear. She wasn't going to wait to find out what he wanted.

Amy was running already, her skirts pulled up to her

knees with one hand while the other held onto her hat.

Rose pulled both skirts up and ran after her. The hat flew from her head. For a second, she turned to pick it up, saw the policeman running towards her and decided to leave it lying in the gutter.

She ran down the street after Amy. It was long and straight with tall, three-storey Georgian houses on either side. A motor car drove past her, blowing its horn. Rose ignored the man driving it and carried on running, the police whistles louder in her ears.

Amy turned right at the corner, not waiting for her. She was heading up Tufton Street. It was what they had arranged last night. By heading this way, they could lose themselves in the crowds near Westminster Abbey.

Rose ran around the corner. As she did, she glanced behind her. The policeman was much closer now, his long legs covering the ground between them quickly. She could see his face. It was the gruff, old policeman she had met on the street.

She increased her pace, must get away, she couldn't face another three months in prison.

Amy was still ahead, crossing Great Peter Street, narrowly avoiding a horse-drawn cab.

Rose looked over her shoulder, the policeman was even closer. She could hear the metallic scraping of his hobnail boots on the pavement, getting nearer and nearer. Up ahead, she could see the tower of Westminster Abbey, a wet grey sanctuary faintly visible through the drizzle.

She wasn't going to make it.

A loud whistle just behind her, followed by a shout, 'Stop her, stop her.'

He was too close. An alley opened on the left. It ran for a short distance before branching left. She ran down it, the ground beneath her feet changing from paving to cobble stones. She stumbled, almost tripping on some rubbish thrown on the ground.

The policeman stopped at the entrance to the alley, deciding which woman to go after. The one in the alley was nearest and she was younger. He ran after her.

Rose took the left-hand fork; the alley became narrower and ran between two tall buildings. She ran down it to the light at the end. She could hear the boots and their staccato rhythm behind her. Which way to go? There seemed to be a street at the end of the left fork, whilst the right fork took her deeper into the maelstrom of buildings.

She ran towards the light, always towards the light. The sound of her teacher's voice came to her. 'It's the quality of light that sets an artist free, Miss Clarke, remember, the quality of light.'

She ran towards the light at the end of the tunnel hoping it would set her free.

Nearly there, nearly at the street.

The sound of the boots was getting louder and louder, closer and closer.

She was nearly there.

A hand grabbed her shoulder, she wriggled out of its grasp and entered the light. It was a small street with an opening at the end where there were people. She must lose herself down there, with them she would be safe.

Two arms circled her waist 'Oh no, you don't.'

She could smell the stale sweat of his uniform and the bitter note of alcohol on his breath. He lifted her up and carried her back into the narrow alley, covering her mouth with his hand.

She kicked out with her heels and bit down on the hand.

He threw her against the wall. Her coat flew open revealing the purple, white and green silk bows and silver medallion with its stern picture. 'Suffragette bitch,' he said as he sucked the flesh of his thumb, a row of red teeth marks livid against the pale skin.

Then a sardonic smile crossed his face and he launched himself at her, pinning his hand over her mouth and leaning all the weight of his body against hers. She struggled but he was too strong.

'Seen your kind before, I has.' His mouth was inches away from her face. She could see the hairs of his ginger moustache bristling against his top lip. She smelt alcohol again, stronger this time.

His spit landed on her cheek and she tried to lift her arms to wipe it off, but couldn't move. He ripped the suffragette badge from her shirt and threw it onto the wet cobblestones.

'Led me a merry dance, you did. 'Fought I wouldn't catch you, but I did. Now it's time for my reward.'

She tried to bite the hand across her mouth but he was cleverer this time, keeping his fingers and palm away from her teeth.

'I always cops a feel from the little suffragettes. My little reward for a job well done, I thinks.'

She felt his hand on her breast, groping for her nipple through the cotton fabric of the shirt. She struggled against him but his body pressed heavily into hers.

'A fcisty one. You're gonna make a man very happy one night.'

His hand began to reach down between her legs, pulling her skirts up.

She closed her eyes. Not this, not this.

Suddenly, she felt the pressure off her body and his hands no longer grasping and clawing at her. There was another man standing there silhouetted against the light.

He grabbed her hand. 'We have to get out of here, there'll be others soon.' She looked down at the policeman lying at her feet. She kicked him between the legs, hearing a loud groan as he curled up into a ball.

'That's done it, we have to run now.'

He bent down and picked something off the floor, grabbed her hand and together they fled down the streets towards the shops. Behind them, the sound of a policeman's whistle, softer now and not as powerful.

Chapter Eleven

Didsbury, Manchester. March 28, 2016.

Jayne rubbed her eyes and switched off the computer. The clock ticked over to 11.30. She went to pour herself another glass of wine but realised the bottle was empty. Where had it all gone? Next to it lay the remains of the packaging of the bar of Amano. A few crumbs of chocolate lay mournfully on the counter. She licked her finger and dabbed them up. 'Waste not, want not.'

She had spent the last three hours trying every permutation of Rose Alexandria Clarke's Christian name and surname, gradually reducing the filters until she was searching the whole of the UK.

Still no marriage details.

At one moment, she thought she had found her in Billericay, Essex, but it turned out this Rose Clarke was 47 years old, already married three times and marrying a fourth husband in the sprightly shape of a 63-year-old. The triumph of hope over experience, she thought.

Then she had moved on to David Russell. Not an easy name in genealogical terms, but she was glad it wasn't a Smith or a Jones. A simple marriage search in the UK for 1916 had led to six results, none of which had involved a Rose Clarke. She expanded it to cover the years of the First World War, 1914-18, and it came back with 33 results, none of which corresponded to her man and none in Scotland. She had searched through each result laboriously, checking and rechecking the names, hoping a Rose Clarke or any sort of Miss Clarke would appear.

Nothing.

Not a sausage.

Nada.

She would probably have to widen the dates up until the old woman entered the asylum in 1923, just to be on the safe side, but the thought of wading through more names defeated her.

Mark Russell was convinced his great grandmother had married at Gretna Green in Scotland. Perhaps the records had been lost or misfiled and that's why they didn't appear on any online search.

Perhaps a visit to the Public Records Office in Scotland and Gretna Green would help. There may have been other records kept by the Justice of the Peace or the registrar which weren't available online. She would have to check.

And then there was David Russell himself. Mark had said his great grandfather was a soldier when he died. If it were true, she would have to look at the army records.

She was tired, tomorrow she would finish it off.

She stood up, stretched and switched off her laptop. Paul suddenly popped into her head. Was he thinking of her, wondering what she was doing? Or was he fast asleep, snoring with his mouth wide open as he usually did?

She thought it was probably the latter.

The cat made a figure of eight through her legs. 'Okay, okay, I know. Time for your night-time rambles.' She walked over and opened the patio doors. Mr Smith darted out through them and vanished into the night. 'Where do you go to every night, Mr Smith?' she said aloud. And then quickly shut the door, locking it and closing the curtains.

The neighbours would think she was some mad cat lady, talking to her familiar before she cast a wicked spell. She placed the empty glass in the sink and the bottle on the counter. She would wash one and put the other in the green bin, tomorrow.

One last look around the kitchen to check all was well. Again, she couldn't shake off her old police training. The ability, instilled in her for the eight years she was a detective, to look at a room and sense where something was wrong or out of place. Her colleagues used to joke she was better than one of the sniffer dogs at finding stuff.

Her instincts had failed her when Dave died. Why didn't she know there was somebody behind the door? It had seemed like a normal enough day. Just following up on a series of burglaries that had happened in the neighbourhood. They received a tip-off the goods were being kept in this walk-up in Moss Side. Dave had gone first, knocking sharply on the frosted glass of the door. She had stopped for a moment to tie her laces.

An ordinary day. Nothing special.

The blast, when it came, ripped through the glass, hitting Dave in the chest. She had jumped up and pushed herself against the wall. Another blast came soon after, hitting him in the back as he lay on the floor. The door had opened and she saw the shotgun peering out.

She had grabbed it, the hot barrel searing her hands. She had hit the man with the butt again and again and again. But however hard she hit the bastard, Dave still lay on the dirty concrete of the corridor, blood pooling around his body.

'ENOUGH,' she shouted, 'enough.'

Before she switched off the light, she glanced across at the picture of the woman topped by its faded ribbons. Who was she and why was she framed in a silver medallion?

She yawned and rubbed her eyes once more. With luck, she would find out tomorrow.

Chapter Twelve

Didsbury, Manchester. March 28, 2016.

Outside on the street, Herbert Small watched as the lights went out on the downstairs floor in the woman's house. A black and white cat crossed the street in front of his car, jumped on top of a wall and vanished into the garden opposite.

Herbert Small poured himself some warm milk from his flask. He could go back to his hotel tonight but he preferred sitting outside in his car, watching.

The lights had gone out upstairs now. 'Good night, Mrs Sinclair. Enjoy your dreams.'

Herbert inhaled the gentle aroma of the warm milk, sipped a little, feeling the warmth slip down his throat and settle in his stomach.

That felt better. Milk was the only drink his stomach would tolerate. Over the years, he had come to appreciate its soft, soothing caresses.

His mother would have consoled him. 'There, there, poor Herbie,' she would have cooed as she poured the warm milk from the pan into his cup, 'tummy not feeling good again?'

He would sit there silently at the kitchen table, never acknowledging her words. She never seemed to mind, it was what she was used to.

She had died from stomach cancer two years ago. Of course, he had run off to the doctor to have himself checked as soon as she told him of her diagnosis. After a series of exhaustive tests and even more exhaustive payments, he had been proclaimed as clear. But what did doctors know? He knew there was something wrong with him, they just couldn't find it. One day, they would, and he would be proven right.

He took another sip of milk. The tree-lined street was quiet in front of him. 'Quite a nice place to live, Mrs Sinclair.'

His own house was in a long terraced row. He had been born there and was going to die there. He could afford something much better, the genealogy work was rewarding and his costs were as small as his name, but what was the point of moving? After his father had left when he was five, he and his mother had continued living in the house, removing every trace of the other man who had once been there.

There was always just the two of them. Until she had left him too.

He settled down into the old leather of the car, twisting the cap back on the flask to ensure the milk remained warm. It was going to be a long night with only the roaming cats for company, but Herbert didn't mind.

He enjoyed watching, it's what he did best.

Chapter Thirteen

Westminster, London. April 25, 1913.

'There was no need to kick the policeman when he was down.' David Russell leant into her so none of the other passengers could hear. They had leapt onto a tram at the end of the street just as it was pulling away, without looking where it was going. The last thing they had seen from their seats at the top of the tram was a group of policeman running into the street still blowing their whistles like demented football referees.

'Excuse me, it was you who attacked him in the first place.'

'You needed rescuing.'

'I did not…,' she shouted.

The passengers in front of them turned round to stare. He smiled back at them sheepishly, whispering an answer. 'No policeman should treat a woman in such a way, even if she…'

'Even if she is a suffragette?'

'I was about to say, even if she had broken the law. What did you do anyway?'

'I broke a window.'

'Not so bad.'

'It was in the house of the Home Secretary. I threw a brick through the glass.'

'Not so good. The man probably deserved it, but still not so good.'

The heavy tramp of the conductor's boots reverberated up the stairs. 'Tickets, please. Let's be havin' your tickets.'

Rose reached down beside her. Her bag, where was her bag? Then she remembered the policeman's rough hand on her breast and the bag sliding off her shoulder. 'My bag,' she said out loud.

'What?'

'I left my bag back there.' She turned towards him. 'We have to go back. My purse… my money…'

The conductor was standing in front of him with his board. 'Your ticket, miss.'

'Where's the terminus?' David asked.

'This tram's goin' to Smithfield Market.' He looked at them suspiciously. 'Why'd you get on board if you don't know where it's goin'?'

'We're exploring London.' David's accent had changed to the broadest Derbyshire drone.

'Nuthin' to see in Smithfield, 'cept the market.'

'The market it is, then.'

The conductor took out two tickets. 'Four pence each.'

David gave him a shilling and received change plus two tickets. The man moved forward, swaying from side to side with the rhythm of the tram. 'Tickets please, let's be havin' your tickets.'

'Thank you,' whispered Rose, 'I'll pay you back as soon as I can.'

'There's no need.' David waved his hand as if the money were no consequence. 'Just answer me one question. Why on earth were you throwing bricks through the windows of the Home Secretary's house?'

'I'm a suffragette…'

'So I gathered.'

'We were protesting the Cat and Mouse Act…'

'And what's that when it's at home?'

She leant away from him and looked shocked. 'You

don't know?'

He shook his head. 'I really don't know.'

'You don't read the papers?'

'Don't trust them.'

'Neither do I, but I still read them with a critical eye.'

'Not much call for reading in my line of work.'

'Which is…?'

'I thought I was supposed to be asking the questions?'

'You were. But here I am, a young woman sitting next to a strange man whom she has never met before, on the top of a tram…'

As if to confirm its presence the tram lurched and rattled as it crossed some points and turned left. Rose was thrown against David. Quickly she pushed herself away and smoothed down her dress, reaching up to adjust her hat and realising it wasn't there.

'As I was saying, I am sitting next to a man whom I know nothing about. You could be Jack the Ripper for all I know.'

'Old Jack was prowling the streets over 20 years ago. I may look old but I'm not quite so old.'

She laughed.

It was the first time he had seen her laugh and he loved her for it.

'You're staring. Don't you know it's not polite to stare?'

'Sorry, sorry.' He looked down at his hands. Large hands with the scar from the sword vivid on the skin. 'There's not much to say really. I'm a soldier with the Derbyshire Fusiliers, seconded to the War Department. I'm from near Bakewell originally but went to boarding school in the South.'

'Hence the ability to do the accent.'

He nodded. 'And you are?'

She thought for a moment. 'A suffragette, protesting the Cat and Mouse Act by throwing stones through the windows of the Home Secretary.'

'I meant what's your name.'

Again, she paused for a moment before answering, 'When I was in prison, I didn't have a name but a number. 10457. I suppose it was to make me feel less human.'

'You were in prison? You don't seem the type.'

She raised her voice. 'And what type is that?'

The passengers turned and looked at them again.

David shrugged his shoulders and whispered, 'You don't look like a person who belongs in prison.'

'Nobody belongs in prison.'

'Except those who break the law.'

'Who makes the laws?'

David shrugged his shoulders once more. 'Parliament? The Government?'

'And who sits in Parliament?'

'MPs. Members of the Government…'

'Men, all of them.'

'I suppose so.'

'We are half the population of this country, yet we have no vote and we have no say. There is not a single female representative in that august body of men…' She almost spat out the last words in disgust.

'And the Cat and Mouse Act?'

'The latest attempt by the men of Parliament to control us, just as they would control a flock of sheep.'

He looked at her quizzically.

'You really don't know, do you?'

He shook his head.

She sighed. 'We refused food in prison to protest our incarceration, so the authorities began force-feeding. Holding us down and pushing a rubber tube up our nose or into our throat...'

'Did it ever happen to you?'

She shook her head. 'I was lucky.' She played with the edge of her sleeve. 'Others were not. Many suffered horribly, and, of course, forcing women to eat led to an awfully bad press for the men of the government.'

'So they passed the Cat and Mouse Act?'

'They plan to let us starve ourselves, until we are weak and feeble, then release us. A week later, after we eat, we will be re-arrested and forced to serve the rest of our sentence.'

She stared into mid-air, lost in thought.

'If you had been arrested today, what would you have done?'

'I would have been sentenced to three months in Holloway and gone on hunger strike immediately.'

He gestured to her dress. 'But there's nothing of you...'

Their conversation was interrupted by a loud squeal from the brakes of the tram and a shout from the conductor. 'Smithfield Market. This is the market.'

She rose to go. 'I believe this is our stop.'

They both walked down the curved stair of the tram. The conductor was waiting at the bottom. 'Don't get many tourists here.'

He pointed to the hustle and bustle of the market. Merchants yelling the price and quality of their vegetables. Old women in shawls bawling even louder as they bargained for a piece of meat. Two market porters in dirty white coats and hats carrying pigs' carcasses on their backs, bellowing to the crowd to get out of the way. A mongrel squealing as it was kicked by one of the traders. And enveloping it all the stench of fish, rotting vegetables, and people, lots of people.

David soaked in the noise and the colourful stew of meat, fruit, vegetables and mankind.

'Aye, lad, one of seven wonders of t'world. Nowt like it in Derbyshire.'

He hooked Rose's arm in his and stepped down from the platform, walking towards Charterhouse Street.

'Nowt like it in Derbyshire,' she whispered in his ear and laughed, her mouth open and her head thrown back.

God, he thought, how he loved her laughter.

They walked to the edge of the main pavement. 'Thank you for your help, but I have to be going home now.'

'Where do you live?'

She pointed vaguely over her shoulder. 'Over there. Not far.'

'But you have no money, and your clothes...'

For the first time she noticed the policeman had ripped her shirt when he had molested her. Her shoes had come unbuttoned and her skirt was covered in mud. Quickly, she pulled her coat around her to hide the torn shirt. 'Don't worry, my father will fix it, he's a haberdasher, better than my mother with a needle and thread.'

'Let me at least take a cab with you.' He turned and his arm shot into the air. 'Taxi.'

A cab appeared as if out of nowhere and pulled to the side of the road. 'Let me escort you home.'

'I can't... I couldn't.'

'You can't walk home in such a state.'

'Do you wanna a cab or not? Can't wait here all day,' the cabby shouted from behind the wheel.

David opened the back door and ushered Rose into the back.

'Where to, miss?'

'Curtain Road, Shoreditch, please.'

'Here's some money for the fare.' He shoved a ten shilling note into her hand.

'It's far too much.'

'You can pay me back when you see me next.'

'I don't even know your name.'

The cab began to pull away from the kerb.

'Lieutenant David Russell. And yours?'

'Rose, Rose Clarke,' she shouted as the cab pulled away, 'Thank you, Lieutenant Russell.'

The cab pulled out into the traffic and moved away down the road, her face framed in the rear window looking back at him. As he lifted his arm to wave goodbye, he felt something in his inside pocket. The medallion and bows he'd picked up from the street.

He ran after the cab waving his arms in the air. But it was moving down Charterhouse Road quickly, pulling further away with every second.

He looked down at the silver-mounted medallion lying in his hand with its purple, white and green bows.

To Rose from E.

Chapter Fourteen

Rusholme, Manchester. March 29, 2016.

Jayne ran through the entrance of the Tea Hive. Maeve Kennedy was already there enjoying tea and a scone. A young woman in her early thirties, with large spectacles and short blonde hair. The very archetype of the professional woman.

'I'm really sorry, Maeve, one day I'll get my act together.'

'No worries. I'm just enjoying a quiet start. I've a presentation to write for this afternoon, and anything I can do to avoid it is a bonus.'

Jayne indicated the counter. 'Can I get you anything?'

'I'm fine,' she said taking a bite out of her scone.

Jayne ordered a latte from the girl and returned to the table. 'How are you, Maeve?'

The woman held her hand out horizontally and let it wobble.

'Still seeing the psychiatrist?'

'Her? Waste of my time.'

Jayne had first met Maeve four years ago. She was a doctoral student at the University of Manchester. On her way home one evening, she had been attacked and robbed by two young thugs on bicycles. Maeve had been shaking and shivering as Jayne had tried to interview her following the incident, unable to remember much about what had happened.

A week later Jayne had gone round to the address she had been given. The young thugs had been arrested and they needed an identification in a line-up. She had been shocked to discover Maeve in her apartment, the curtains closed and the lights switched off. The young woman was just sitting there staring at the wall. A phone call to the university revealed Maeve hadn't been in to the department since the attack. Hadn't been anywhere at all.

'It takes time, you know, getting over what you endured.'

'It's been four years, Jayne.'

'There's no time limit on it.' The girl came over with her latte and put it down next to her. 'PTSD is not something that's there one moment and cured the next. Talking helps. It's what the psychiatrist is for. Someone to talk to.'

'I'm fine most of the time, just occasionally, when I'm alone in bed at night…' Her voice trailed off.

Jayne nodded. 'For me, it's loud noises. One moment I'm as right as can be, the next I'm a gibbering mess. It meant I couldn't do the work any more.'

'That's why you left the police?'

'After Dave was killed. Useless I was. Six months on leave. Then I went back and two days later resigned. I couldn't risk it, you see. Couldn't risk letting another copper down.'

Maeve took a sip of her tea. 'The psychiatrist says not to blame myself, but I do. I shouldn't have been so stupid, those men…'

'The psychiatrist is right. And those men will be spending another seven years inside. You weren't the only victim.'

Maeve nodded. 'I know, but…'

'It doesn't help?'

'Not much.' Maeve took another sip of tea. 'What are you doing now, if you've left the police?'

'That's what I'm here for. I need to pick your brains.'

'Pick away.'

Jayne pulled out the two envelopes from their acetate folder. She opened up the first envelope and held the medallion and its ribbons in the palm of her hand.

Maeve's eyes lit up. 'Oooh, I haven't seen one of those for a long time.'

'What is it?'

'You don't know?'

Jayne shook her head. 'Haven't a clue. I'm researching the family background of one of my clients and this belonged to his great grandmother.'

Maeve picked up the medallion and read the inscription on the back. 'To Rose from E.'

'Rose was the name of my client's great grandmother.'

Maeve whistled. A strange sound coming from such a quiet academic. 'The inscription confirms it for me. This is a picture of one of Manchester's most famous daughters.'

'Who is it?'

'I'm amazed you don't know, Jayne.'

Chapter Fifteen

Shoreditch, London. May 2, 1913.

The week passed quickly for David Russell in the time following his meeting with Rose Clarke. As a lowly lieutenant, his duties at the War Office were hardly onerous. Mostly they involved escorting visiting dignitaries into meetings with illustrious personages such as Lord Kitchener. That week, a delegation from the General Staff of the German High Command had been paying one of their visits.

The Germans were so much easier to handle than the French. At least they were always punctual.

All week as he escorted the various stubble-haired Germans through the long corridors from meeting to meeting, David had carried the medallion and its ribbons in his jacket pocket, a constant reminder of Rose and her smile.

On Saturday, a day off for him when so many others were working, he dressed in his best Anderson and Sheppard suit and set off for Curtain Road. He didn't know exactly where she lived but thought it shouldn't be too difficult to find. He asked the porter in his club to call a taxi and waited just inside for the man to come and fetch him.

At this time in the morning, just after 10.30, the club was empty, the only sounds the gentle swish of the pendulum of the grandfather clock and the soft scratch of the concierge's pen in his ledger.

The porter arrived and David deposited sixpence in his hand. 'Where shall I tell him you're going, sir?'

'Curtain Road, Shoreditch.'

'Are you sure, sir? Not many people go near that end of town at this time in the morning.'

'I'm sure,' David said firmly.

The young porter shrugged his shoulders. 'Right you are, sir.'

The same questions were repeated by the cabbie. 'Are you sure you wanna go 'dere, sir?'

What was wrong with these men? 'Of course I am, just take me,' he snapped.

The cabbie also shrugged, put the car in gear and double de-clutched to move the taxi forward.

David had just learnt to drive in Derbyshire last year, so he watched each move of the cabbie with interest. The casual way he drove with his left hand resting on the gear stick, the eyes flicking up every few seconds to check the rear view mirror, the casual adjustment of the pace of the vehicle as it approached each junction.

'Do you drive, sir?'

'Learnt last year in the country.'

'Different from driving in London, sir.'

'It does seem so.'

'You gots to keep yer eyes open in London. Them pedestrians are the worst, always crossing the road without a care in the world...'

As if hearing the cabbie speak, an old man stepped off the pavement in front of him. The cabbie reached out and squeezed the horn, causing the old man to look up in surprise and jump back with all the agility of a 20-year-old.

'I do likes to give 'em a fright, sir. Only bit of amusement I gets, sir.'

'What make of car is this?'

'It's a Unic four cylinder, type C9, 14 horsepower, brand new, sir. Them frogs knows how to build a cab. Faster than an 'oss, sir. And you don't have to feed it oats. But expensive to run, sir. You don't know the money I have to pay out. Only last week…'

David switched off as the driver talked in detail about some obscure engine part. Would he be able to find Rose? And if he did, would she be pleased to see him?

For the last week, her face had continually popped into his mind at the most inopportune moments. He had been so distracted, he spilt tea on the uniform of a German general. Another time, he lost his way in the labyrinthine corridors of the War Ministry whilst escorting a group of staff officers. Luckily, they didn't realise he had led them astray.

He had to find her again, even if she told him to go away. At least then, he would know he had tried. He took out the medallion once more and looked at it. The stern face stared back at him. His excuse for going to her home was to return this to her. Not much of an excuse, he knew.

The cab screeched to a halt.

'Curtain Road, it is, sir. Don't normally take toffs like yourself to places like this. You want me to wait?'

'No, this is fine.' He handed over the fare and added a shilling as a tip, receiving an extravagant salute in return from the driver.

David stepped out of the cab. Which way should he go? The road stretched endlessly to both right and left. Rose had given him a clue when she said her father was a haberdasher. He must have a shop somewhere along here. But, he hadn't realised the road was so long. She could be anywhere on it.

The cab pulled away in a haze of blue fumes pouring from the exhaust. He looked up into the sky. The sun was a faded yellow glow behind a mist of coal smoke. It was fairly high in the sky, if he headed to his right he would be going away from town, to his left, towards town.

People were everywhere, out for their Saturday morning shopping. Most were poorly dressed in the roughest of clothes. A few stared at him rudely as he decided which way to go. One man, a rough-looking fellow in a cap and homespun trousers looked him up and down.

'Ye wan' anyfing?'

David ignored him.

The man persisted. 'Wha' ye wan'?'

David turned to face his questioner. 'I'm looking for Clarke's Haberdashery. Do you know where it is?'

The man nudged another thug standing next to him. 'Bert, 'ark at 'im. Clarke's? Never 'eard of it, chum.'

His mate touched a bent finger to his forelock. 'Dahn that a way, sir. But the likes of you won't find nuffin' 'dere. It's not what you might call a gentleman's place.'

David lifted his hat. 'Thank you anyway.'

He headed east, the way the man had pointed, away from town.

The further he went away from the centre of the city, the thicker the crowds became, and the more shabbily dressed. On each side of the road, he passed small alleyways leading to vast tenements. These must be the infamous Shoreditch rookeries. Areas full of thieves and vagabonds, where no police were allowed to enter.

Outside each one, young men lounged against the walls smoking. A few stared at him as he walked past, obviously wondering what a man dressed like him was doing in such a place.

He walked for 15 minutes and still the road stretched to the east. He was about to stop and turn around when he saw a large painted sign over a shop with two mannequins in the window. One was of a man and the other a woman.

Both were dressed in clothes fashionable in the old queen's reign. The sign said Clarke's in a golden cursive script. Beneath the name was the description: *Ladies' Haberdashery and Gentlemen's Outfitters. Founded 1890.*

The shop was cleaner and smarter than the rest in its row, with a new awning sheltering passers-by from the rain or occasional sun.

He crossed the street, took a deep breath and opened the door. A bell above his head rang.

The shop was empty.

Then, out of nowhere, popped a thin man wearing a bowler hat with a tape measure draped around his neck. 'Good morning, sir. How may I help you?' he asked in a pronounced European accent.

David hadn't prepared for this. He had imagined walking into the shop and seeing Rose there. She would immediately recognise him and they would begin to talk. But this wasn't the lovely Rose, but a rather plain old man with a walrus moustache and an extravagant bowler hat.

'How may I help you?' the man repeated.

'D-Do you sell ladies' gloves?' David blurted out. He didn't know why he asked for them. It was the first thing that popped into his mind.

'Of course, sir. Leather, cotton or silk?'

Leather, cotton or silk? Which one? He didn't know. 'Leather,' he finally said.

The man looked at him strangely. 'Rose, could you bring the ladies' leather gloves to me, please.'

A voice from the back answered immediately, 'Brown or black, Father?'

'Brown or black, sir?' the man repeated as if David had been unable to hear the words.

'Black, I think.'

'Or would you like to look at both, sir?'

David pretended to think. 'No, just the black will be fine.'

'Please bring the black ladies' gloves, Rose.'

'Yes, Fath…'

She stepped out from behind a curtain at the end of the shop carrying a wooden box filled with black ladies' gloves.

David took off his hat and made a small bow. 'Good morning, Miss Clarke.'

The father looked from Rose and back to David. 'You know this gentlemen, Rose?'

She recovered herself quickly from the shock of seeing David in her shop. 'This is Mr Russell, father. He was the kind gentleman I told you about. The one who escorted me away from the trouble last Sunday.'

The man came out from behind the counter and shook David's hand. 'Thank you very much, sir. I am most thankful. The police can be extremely rough with the demonstrators these days.'

David looked surprised as the man shook his hand.

'Don't be shocked, Mr Russell, my father is supportive of my activities in the movement.'

'Indeed I am,' said her father still shaking David's hand, 'Rose's mother, God rest her soul, would be proud of her daughter, as is her father. It is only right women should have the vote as well as men, don't you agree, sir?'

Rose stared at David. 'Father always supports me going on demonstrations, don't you Father?'

'Of course, Rose, but I don't agree with the planting of bombs in letter boxes and throwing stones through windows. That's going too far, far too far.' He glanced across at his daughter. 'After the last time, Rose promised me no more of those shenanigans, didn't you, Rose? All demonstrations should be peaceful, don't you agree, Mr Russell?'

The man finally let go of David's hand. 'I don't know what to think, Mr Clarke.' He patted the inside pocket of his jacket. 'I actually came to return this to your daughter.' He pulled out the silver medallion and the ribbons. 'She dropped it when the policeman attacked her.'

'Oh, bless you, sir. It's Rose's medallion, given to her by Mrs Pankhurst, her prize possession.'

David passed the medallion to Rose.

'Thank you, Mr Russell, it's kind of you to take the trouble to return it to me.'

'It's no trouble, Miss Clarke, it's the least I could do. And, whilst I'm here, let me buy some of your wonderful leather gloves. For my mother, of course.'

As he was speaking, the bell above the door rang again and an old man stepped into the shop.

'Please serve Mr Russell, Rose, whilst I deal with this customer.'

Rose placed the box on the counter. David walked over and pretended to sort through the gloves.

'How did you find me?' she whispered.

'You told the cabbie the name of your road, it was easy to find a shop with your surname.'

'You are too bold, Mr Russell,' she whispered before raising her head and saying, 'Perhaps this pair would suit your mother, Mr Russell. It's calf skin from Ireland.'

David smiled. Out loud he said, 'I'm afraid my mother's hands are much larger.' Turning his face away from her father, he whispered. 'I'm a soldier, remember? I'm meant to be bold.'

'But coming into the shop?'

'I wanted to see you again.'

'Perhaps this size would suit her better?' Rose shouted so her father could hear. The man looked up from serving his customer and smiled.

'Perfect, Miss Clarke.' David wasn't looking at the gloves but at Rose.

'Are you sure, Mr Russell? They might be a little tight for your mother.' She leant in and whispered once more. 'You're embarrassing me.'

'I didn't mean to, Rose.'

'You shouldn't have come.'

The father appeared beside them 'Don't worry, see if they fit your mother. If they are too small, just return them and we'll find a bigger size.'

'Sounds perfect, Mr Clarke. I'll take them.'

'Very good, Lieutenant Russell. Please wrap them for the customer, Rose.'

Rose glared at him but began to wrap the gloves. 'That will be 30 shillings.'

David fished for the money in his wallet, finally finding two notes and giving them to Rose.

The father handed over the wrapped parcel. 'I do hope your mother likes the gloves, Mr Russell. They are made by the late Queen's glove maker in Dublin. Wonderful quality even if I do say so myself. Now, remember to bring them back if they are too small.'

'I will, Mr Clarke, and I thank yourself and your daughter for your excellent service.'

'And I thank you, Mr Russell, for the service you did my daughter. Women must have the vote, Mr Russell, and we must help them in any way we can, don't you agree?'

David bowed slightly in the direction of Rose and placed his hat on his head and the parcel of gloves under his arm.

'Come again, if they are too small.'

So David went back the following week. And the week after. And the week after that. He hadn't meant to of course. But he found Rose's face and smile haunted his thoughts.

At first, she wasn't pleased to see him, positively cold in her attitude. But gradually, she warmed up, until he realised she began to look forward to his Saturday morning visits almost as much as he enjoyed making them.

The father always seemed pleased to see him, especially as each time he bought something new for his mother, gradually building up a whole cabinet of ladies' accessories in his room at the club. Anybody finding them there would have thought he was quite peculiar.

One day, he summoned up all his courage. Over a tray of tortoiseshell hair clips, he finally asked her. 'Would you like to go for tea with me tomorrow?'

'I'm afraid I'm busy,' she whispered.

'All day?'

She nodded. 'Haven't you read the news?'

'Remember, I never read the papers.'

She snorted. 'You don't know about Emily Davison's death?'

Her father looked up from serving a customer.

'Who is she?' asked David.

'A suffragette, killed by the King's horse at Epsom. Her memorial service is tomorrow at St George's. We have arranged a procession to escort her hearse to the station for the last journey to her home in Morpeth.'

'Can I escort you to the procession?'

Rose smiled and lifted her head. 'Father, Mr Russell would like to escort me to the funeral procession tomorrow.'

'I feel your daughter needs protection… just in case the

police attack again, Mr Clarke.'

The man looked up from serving his customer. 'My daughter needs no protection, Mr Russell, but she, and other women, need support.'

Rose looked at David. 'There you have it, Mr Russell. Will you give me, and the other women, your support tomorrow?'

David smiled. 'Of course, Miss Clarke, you will always have my support.'

Chapter Sixteen

Rusholme, Manchester. March 29, 2016.

Maeve held the medallion up to show Jayne the woman's picture. 'I thought you would have recognised Emmeline Pankhurst.'

'Votes for women and all that?'

'The one and only. And you see the colours of the ribbons?'

'Purple, white and green.'

'These colours appear on all of the suffragettes' emblems. I forget what they're supposed to represent. Purple was dignity, white purity and green was hope, I think.'

'So, let me get this right, my client's great grandmother was a suffragette?'

Maeve nodded. 'Probably. These medallions are extremely rare. I've only seen one other like it, in the Museum of London. It was probably given to her for a service she had performed.'

'Such as…?'

'Such as being imprisoned, or arrested. Or worst of all, being one of their hunger strikers.'

'Why do you say "worst of all"?'

'The government of the day instituted force-feeding for many of the women. A tube was inserted up into their nostrils and soup poured down it into their stomachs. Many suffered lasting trauma for years afterwards, both physical and mental. It makes our PTSD look like a walk in the park.'

'Don't do that.'

'Don't do what?'

'Don't minimise your suffering. Listen Maeve, you were the victim of a horrendous attack. Nothing and nobody, least of all you, should ever trivialise your suffering. Do you understand?'

Maeve nodded.

'There's something else troubling me about my client's great grandmother, Rose Clarke. I can't find her on the census. She may have been outside London, I guess. Or travelling. But somehow I doubt it.'

'I can help you there. Many of the women boycotted the census. Their slogan was "I don't count so I won't be counted". Some spoiled their papers with slogans such as "No persons here, only women!"; they gave their occupations as "suffragette", and listed their "disenfranchisement" in a column headed "Infirmity". There was even a mass demonstration in Trafalgar Square against completing the form.'

'So our Rose Clarke could have been one of those women?'

'Possibly.' Maeve looked at the medallion, turning it over to read the inscription once again. 'I will tell you though, this Rose was an extremely brave and determined woman.'

'Not the sort to end up in an asylum for the rest of her life?'

'These women were angry, not mad.'

Jayne put the medallion back in its envelope and unfolded the drawing of the young woman from the other envelope.

She passed it over to Maeve who adjusted her glasses and stared at the picture. 'Who is she?'

'I don't know. I was going to ask you the same question. This drawing is one of the only possessions left by my client's great grandmother.'

Maeve turned the picture over. 'Doesn't say who she is. Could be anybody.' She brought the picture closer to her face. 'Is she wearing a uniform? Can't recognise it, if she is.'

'Did the suffragettes wear a uniform?'

'I don't think so. There were many different organisations involved in the fight for women's suffrage, Emmeline Pankhurst was the head of the most militant section. The Woman's Social and Political Union.'

'Most militant?'

Maeve laughed. 'They were the ones who planted bombs in letter boxes, chained themselves to railings and smashed windows.'

'Proper little anarchists.'

'They were committed to the cause and prepared to fight for it. Funny thing is, today we don't remember all the women who protested peacefully, we just remember those who broke the law.'

'So you don't recognise this woman?'

Maeve laughed again. 'Sounds like the sort of thing you asked me four years ago in the identity parade.'

'You remember?'

Maeve put the picture down and picked up her cup of tea. Jayne noticed her hands were shaking as she brought the cup to her mouth. 'I remember it every day of my life, Jayne. But to answer your question, no, I don't recognise her.'

Jayne took that moment to put the drawing back in its envelope. Maeve slowly sipped her tea.

'You should make an appointment to see the psychiatrist again. She could help, you know.'

Maeve looked over the top of her cup. Her eggshell blue

eyes were clear and piercing. 'And you, Jayne, do you still see your counsellor?'

Jayne shook her head. 'I don't need her any more.

'Are you so sure?'

Chapter Seventeen

Buckingham Palace Road, London. June 14, 1913.

The mood was sombre as the women assembled to form the cortege at Emily Davison's funeral. David had taken a taxi to Shoreditch that morning to pick up Rose from her father's shop. She was waiting outside dressed in white with a purple sash across her right shoulder.

'I'm glad you've come,' she said as he approached her.

'I said I would support you, so here I am.'

They both jumped into the back of the waiting taxi.

'Is this your uniform?'

'Not really. I'm to be one of the women walking behind the bier with the coffin. Emmeline has asked us all to dress in white.'

'A strange colour for a funeral.'

'But not a strange colour for a suffragette.'

The taxi weaved its way through the streets of London, packed with shoppers as it always was on a Saturday at midday.

Rose was in a quiet mood, staring out of the window at the crowds.

'Did you know Emily Davison well?'

'I met her a few times at meetings and she was in prison at the same time as I was. A quiet, intense woman, born in the north of England. She didn't talk much. A doer not a talker.'

'Was she on hunger strike?'

'Nine times, I believe. Emmeline told me they force-fed her more than 30 times.'

'A brave woman.'

'More than brave, I think.'

She lapsed into silence again. The taxi turned onto Buckingham Palace Road. They could see the funeral procession already beginning to form. Horses were being jostled into position. Women dressed in white assembled. A row of clergy, robes blowing in the breeze, were being chivvied into their place behind the coffin by a tiny woman wearing an immense hat. A funeral of undertakers marched past in a column, and everywhere, purple, white and green flowers, strewn on lorries, in the manes of horses, and lying in piles along the side of the road.

'You can stop here,' Rose told the taxi driver. David paid the driver and they stepped out.

Rose took David by the arm. 'Come on, I'll introduce you to Emmeline.'

'Mrs Pankhurst? Are you sure?'

'Of course, she'd love to meet our latest supporter, come on.'

Rose hustled a reluctant David across the road to where a tall, elegantly dressed woman was barking rapid orders to a crowd of white-robed women.

'Mary, have you checked if the London delegation is ready?'

'Rachel, do tell the Reverend Baumgarten where he needs to stand when we reach St. George's.'

'Helen, have you passed out the Madonna Lilies yet?'

The tall woman spotted Rose in the crowd, waved and beckoned her forward.

Rose edged through the crowd, holding David's arm tightly.

'You're a little late, Rose.'

'Sorry, Emmeline, the traffic was heavy.'

The voice was patrician and commanding. 'Well, dear, now you're here, you need to find Miss Tyson. You're in section D, walking in front of the hearse.' Emmeline Pankhurst finally appeared to notice David. 'And who do we have here?'

'Mrs Pankhurst, let me introduce our latest supporter, Lieutenant David Russell.'

The tall woman held out a gloved hand. David didn't know whether he was supposed to kiss it or shake it. He decided the latter was probably the correct course of action and took the gloved fingers gently in his own hand.

Mrs Pankhurst stared down at him. 'Russell, you wouldn't be one of the Holton Hall Russells, would you?'

'Lord Lappiter is my father, Mrs Pankhurst.'

Rose stared at him directly, her eyebrows raised.

'A lovely man, your father, and a wonderful botanist. You know he sends the Manchester branch ten pounds every year to support our work.'

David was surprised. 'I didn't know...' he stammered.

'Your mother however, is not a friend of the cause. I asked for her help three years ago and she rejected me quite rudely.'

'My mother is a law unto herself.'

'Hmmm,' was Mrs Pankhurst's reply, 'well, at least you are taking after your father.' She checked the programme in her hand. 'Supporters walk in Section J under Miss Virtue, a woman whose name describes her perfectly.' She held out her hand once more. 'I hope we meet again, Lieutenant Russell, and please give my regards to your father.'

She turned away to bark more instructions at the women dressed in white.

Rose led him away. 'You didn't tell me you were a Lord,' she whispered.

'I'm not, my father is.'

'You should have told me.'

'I wanted to but it was never the right time.'

A woman waved her arm and shouted at Rose. 'You're in my section, Rose, we're ready to move.'

'We need to talk, later...' she said as she ran off to take her place at the front of the procession.

Within a few minutes, the funeral cortege had formed itself into a coherent organisation and begun to move off.

At the front, a large banner read 'Fight on and God will give the victory.' This was followed by sections of women dressed in white carrying a single flower, each separated by carriages filled with purple, white and green blooms. The clergy came next, their robes still blowing in the wind.

David saluted as the hearse passed him, its pale wood draped with a suffragette flag and festooned with more blooms. Following it was Mrs Pankhurst herself, head erect, walking proudly, surrounded by what David presumed were Emily Davison's relatives. Above them another banner proclaimed 'Dulce et decorum est pro patria mori.'

A woman walked past and put a programme of the day's events into David's hands. At the top, a headline in block capitals: 'SHE DIED FOR WOMEN' and at the bottom a quote David recognised from the bible: 'Greater love hath no man than this, that he lay down his life for his friends.' The procession itself was ordered with military precision. Indeed, David believed the trooping of the colour itself was not as well organised.

The procession drifted past him, more women walking behind the hearse, some in white, some in black, others wearing their university gowns.

Crowds had already begun to form at the side of the street; policemen lined up to clear the way on either side.

A woman at the head of one of the sections in the rear waved at David. 'Lieutenant Russell, cooeee, Lieutenant Russell.'

David walked over to her as she marched at the head of her section.

'Mrs Pankhurst said you were to join my group.'

'It would be my honour, Miss Virtue.'

The elderly woman blushed a bright crimson. 'As you can see there are a lot of us today.'

'More than I thought.'

'Mrs Pankhurst wanted to make it a special occasion. It's a wonderful sight, don't you agree?'

'I do, Miss Virtue, a wonderful sight.'

David let himself drop back to join the rest of the mourners behind Miss Virtue. There were a mixture of men and women from all social classes, but all with their heads held up, walking proudly in the procession.

As they marched through Piccadilly and down Shaftesbury Avenue, the crowds on either side increased, sometimes swamping the policemen with their numbers. At one point, the watchers were standing ten deep on either side of the road. Most, if not all, were men, jostling with each other to get a better view of the women as they marched behind the hearse. A few shouted obscenities, but most were intent on seeing these strange creatures who were fighting for the right to vote.

David ignored these men, finding a strange camaraderie in being in the group with Miss Virtue. People didn't talk much, respecting the solemnity of the occasion, but there was a sense of unity and purpose. It was as if he were marching in a parade with his men, all together, all united as one; an army on the march.

As they neared St George's Church, the crowds became

even more numerous, breaking through the police cordon and stumbling into the paths of the mourners.

David's section halted as the coffin was removed from the hearse and carried by the undertakers into the church. He saw Rose and waved.

She didn't wave back.

The rest of the day passed in a blur for David. He waited outside while the service was in progress, casually smoking a cigarette. After half an hour, the coffin was carried out of the church and remounted on its bier.

The procession formed up once more and moved off through Bloomsbury to King's Cross where the coffin was to board a train to Morpeth in Northumbria.

The crowds became even denser, shoving the police as they spilled out from the pavement. The mourners, though, just carried on walking behind the hearse, heads held high.

When the coffin was finally unloaded and carried through an honour guard of white-robed women into King's Cross, David went looking for Rose. He found her sitting all alone on a bench.

'It was a moving occasion. The women should be proud,' he said.

Rose looked up at him. 'We are.'

He sat down beside her. 'What's the matter, Rose?'

She thought for a moment before speaking, her teeth pulling at the skin of her bottom lip. 'Why didn't you tell me you were the son of a Lord?'

'I was going to, Rose, but it never came up, or it never seemed the right time.'

'You kept coming to my father's shop, buying things for your mother, was it all just a joke? A silly tale you could tell your friends and laugh about at our expense?'

'Of course it wasn't.'

'But why, why did you keep coming?'

'I thought it was obvious, Rose.'

'But why me? I'm just a shopgirl from Shoreditch.'

He took hold of her hand. 'To me, you're much more than that, you're Rose, my Rose.'

'But we're so different, from different backgrounds, different lives, different everything.'

He looked down at his hand holding hers. 'There's just you and me, Rose and David. Two people, who have become more than friends, who support each other. Whatever you face, I will face. For good or ill, in happiness or sadness, come riches or poverty. All we should have together is the deepest joy.'

Rose smiled. 'You're not a common kind of soldier, are you, Lieutenant Russell?'

David noticed the time on the station clock. 'We should be off. Your father will begin to worry.' He stood up and hailed a taxi.

On the short drive back to Shoreditch, they held each other's hand out of sight of the driver, enjoying the closeness between them and the absence of any necessity to speak. As they got closer to Curtain Road, it was David who finally spoke. 'I meant every word I said tonight..'

She just nodded. 'I know, it's just neither of us can escape out pasts, it's who we are and where we came from.'

'It's not our pasts I'm interested in, it's our future…'

He began to say more, but she placed her finger across his mouth to stop him. 'Let's just enjoy being together for now.'

And with those words, she rested her head on his shoulder, leaving it there until the cab jerked to a stop outside her father's shop on Curtain Road.

Chapter Eighteen

Bakewell, Derbyshire. March 29, 2016.

'I'm a busy man, Mr Small, what do you want to see me about?'

Eamon Dunphy hadn't greeted him when he was shown into the man's office. There was no offer of tea or biscuits. No preliminary chat to make him feel at ease. Dunphy just carried on writing without looking up. Well, two could play at that game.

Herbert Small took off his hat and unwound the scarf from around his throat. He always wore one when he travelled out into the countryside, one couldn't be too careful these days. He paused for a moment before saying, 'Would you like to save millions of pounds, Mr Dunphy?'

The man stopped writing and looked up. 'And I suppose you're going to tell me exactly how I can save the money?'

'I am, Mr Dunphy. And I will need more than 15 minutes to do it.'

The property developer sat back in his leather executive chair, bought by his wife for a small fortune.

Herbert Small took off his coat, laying it next to his hat and scarf on the couch. He sat down opposite the property developer. 'My name is Herbert Small...'

'I already know.'

Herbert continued anyway, '...I specialise in genealogical investigations on the unclaimed estates list.'

'What's it to do with me?'

'You have an interest in Holton Hall, I believe?'

'It's no secret, I'm planning to develop the site. People

are looking to escape the cities and return to a quieter, safer, more rural way of life. I offer them a chance to enjoy a rural lifestyle with all the amenities of a city.'

'You have spent a lot of money on your plans, Mr Dunphy. Four million pounds is the figure I heard.'

The skin around Dunphy's eyes tightened and a growl entered his voice. 'That information is confidential, Mr Small, how did you...?'

'My sources do not matter, Mr Dunphy. What matters is you are about to lose everything you have invested so far.'

Eamon Dunphy sat forward. Herbert knew he had his attention now. Money was always the clincher for these kind of people.

'But before I tell you my story, I wonder if your secretary could make me a pot of warm milk. It was such a long drive out to see you here today.'

Chapter Nineteen

Manchester Airport. March 29, 2016.

'Did you wait long?' Paul gave his wife a hug. He had put on weight in his time in Brussels.

'Not too long.'

'I had to wait ages for the bags. Two flights just came in from the Canaries. I was surrounded by drunken suntanned people, wearing white vests and tattoos. I often wonder what the poor Spanish must think of us.'

'I think they probably see the wallet rather than the person.'

Her husband attempted another hug. Strangely, she was glad to see him, realising she had missed him the last couple of months. She attempted to pick up his bag, but he took her hand instead. Together, they walked to the car park.

'How long are you here for?'

'Trying to get rid of me already?'

Why did it have to start like this? The constant bickering between the two of them. She remembered when she loved him. When they were first married, they had spent all their time together, resenting the intrusion of others into their lives. And when she had been on leave from the police, after Dave's death, Paul had been her rock. Listening to her, caring for her, holding her. It was as if he preferred her dependent on him, not an individual with her own wants and needs.

She put some coins in the car park machine. 'You didn't need to be so blunt.'

'I've only just arrived and you're asking when I'm leaving.'

'I didn't mean it like that.'

A silence descended between them as they walked to the car and it continued as they drove home. It was another thing that annoyed her about him. The constant melodrama. He always knew how to turn a drama into a crisis. Jayne blamed his mother. A diva if ever she saw one. His mother hadn't been amused when Paul had announced he was going to marry a lowly copper. Oh no, her beloved son deserved somebody far better and far more refined than a bloody plod.

Of course, the old harridan hadn't come out and said it as such, but she had insinuated it in so many ways. Ways in which Paul, blind to her faults, could not possibly see. The old witch had passed away five years ago, so she shouldn't speak ill of the dead, but if her grave was in Manchester, not down south, Jayne would have gone once a year to dance on it.

He finally broke the silence as they neared the house. 'As you're interested, I'm here until Monday. I've a meeting with a prospective client in London on Friday; I may be up for a promotion. But the weekend is free. I was thinking we could spend it together. In London. Take in a few shows, eat at a few good restaurants. Just the two of us, like it used to be.'

Jayne thought of her client. They had till next Tuesday to discover the truth about his great grandmother. After then, the inheritance would pass to the crown. 'Sounds like a plan,' she finally answered, 'but I have a client at the moment...'

'Another one of your bloody genealogy clients? It's not a job, Jayne, it's a hobby.'

She gripped the wheel tighter. Why was he so discouraging about the work she loved? 'It is a job. It's my job.'

'Look, Jayne, trust me, looking into people's past lives is not a proper job. You'd miss the chance of a weekend in London, just to research someone's family tree?'

'I promised I would finish by next Tuesday…'

'The family isn't going anywhere. If it's an old ancestor, they'll still be dead next Tuesday, whatever you come up with.'

She glanced across at him, anger burning in her eyes. 'So your work matters and mine doesn't?'

He put his hand on her shoulder. 'Jayne, it's just we don't see each other often and now we have a chance to spend a weekend together in London. Doesn't your husband deserve a little time with you?'

There it was again. His poor little-boy voice. God, it annoyed her. She didn't answer him, just stared at the road ahead, her fingers gripping the wheel tightly.

Chapter Twenty

Didsbury, Manchester. March 29, 2016.

Jayne was alone in the kitchen, Paul had gone to bed in the spare room.

They had decided to go for a meal in Azzurro on Burton Road, and all had been well, they had chatted inconsequentially for most of the meal, both ignoring the one subject they knew they had to talk about.

It was Paul who broached it as the limoncello arrived. 'Where are we going with this, Jayne?'

There it was, the question both of them had been avoiding all evening. It was time for her to be honest. 'I don't know. I thought I would know when I saw you, but I didn't.'

'Have you missed me at all?'

It was the time for truth. 'I've missed you being around the house and going for meals and…'

'But have you missed me?' he interrupted.

Why was she such a coward about these things? Why did she avoid telling him? In her professional life, she prized honesty above everything. She'd had no problems telling a colleague he was an arsehole when she was in the police. She had no difficulty telling a client the truth, so why did she avoid it now?

Paul was looking straight at her, waiting for an answer.

'I've been so busy recently, what with the new case and tying up all the loose ends on the Hughes investigation…'

Paul smiled. 'I think you've given me my answer.'

The walk home had been made in silence. Inside the house, Paul had stretched, yawned and said, 'I'm off to bed, lots to do tomorrow. I think it's best if I sleep in the spare room, don't you?'

Before she could answer, he had already launched himself up the stairs.

She sat in front of her computer for a long while, staring into mid-air, before the loud miaows of Mr Smith, begging to be let out, brought her back to the present.

She opened the patio door and he hurried out, desperate to be away from the house. If only it were as easy for her, she thought.

She went back and switched on the computer. While it booted up, she poured herself a glass of water. No wine, not tonight.

Something Maeve had said stuck in her mind. If Rose had been a member of the WSPU, the militant arm of the suffrage movement, perhaps she had been arrested at some time in the past?

She logged onto Find My Past and immediately went into the courts and legal section, typing in Rose Clarke's name. As she waited for the results to appear, she thought about the certainties of research. Everything was cut and dry; either there was a record or there wasn't. So unlike the problems of being married. Here, she was always bedevilled with the unpredictability of other people, the difficulty of understanding what somebody else wanted. She would have to tell her father what had happened tomorrow, he would know what to do.

Two results appeared for a Rose Clarke before 1914. Jayne clicked on the first in 1912 and then on the icon of a camera on the far right. After a few seconds a page from an old ledger appeared on her screen. Rose's name was in the left column in the middle of a group of other women, some arrested for similar offences, others for theft or prostitution.

Her age was given as 19 so this was definitely the Rose Clarke she was looking for. Jayne read the rest of the details on the prison sheet.

Name:	**Rose Clarke, 19, shop assistant**
Education:	**V11**
Magistrate:	**H. M. Bennett. Bow St Police Ct.**
Warrant:	**March 2, 1912.**
Custody date:	**March 2, 1912.**
Offence:	**Maliciously damaging one glass window, the property of Philip Dunne, to the amount of 15 pounds.**
Trial Judge:	**L. Wallace Esq., March 13, 1912.**
Verdict:	**Guilty**
Sentence:	**Three months imprisonment inside Holloway Prison. (Sentence to start from March 5, 1912.)**

'Well, well, Miss Clarke, you were a militant. But I'm sure Holloway wasn't easy jail time in those days.'

She went back to Find My Past and clicked the second result. Another prison record appeared, much like the first.

Name:	**Rose Clarke, 21, shop assistant**
Education:	**V11**
Magistrate:	**R. T Alderson, Esq.**
Warrant:	**May 22, 1914.**
Custody date:	**May 22, 1914.**
Offence:	**Obstructing an on-duty officer, Constable M. Talon in the course of his duty.**

Trial Judge:	**P Creichton Esq. May 29, 1914.**
Verdict:	**Guilty**
Sentence:	**Six months imprisonment inside Holloway Prison. (Sentence to start from May 25, 1914.)**

Jayne smiled. Obstruction. The classic police charge when an offender couldn't be charged with anything else. Standing in front of a policeman was obstruction. Breathing whilst in front of a policeman was obstruction. Anything was obstruction as long as it was said to be obstruction by the police. It was a great Catch 22 of a charge.

Jayne checked the sentence once more. Six months. They must have wanted to teach her a lesson.

She opened another window and typed in the date of the offence and the word 'suffragette'. An article from the Daily Mirror appeared, accompanied by photographs, dated May 22, 1914. It was a special edition, priced at one halfpenny. The headline shouted out in bold capitals:

MRS PANKHURST ARRESTED AT THE GATES OF BUCKINGHAM PALACE IN TRYING TO PRESENT A PETITION TO THE KING.

Jayne checked out the pictures. A police horse and constables pushing into the crowd had a caption beneath saying 'Forcing back the women at Constitution Hill.' Another had a woman on her back lying on the ground. 'Suffragette faints after a scuffle', but it looked to Jayne like she had been hit over the head rather than having fainted. The third picture had a burly copper with both his arms around an older woman, and a plain clothes detective wearing a natty straw hat, holding on to her arm. The caption read 'Chief Inspector Rolfe arrests Mrs Pankhurst.'

Jayne looked closely at the woman in the picture. She was sure it was the same woman on the medallion. It was Emmeline Pankhurst.

'Maeve was right. Perhaps there's more,' she said out loud. She looked up from the screen, suddenly aware she was talking to herself. The only answer was the slow ticking of the clock. 1.30 in the morning.

One last search.

She typed 'Rose Clarke, suffragette' into Google. As ever, the time of the result was trumpeted with pride. 0.17 seconds.

If only all her searches were as quick. She scanned the results. Most seemed to be mentions in academic books for active suffragettes at the time. But then she noticed a Google Images result.

She clicked on the page and a picture of a single dishevelled woman dressed in rough linen and a white apron with dark prison arrows on it appeared.

The photograph was taken from a distance, but, despite the roughness of the clothes, Jayne could see the pride, bearing and defiance in the posture.

The caption read, 'Surveillance picture of Rose Clarke, suffragette, taken in the exercise yard of Holloway Prison, 1912.'

Jayne clapped her hand across her mouth. 'Oh, my God.' Quickly, she scrambled for the acetate file. She opened the envelope inside and took out the pencil drawing. It was her. The drawing was definitely Rose Clarke. But a happier, more contented woman, not the gaunt, sad, prisoner in the surveillance photograph.

Jayne stared at the picture for a long time, drawn to the

strength in the woman's eyes.

She was going to find out what happened to Rose Clarke, with or without the help of the Russells. She owed this woman something for all she had suffered in her fight for other women. Even now, over 100 years later, Jayne felt she could still right the wrongs of the past. It was why she did what she did.

Chapter Twenty-One

Holloway Prison, London. July 23, 1914.

David walked through the gates of the prison carrying his bouquet of flowers. It was Rose's birthday today and he desperately wanted to talk to her before he returned to his regiment in the North. He had visited her every Saturday morning since her imprisonment. His commanding officer didn't approve, but he didn't care. Rose meant more to him than anything, including his career in the army.

The iron doors slammed behind him. The place smelt of boiled cabbage and humans, lots of humans. A male warder rattled a large bunch of keys and let him into a waiting area, full of men and children. Some of the men were smoking, others reading newspapers, still more just sitting staring into mid-air, a lost look in their eyes.

He sat down on a rough wooden bench against the wall as he had done every weekend since Rose had been imprisoned.

He had asked her, pleaded with her, not to go to the demonstration outside Buckingham Palace.

'They're going to be waiting for you there.'

'We know.'

'They want to make an example of you all. Teach you a lesson. The papers have all been asked to be there with photographers.'

'We know. But how do you know?'

David threw up his hands. 'A demonstration outside Buckingham Palace and you don't think the army will be warned? It's a set-up, Rose, you're all going to be arrested.'

Rose looked down. 'We know.'

'And you're still going?'

'I have to, Mrs Pankhurst wants me to be with her.'

'And what about me, don't I have a say in this?'

Rose looked back up at him, her eyes burning with anger. 'David, I have to go. You promised me your support; now is the time to deliver your promise.'

'Of course, I support votes for women, but…'

'There are no buts, David.'

It was his turn to look down. 'You know I can't be with you, Rose, as a soldier, not outside the Palace.'

She took his hands in hers. 'I know, but I have to go. Mrs Pankhurst needs me.'

Of course, she had been one of the first to be arrested. The trial had been quick and brutal, the revenge of the stubborn men in Parliament complete.

A clock on the wall chimed the hour, 10 a.m. Immediately, the mass of men and children stood up. A female warder opened a door at the side and the people all rushed, pushing and shoving, to enter.

David hung back, letting the crowd sort itself out before finally walking through the door.

The female warder stopped him with her arm. 'You can't take flowers in there.'

'But they're for my friend.'

'I don't care if they're for the Queen, you can't take them in. Nuffin' allowed in 'e prison 'all.'

David thought about arguing, but saw the intransigence on the woman's face. 'Here, you have them instead. A present for all your good work.'

He gave the bouquet to her and walked through the door. A large cavernous hall with high ceilings and small desks scattered throughout its length greeted him. Women prisoners were sat behind the desks, all wearing the same dirty brown prison clothes and white pinafores. Most had men and children in front of them, talking in subdued voices.

In the far corner, a woman sat by herself, looking out of the large picture window up into the grey sky. David walked towards her, avoiding all the other visitors and their children.

'Hello,' he said.

Rose turned towards him. Her face was thin, almost haggard. A thin strand of lank hair hung down from the grey cap on her head.

She didn't say anything.

He pulled out the rickety hard-backed chair and sat down opposite her. Her hands lay on the table in front of her, the sharp edge of her wrist bones pushing through her shirt sleeves. He couldn't think of anything to say. 'How are you?' eventually came out of his mouth.

She shrugged her shoulders. 'As well as can be expected.'

'Happy Birthday.'

For a moment he saw the old sparkle in her eyes. 'What day is it? July 23rd already?'

He nodded.

'22 years old today.' She lapsed back into silence.

'Are you on hunger strike?' he asked.

'I look so thin?'

'N-no, I meant...'

She reached out and touched his hand. He felt how cold and slight the touch was.

'No, not yet. Not my turn yet.'

'You're going on strike too.'

'Eventually. They still won't give us Category One Status.'

'But you'll just starve yourself and then they'll release you, arresting you again when you've recovered your health.'

She shrugged her shoulders again. 'It's the game they play…'

'Cat and Mouse.'

She smiled. 'You're catching on.'

'I'm also reading the papers.'

'And what do they tell you?'

'There's a war coming soon.' He took a deep breath. 'I've been recalled to my regiment in the country.'

Her face fell. 'So you won't be coming any more?'

'I don't know. I'll try…'

The silence lay between them.

It was David who spoke first. 'When you are released…'

'Don't talk about getting out of here, I can't think so far ahead. Just one day at a time. One night at a time.'

'When you are released,' he continued, 'I want us to get married.'

She took her hand away. 'No,' she answered firmly.

'Why not? I…'

'Your family would never agree. The next Lord Lappiter, marry a shopgirl? Never. And especially not one who had been in prison. Twice.'

'I'll talk to them, they'll come round. You'll see…'

'The answer is no, David. I don't want to marry you. Not now. We're too different, coming from different worlds. It wouldn't work.'

He reached for her hand again. 'It would work. We would make it work. My family doesn't matter, you're all that matters to me, Rose.'

A warder rapped the table between them with a truncheon. 'No contact with prisoners.'

They both stared at her. She rapped the table again, this time harder. 'No contact with prisoners,' she repeated.

Rose pulled her hand away.

The warder strolled away, keeping her eyes on them all the time.

'David, you have to understand. You're going off to war and I am locked up in here with no hope of release for another four months. I can't plan so far ahead. I survive today, hope to be alive tomorrow, not thinking about the day after. You can't ask me to marry you now, not here.'

'But, Rose...'

She stood up. 'Perhaps, when all this ends and we have the vote and the war is over. But not now, not now.' She stood up without looking at him and walked away from the table with her head held high.

David sat still, ignoring the noise of the children as they played around him, watching her approach the warder and pass through the door into the prison without looking back.

He didn't see the tears in her eyes as she went through the doors. He didn't see her collapse against the wall on the other side of the door. He didn't know she spent the night on her bunk huddled with her knees pressed into her chest, rocking herself to sleep.

He sat there on his own, staring into mid-air until a warder finally tapped him on the shoulder.

'Visiting time's over, sir. Time to go.'

He stood up slowly and went out of the door on the opposite side of the room. Down the long corridor with its stench of cabbage and carbolic soap, under the stone gateway and out through the iron gates, into the fresh, coal-soaked air of London.

Up above, the sky was a dull, lukewarm grey. He put his hat on his head and walked down the street in a daze, ignoring the newspaper boy at the corner.

'**AUSTRIA-HUNGARY ULTIMATUM TO SERBIA**' was the headline on the Evening Standard in the boy's hands.

Chapter Twenty-Two

Didsbury, Manchester. March 29, 2016.

Jayne stretched and blinked her eyes three times. The computer screen was beginning to go in and out of focus. After her discovery of the surveillance photograph, she had pushed herself even harder to find out as much as she could.

Paul had vanished into the spare room three hours ago. She decided to climb the stairs to listen at the door, thinking it wouldn't hurt to talk a little more. As her dad said, 'Never go to bed angry, lass. Screws up the bowels it does, anger.'

But just before she knocked on the door, she heard a loud snuffle, followed by a long, rickety snore.

He was fast asleep. So much for being upset.

She crept back down the stairs and made herself a cup of tea. Despite the tension with Paul, she felt she had made a breakthrough with her research. She still hadn't discovered the marriage certificate, but she felt she was getting to know, and like, Rose Clarke.

She sat down at her laptop; just one more search to complete before she would have to climb upstairs to bed.

She went the 'London Gazette' website to find the records of serving officers in the First World War and typed in 'David Russell'. Three records popped up immediately.

The first recounted his promotion to Captain on May 1st, 1915. The second detailed his award of the Military Cross for Bravery in September 1915. The citation read *'For conspicuous gallantry in action. He led forward to their final objectives companies who had lost their officers. Later, while consolidating his position, he was severely wounded, but remained at his post directing the fire of his men to repel the enemy.'*

A brave man, she thought. The third and last entry was spare in its simplicity. 'Captain, the Honourable, D W J Russell, to Brevet Major (since killed).'

The two little words in brackets punched Jayne in the stomach; 'Since Killed'. She checked the date – 8th July 1916. 'It makes sense,' she said out loud. 'Mark said he was killed on the first day of the Somme.'

She logged out of the London Gazette and into Find My Past. In the section entitled, 'Soldiers, died in the Great War' she typed David's name.

The result came up and she clicked on it.

First name(s):	**DAVID WILLIAM JOHN**
Last name:	**RUSSELL**
Service number:	**9603**
Rank:	**CAPTAIN**
Regiment:	**DERBYSHIRE FUSILIERS**
Battalion:	**1st Battalion**
Birth place:	**Bakewell, Derbyshire**
Residence:	**Holton Hall, Derbyshire**
Enlistment place	
Death year:	**1916**
Death day:	**01**
Death month:	**07**
Cause of death:	**Killed in action**
Death place:	**France & the Somme**
Theatre of war:	**Western European Theatre**
Notes:	**Body not recovered**

There it was. Captain David Russell had died on the first day of the Battle of the Somme. End of story.

Had he married Rose Clarke before he died? The Russells believed it was a possibility, but there was no proof. Her searches had discovered nothing. And certainly, when the last Lord Lappiter died, the heir-hunting firms had discovered nothing either.

But there was something missing, something bothering Jayne. Why did Herbert Small have such a gloatingly smug look on his face? And why did Rose Clarke insist till the day she died that she had married Captain David Russell in Gretna Green?

Jayne closed the lid of her laptop. She knew what she had to do. Paul wouldn't be happy of course, but she had to go through with it, whatever happened. She owed it to the old woman who had spent 50 years in an asylum.

Chapter Twenty-Three

Didsbury, Manchester. March 30, 2016.

The following morning, Paul left the house early for his meeting without saying a word, ignoring Jayne completely.

She tried to break the ice, hoping he would respond. 'Did you sleep well?' she asked.

There was no answer.

Instead, a few moments later, she heard the door slam as he left. She would try to talk to him tonight, perhaps he would be in a better mood then.

She glanced at the Ikea clock. Its big red numbers shouted 9.45 at her.

'Shit, shit, shit.'

She grabbed the acetate folder with the two envelopes inside, snatched her car keys from the hook beside the door, and ran out of the kitchen, returning a few seconds later to check Mr Smith had some water and some nibbles. He liked to snack when she wasn't there, in between naps, saving his main meal for when she arrived home.

Both bowls were full.

Jayne met Mark and his father in the same cafe as before. They were already waiting for her when she arrived and their body language was stiff and formal towards each other. Another couple in the middle of an argument.

After ordering a latte, she joined them at the table.

'How's the research?' asked Mark before she had even sat down.

Jayne put her bag on the chair next to her and took off her coat. 'It's moving forward, I've had some success.'

'You've found the marriage certificate?'

'Not yet, but...'

'What did I tell you?' interrupted the father. 'These people are just stringing you along, making money out of you.'

Jayne put her hands on the table. 'May I remind you, Mr Russell, I am performing this research for nothing. You only pay me if I find something proving they were married.'

The old man scowled and looked down at his tea.

'You were saying, Jayne...'

The woman arrived with the latte. Jayne took a sip and began talking. 'I'm afraid I've checked all the online records and I can't find any proof or certificate of the marriage.'

'We already told you,' sneered the father.

'But what I did find was your great grandmother was a suffragette, one of the more militant ones.' Jayne showed them printouts of the newspaper articles and the prison records. 'Prison was tough in those days. Many women were force-fed after they decided to hunger strike. Not a pleasant experience.'

'Good old Rose. And I thought you were just an Edwardian wallflower,' Mark said.

Jayne pulled out the medallion and ribbon. 'This led me to her. Apparently, the colours are specific to the suffragettes. My source tells me it's quite valuable.'

The father interrupted Jayne. 'She always kept it locked away in a small case. Wouldn't let me see it when I visited her in the hospital. She became upset whenever I went near the case.' Richard Russell stared off into mid-air as if reliving his time as a young boy, visiting his grandmother in her hospital. 'Used to hate going there, I did. Stank of piss and disinfectant. There was one woman, in the cell next to my grandmother, who spent the whole time screaming for her lost baby. She never stopped, on and on and on.' The old man shivered. 'Gives me the creeps just thinking about it.'

Mark turned back towards her. 'Did you find out anything else, Jayne?'

'Well, there is this.' She pulled out the surveillance picture of Rose. 'This is your great grandmother in Holloway prison in 1912, the first time she was imprisoned.'

Mark looked at the picture. 'She looks so thin, yet with so much dignity and strength.' Then, just like Jayne, he did a second take. 'But, that's…'

Jayne nodded and produced the drawing. 'I'm pretty certain it's the same woman.'

Mark placed the two pictures side by side. 'It is the same woman, but here she looks happy and content.' He pointed to the drawing.

The father snorted and looked away.

Jayne ignored him. 'I agree, a happy woman, at ease with herself. It's almost as if she is in love.'

Mark passed the surveillance picture to his father.

'Is that her? She looked so much older when I met her. I didn't recognise the drawing at all.'

'The picture is fascinating, Jayne. At last, we are beginning to discover a little about my great grandmother.'

The old man snorted again. 'Have you found anything to prove she married David Russell?' he asked Jayne directly.

Jayne shook her head. 'Not yet.'

'Told you these genealogists were hopeless. We've only got five days left after today.'

'I am aware of the timing, Mr Russell, but it's a difficult case.'

'Any next steps?' asked Mark quickly.

Jayne thought for a moment. She knew the choice she

had to make but Paul wasn't going to be happy. 'I think I have to go to Gretna Green,' she finally said. 'Sometimes records get misfiled or mislaid. It's a long shot but it's worth a visit.'

'A little trip on our money, huh?'

Jayne ignored the old man.

'I'll drive up tomorrow.' Jayne wondered how she was going to tell Paul. It wasn't going to be an easy conversation.

'Sounds good. What time are you leaving?'

'Why?' asked Jayne.

'I'd like to go with you.'

'I don't think it's a good idea.'

'Why not?'

'I-I-I like to work alone. You'd just slow me down.'

'That's a bit insulting, Mrs Sinclair.'

Jayne couldn't tell him the real reason. She just wanted to be away from men, all men, for a short while. 'I'm sorry, Mr Russell, I didn't mean it in that way, it's just...'

'Good, what time do we leave?'

Jayne shrugged her shoulders. 'You're my client, Mr Russell, I can't stop you from accompanying me, but...'

'That's settled then. I'll see you at eight tomorrow morning.'

Jayne nodded her head. He was the client and it was his family she was researching, but here was another man who didn't listen. Would she ever meet one who did?

Chapter Twenty-Four

Buxton, near Manchester. March 30, 2016.

After the meeting with the Russells, Jayne decided to drive slowly down the A6 to Buxton to see her father.

'How's he been?' she asked the receptionist.

'Not bad. Still a little grumpy and he called Mrs Guthrie an old cow, but other than that, not bad. No more midnight rambles, I'm happy to say.'

Her father was sitting in his usual place, in front of the picture window, facing the old oak tree dominating the garden.

'Squirrels have been fighting again.' He pointed up into the tree. 'It's the time of year. And how are you, lass?'

Jayne could see one grey squirrel chasing another through the branches. 'Not bad,' she answered noncommittally, and then continued, 'Dad, you should know, Paul's come back.'

'Thought he would, men always do.'

'You knew.'

'Hard not to know, lass. Marriage is hard, you have to make a lot of compromises. And compromise isn't your strong suit.'

'So you think it's my fault.'

'I don't care whose fault it is, lass. None of my business. But I can see when you're not happy.'

'Dad, can I ask you something? How did you manage to stay with my mum for so long?'

Her father scratched his nose. She could see the wrinkled, liver-spotted hands and the thick nail at the end of the index finger.

'It wasn't easy, I'll tell you. She weren't an easy woman your mother.'

'I know more than most.'

'But I did love her and she loved me, even if she weren't very good at showing it.' Then he looked up at her. 'And there was always you to keep us together.'

'But I wasn't even your child.'

'Of course you were. Just because you weren't my biological daughter doesn't make our relationship any weaker. I always thought of you as my daughter.'

Jayne put her arms around him, feeling the bristle of his chin against her face and the thinness of his body. He pretended to push her away. 'Don't go all soft on me now, lass. Not what I raised you to do.'

She leant away from him. He picked up the Guardian from the table; she could see the crossword was half-finished.

'How's the investigation going?' he asked.

She sighed. 'Not so good. I've found out a lot about my client's great grandmother but nothing about any supposed marriage to a David Russell. She was a suffragette.'

'Brave woman. Did she go to jail?'

Jayne showed her father the surveillance picture.

'What they did to those women was terrible, lass. Force-feeding them... and then there was the poor woman who threw herself under the King's horse.'

'Emily Davison.'

'That's her. Horrible way to die.' Her father looked down at his liver-spotted hands.

Jayne decided to change the subject quickly. 'I need to find out if a marriage took place nearly 100 years ago, but there are no records of it ever happening.'

His head lifted up and the old spark appeared in his eyes. 'Where?'

'Gretna Green.'

'Oh, one of those sort of marriages,' he said with an arch look.

'The bride was over 21 so there can't have been any objection from her family, and the groom was a soldier.'

'Perhaps they just didn't want to wait. Stranger things have happened in wartime.'

'True. But, I get the feeling there's more to it.'

'You've checked all the Scottish records?'

She nodded. 'Nothing.'

'You know, it was wartime. Records get lost or they get misfiled. A lot of the regular clerks had joined up by 1916, so they were using young boys and old men as registrars - mistakes were made.'

'But how would I know?'

'Only one way, lass.'

'I know, it's something you always tell me.'

'Nothing beats going there,' they both said at the same time.

'The computer's great, lass, but there's always human error. The only way is to go through the files yourself.'

'Looks like I'm going to Scotland.'

'Have a glass of whisky for me. Nothing beats a drop of Scotch in Scotland. Can't stand the stuff anywhere else.'

Jayne took out the drawing of Rose Clarke. 'This is the client's great grandmother. I'm beginning to find out she was a hell of a woman.'

'So this is the woman you're chasing?'

Jayne nodded.

'She was a nurse?'

'A what?'

'A nurse. She's wearing the uniform of one of the VAD.'

'VAD?'

'Volunteer Aid Detachment. They were nurses, order-lies, drivers and such things during the First World War, I recognise the uniform. My auntie on my mother's side was one. She drove a General all over France. Kept getting lost, she told me, signs were all in French and she didn't speak a word.'

Jayne leant forward and kissed her father on the top of his head. 'You're a godsend, Dad. I don't know what I'd do without you.'

'See, us old codgers can be of use sometimes. You can bring me back a bottle of Scotch from Gretna Green if you like. I might take up drinking again, just to annoy that bloody Matron.'

Chapter Twenty-Five

Royal Herbert Hospital, London. May 28, 1915.

Her feet were aching, aching, aching. She slipped off the sensible shoes and wiggled her toes, flexing her arches. She noticed a small gravy stain on her starched apron and quickly took a cloth to sponge it off before she had to return to duty at six. Officially, this was her dining break, but she rarely ate. A quick wash and a quiet nap were infinitely preferable to eating.

The stain was still faintly there. Maybe Sister wouldn't notice. Perhaps she would be too taken up by the impending arrival of a new intake of men from France to worry about such a small thing as a gravy stain.

She wondered even during her training why they dressed in white. It was a nonsensical colour for a nurse, let alone a VAD: a starched white bib with a small red cross in the centre covered a white cotton ankle-length dress, all topped by a stiff white collar and an even stiffer white cap. She supposed it was supposed to represent purity and cleanliness, but for her it made them look like preternaturally thriving schoolgirls.

She had gone along to the headquarters in Piccadilly at the end of the year. Her father had died soon after the outbreak of war and living with a maiden aunt in Worthing had been trying. Her aunt was a good person but so set in her ways; the tobacconist opened at 8 a.m., luncheon was at 12.30, afternoon tea at 3.30, the evening meal was at 6 p.m., and bedtime was at 9.00. In between, stultifying attempts at conversation were the only method of breaking up her boredom.

Inevitably, her thoughts turned to David. Had she been right to reject him? Where was he now? Why hadn't he written to her? As she read the news from France, with its increasingly long lists of dead and wounded, she realised she couldn't sit with her aunt any more and drink tea.

'Auntie May,' she announced one afternoon, 'I'm going to London to join the Voluntary Aid Detachment.'

Her aunt put down her china cup in its saucer and stared at her. 'You must do what you think is right, dear.' Then she had picked up the cup and began talking about the weather.

Rose realised her aunt was as sick of her presence as Rose was of being present. The next day she had taken the train up to London and presented herself at the headquarters of the Voluntary Aid Detachment in Piccadilly.

The interview, undertaken by a neatly coiffeured spinster with a strong Home Counties accent, was perfunctory. 'You were studying Art?'

'That's correct.'

'Any experience of nursing?'

'None. Other than nursing a sick mother when I was 13.'

'It doesn't really count. Can you drive?'

'I'm afraid not.'

'Not to worry. You'll receive some basic training in first aid and home nursing, then we'll let you loose in one of the hospitals. Under the supervision of a trained sister, of course.'

'Of course.'

'I see from your birth date you'll be eligible for service in France next year.'

Rose lifted her eyebrow.

'You need to be over 23 to serve overseas. We have to

make sure our girls have a certain level of maturity before we let them anywhere near the front.'

Girls was pronounced 'Gels' as if they were members of some horribly athletic hockey team. The woman, Rose never heard her name, stamped the form in triplicate, obviously enjoying the process. 'Go down the corridor on the left and we'll measure you for the uniform.'

'That's it?'

'All done. Welcome to the VAD, Miss Clarke.'

After training for two weeks, which consisted of attending a series of lectures from medical officers, listening to aging matrons, and spending hours working out how to wear the uniform, she was posted to the Royal Herbert Hospital in Woolwich.

A sharp-faced, thin-lipped sister greeted her on her first day. 'You the new VAD?'

Rose nodded.

'In my experience, there are three types of VAD: the enthusiastic but hopeless, the hopeless but enthusiastic, and the bloody hopeless. Which are you Miss Clarke?'

'Enthusiastic and useful, I hope, Sister.'

The sister snorted. 'We'll see. And rid yourself now of any dreams of tenderly caring for beloved wounded heroes, wiping their brows, reading letters from home, comforting them in their hour of need. You'll be emptying bedpans, cleaning bandages, mopping floors and shovelling shit. Do I make myself clear?'

The sister sniffed and, with a swirl of her cape, turned to go. The greeting was finished.

Rose ran after her. 'Where do I go, Sister?'

'Ward 12 needs the bedpans emptied. I would go there if I were you.'

Rose shuffled down the long, dim corridor looking for

Ward 12. On the walls, the gas lighting was turned down so low it threw shadows rather than light. And all the corridors were painted the same colour; a peculiar shade of sickly green which inhabited every government office and hospital.

Eventually she found the ward after asking three different nurses and VADs, all of whom had pointed vaguely down the corridor before saying 'Over there' and rushing off to do something far more important than waste time with one of the new 'gels'.

The ward itself was two long rows of beds on either side of a central aisle. The opening of each pillow case faced the door. Eighteen fern plants sat in identical pots on tables next to the beds. A larger fern sat on a table at the entrance, greeting visitors. The lighting was almost as dim as in the corridor; small lamps between the beds gave off a subdued glow.

Each bed had a man in it, and each man turned to look at her as she entered, before returning to whatever it was they were doing. She took two steps inside.

'Are you the new VAD?' a voice asked from behind her.

A sister stepped out from a room hidden to one side. Rose could see a couple of bunks, a small table and a desk light but nothing else. To describe it as sparsely furnished would be an understatement.

'Rose Clarke.' She held out her hand.

The sister smiled and shook it. 'Good, I've been waiting for you, lots to do. You can start by emptying all the bedpans.'

And so life began for Rose. She didn't mind the hard work; the first two weeks she seemed solely involved with cleaning; toilets, floors, walls, ferns, windows, tables, more bedpans. If it didn't move, it was to be wiped down with disinfectant twice a day. The first sister she worked for was a lovely person, always willing to teach and help her become better, showing her how to perform her cleaning duties quickly and efficiently.

After this baptism of cleanliness, she graduated to making beds. All the sheets had to be folded in the prescribed fashion; openings of pillowcases were to be facing the door; covers turned down one-fifth to two-fifths; sheets tucked under and folded back at a 60-degree angle; blanket lines centred exactly. Woe betide her if she made a mistake; the sting of the nursing sister's disappointment was not something she wanted to invoke.

Making the beds gave her more opportunity to talk to the men. They were all officers, in this section of the hospital. Most weren't regulars but volunteers in the first mad days of August 1914. She met goldsmiths, haberdashers, bank clerks, sales reps, public school boys, engineers, jewellers, actors, watch makers and even one MP. They didn't say much to her, too shy or too embarrassed to hold a real conversation. Most turned away from her as they spoke, hiding their wounds or their scars as if ashamed by them.

She didn't get to know them well, calling them by bed numbers rather than names. The hospital concentrated on surgery and post-operative care. Except for a few cases, they weren't in the ward for long, before they were sent out to nursing homes around the country.

Her ward was for the least serious cases, the men whose injuries were certain to be cured with time, and who would then be sent back to rejoin their regiment on the front lines. This knowledge seemed to hang over them like a shroud; quietening conversation, discouraging intimacy.

After three months, she was put in charge of trays for four wards. There was a wonderful mind-numbing structure in her work now; 64 trays each with 12 different components, from knives and forks to salt cellars and napkins, had to be assembled for four meals a day. Each time she did it she counted out the 768 different pieces for the trays, making sure knives were in the correct position facing 12 o'clock, salt cellars were on the left, water glasses on the right. She pushed her loaded trays to the kitchen where one of the cooks placed plates of food in the centres and covered them with thin aluminium cloches.

And she was off down the dimly lit corridor, the hushed roll of rubber wheels and the rattle of plates the only accompaniments to her journey. The men were generally happy to see her. As one of them said one day: 'Nurse, I either sit in bed all day doing nothing, or I get up and do nothing.' Even the hospital food was a break from the monotony.

She grew to love her trips down the endless corridors; the whisper of secrets in the walls, the shuffle of men as they sat up in bed when she arrived, the rattle of the trolley, the way the dim gas light centred in the gleam of the trays; metal salt-cellars, yellow butters, cylinders of fluted glass. She loved the institutionalism of every minute, of every hour, of every day. A regularity that wasn't to be changed even by death.

And she did see death. The placing of screens around a bed. The arrival of a stretcher, the same stretcher they had been brought in on. The covering of the body with a flag. And the way all the men stood, or at least those who were able to, as the stretcher was carried quietly out of the ward to be buried on the hill behind the hospital.

She had seen death and wasn't afraid of it any more. It was a part of life.

After Sister Thomas in her first ward, she never bothered to get to know any of the other sisters. They were a race above, gods in their own kingdom on earth, looking down on the lesser beings such as the VADs. Some were friendly, but most were standoffish, almost cold; as if allowing the smallest sense of human companionship into their lives would make them vulnerable. Vulnerable to what she had asked herself at the beginning. After a while, she realised it was vulnerable to feelings, to sympathy, to empathy with some of these men who would die. Or never walk properly again. Or see. Or speak. Or hear.

She vowed she would never become like them.

She stoked the fire in her room, finished the last of her hot, sweet tea and smoothed the uniform down with her hands. The gravy stain was still on her apron, but hopefully this sister wouldn't notice. She took one last look at the room before closing the door.

The quiet of the ward and the soft snores of the men greeted her. Votes for women seemed so far away now, another life.

Nothing mattered any more except looking after herself and looking after the men in her care.

But often, in the middle of preparing her trays, she would stop and wonder. Where was David? What was he doing now?

Chapter Twenty-Six

Didsbury, Manchester. March 30, 2016.

She couldn't postpone it much longer.

Paul was bustling about the kitchen getting himself ready before they went out for dinner. She had arrived home from Buxton to find him sitting in the kitchen with a big smile on his face, their argument forgotten.

'The meeting was great. Looks like my portfolio is expanding and I'm being promoted; let's go out to celebrate.'

Jayne was tired and had to prepare for the trip to Scotland, but she agreed to go out.

Now, it was close to 7 o'clock, she couldn't leave it any longer before telling him. 'Paul, I need to go to Scotland tomorrow,' she blurted out.

He stopped what he was doing and turned slowly towards her. 'But I thought we were going to London this weekend, just me and you. I booked the train tickets and a hotel for us. Even managed to get tickets to see Les Mis, you know you've always wanted to see it.'

'I'm sorry, it's just the client. We need to go to Gretna Green to check the registers.'

'We?'

Jayne knew she was digging herself deeper into a hole but she had to carry on. 'His name is Mark Russell. He's commissioned me to search for the marriage of his great grandmother.'

'You're going to Scotland with another man and you didn't think to tell me?'

'I'm telling you now. And it isn't "another man", it's a client.'

Paul ran his hand through what remained of his hair. Jayne knew what was coming next and she wished he wouldn't do it.

'Jayne, we haven't seen each other for two months. I'm only back for a weekend and I've arranged for us to enjoy a short time in London together, just me and you. And now you tell me you don't want to go.'

There it was again, the little-boy-lost voice, the hard done victim. God, she hated it when he spoke like this. All it showed was weakness and she hated weakness in men. He wasn't like this before. When Dave Gilmour had been shot, he was her rock, a tower of strength. Looking at him now, all she could see was a weak, flabby man with a receding hairline and a belly hanging over his trousers. Is this where all love ends? In disdain and disappointment and disillusion?

'Well?'

He was waiting for an answer.

'There's nothing I can do. I need to go to Scotland tomorrow.'

She could have explained more. Told him how they only had four more days to solve the case. She could have told him the story of the woman locked up in an asylum for 50 years. Or how a brave man had died in a pointless battle in the middle of a pointless war.

But she didn't.

'That's it then. Jayne Sinclair has decided her career is more important than her marriage. A choice she's made over and over again. Well, I won't put up with it any more, Jayne, I've had enough.'

He pushed past her and ran upstairs. She heard his feet

stomp across the ceiling and the slamming of wardrobe and cupboard doors. Five minutes later, he was standing in front of her carrying an overnight bag.

'If you change your mind, I'll be staying at the Britannia.' With those last words, he left the house, closing the door behind himself quietly.

Jayne was left alone in the kitchen with only the cat to comfort her.

Chapter Twenty-Seven

**No.11 General Hospital, Boulogne, France.
September 19, 1915.**

Rose was carrying the soiled bandages to the laundry room. They were so short of equipment they were having to wash old bandages made from sheets and re-use them.

'Clarke.' The Matron's voice echoed down the hallway. A beckoning finger ordered her to come. 'What's this?'

At Matron's feet was a short piece of bandage covered in dried blood and greenish pus. Its ugliness a stark contrast to the beauty of the marble floor.

'It's a bandage, Matron.'

'And what's it doing on the floor?'

'I'll pick it up.' As she did, more bandages tumbled from her arms. Matron stood over her, the starched white uniform leading to a perpetual scowl. 'Clarke, we are short of bandages and you see fit to discard them all over the hospital?'

'No, Matron.'

'You contradict me?'

'No, Matron.' Rose immediately realised the trap she had fallen into. The Matron smiled. Not a nice smile, a mean smile, one of utter contempt for an amateur doing a professional's job.

'When you have quite finished discarding precious bandages,' the accent was more pronounced now, Ulster at its most devout, 'please go to the new arrival in Room 112. He needs to be completely cleaned before the doctors see him.'

'Yes, Matron.'

'Well, what are you waiting for girl? The vote?'

Rose picked up the bandages and scurried away before more retribution was visited upon her head. The matron knew she had been a suffragette before the war and seemed to think ill of her for it; as if fighting for the right to vote made her less of a woman in the matron's eyes.

Rose had only been in the hospital for three weeks but already the Matron had made life difficult for her. She transferred from the Royal Herbert after nine months on the wards: a time when she learnt everything there was to know about bed pans and piss bottles, about cleaning toilets and men's backsides, setting trays and setting bones.

As soon as she had her 23rd birthday, she applied for a job in a hospital in France. Her first few weeks were difficult, but she realised it was going to be the same wherever she went. At least here, the men needed her, even if the women didn't.

Rose opened the door to the laundry. A cloud of steam and moisture immediately drenched her. Beads of sweat formed on her forehead beneath her cap. Terry was already there, stirring the vast copper pot with a long oar they had borrowed from one of the fishermen.

Terry was Theresa and she suffered even more under the unforgiving gaze of Matron. Not because she was a former suffragette, but because she was a Catholic; a more heinous sin.

Rose added her handful of soiled bandages to the already brimming pot. On its surface was a thick scab of crusty scum composed of blood, mud, dirt, pus, excrement and anything else the poor soldiers had managed to pick up in the trenches. Terry stirred the used bandages into the mixture, hardly disturbing the scum. 'Double, double, toil and trouble; fire burn and cauldron bubble,' she sang as she imitated Macbeth's witches.

'Are you concocting an anti-Matron potion?'

'No, not at all, but it keeps me going as I stir the pot.'

'How long do you have left to go?'

Terry wiped her sweat-dripping forehead with the back of her hand, fixing one dark, sodden curl back under her cap. 'Not long, just six more hours. Sure before you know, it will be time for tea.'

Terry was perpetually happy; despite all the indignities heaped upon her by Matron, she continued to smile and do whatever she was told.

'I have to push off, Room 112.' Rose indicated towards the door with her thumb.

'Ye poor man's been screaming all morning with the pain. No more morphine the doctor said.'

'The Matron really has it in for me. I've to blanket wash him.'

Terry carried on stirring her pot of filth with the paddle. 'Ah, she's not a bad sort. Wants the best for the men.'

'She's an old scheming harridan with the face like tomorrow and a body like the back end of a tram.'

Terry quickly made the sign of the cross with her free hand. 'Please forgive her, Lord.'

Rose left the laundry with Terry's prayers echoing in her head. She turned left down the long corridor past the small ward on the right. The hospital had once been a rich merchant's chateau and the money lavished on the fixtures and fittings was evident everywhere. Shame nobody appreciated them any more except Rose.

She had made a few sketches of the plaster mouldings on the ceiling and the carvings above the doors, but usually she was so tired she just slept or lay on her bunk staring into the air.

After turning a corner at the end of the corridor, she stood in front of the door to Room 112, took a deep breath and entered without knocking. The single rooms were saved for the worst cases; men who were the most badly injured. The patient was lying away from her, his face to the wall. At least he isn't screaming, she thought. That would come later when she had to clean his wounds of dirt and shit and pus.

She drew the curtains and turned on the lamp beside the bed.

No light.

The chateau had been modernised just before the war but many of the lights either worked sporadically or not at all. Each room had an oil lamp to compensate. She lit it.

There was no reaction from her patient, he just stayed where he was; facing the wall, his head buried into the once white sheets as if hiding himself in their cleanliness.

Rose poured water into the washstand in the corner, adding two rolls of dry cotton cloth and placing the carbolic lotion beside the bowl. The liquid would sting but at least it ensured the wound was clean. Afterwards, she would bipp the wound, coating it with bismuth iodoform paraffin paste.

Most of the soldiers had had their wounds dressed at the casualty clearing station before being moved to the hospital, but this was often done quickly and clumsily. It was their first job to change the dressing.

Rose took the bowl and its water over to the table beside the bed and placed it under the light. 'I'm going to have to clean your wound and the rest of your body before the doctors come on their rounds.' She took a length of cloth and squeezed all the water out of it. 'It may hurt at times, but I'll try to be as gentle as I can. Please realise I must do this. It's important your wound is clean.'

It was a speech she had given many times since she had joined the VAD. Too many times.

The soldier didn't answer. Was he asleep?

She touched his shoulder and felt him flinch beneath her fingers. 'I'm sorry, it has to be done.' She began to roll the sheet off his body, folding it back to the bottom of the bed.

He didn't move.

Beneath the sheet he was completely naked, his bony shoulders jutting through a thin white skin. Patches of mud and soil stuck to the body from the neckline downwards as if they had somehow seeped through the uniform and embraced the raw human beneath.

From the bottom of his ribs to the top of his left thigh, a large pad of cotton was taped, hiding his hips. The cotton was no longer white but had transformed into a camouflaged pattern of deep red in the centre, surrounded by a light green, spreading into a dirty mud-coloured brown sludge.

Incongruously, a large red thumbprint sealed the edge of the tape where it joined the skin. It was almost as if the surgeon at the casualty clearing station had signed his work.

She began to slowly lift the tape where it had stuck, prising it from the skin. She let the man take a deep intake of breath, waiting for the pain that was sure to come. She removed the other tape at the corner and peeled back the dirty pad. The inside, where the gauze had touched the skin, was covered in globules of dark red blood, green pus and a thick, white snot-like slime.

The patient groaned as the cold air touched the open wound. The surgeon had done the best he could to clean out the shrapnel and bits of metal buried in the open flesh.

Rose could see the curve of muscle as it reached over the hip, the flesh inside, chopped and shredded. The skin had vanished, no doubt cut away by the surgeon. She wondered if the wound was deep and if shrapnel fragments still lay beneath the tortured flesh.

'This may hurt a little,' she said as gently as she could.

She took up the damp cloth and dabbed at the edge of the skin were it met the wound, cleaning away dried blood and bits of crusted flesh. He flinched as soon as the cloth touched his skin, but then relaxed, giving himself up to his fate like a sacrificial victim at some awful pagan rite.

Rose carried on speaking as she cleaned the outside of the wound. At first, she thought it was to comfort the injured, but later, she realised it was actually to comfort herself. To give her brain something to do, rather than focus on the pain of the individual beneath her.

'My name's Rose, by the way. We'll be seeing a lot of each other.' She cleaned the edge of the wound itself now. The patient flinched away from the cloth, mumbling something in answer to her.

'What was that?' She took the cloth and dunked it in the water, squeezing it out like she had done before.

'I knew a R-R-Rose once,' the patient mumbled.

'Did it have prickly thorns?' She dabbed the wound directly. The patient jerked his legs and let out a howl of pain. 'Sorry, I have to do it. If you lie still, it will all be over soon, I promise.'

The man mumbled something again.

Rose dabbed the wound. He flinched a little, but otherwise stayed still. His breath became shallower and he gritted his teeth, repeating the phrase to the wall. 'No thorns. No thorns. No thorns. No thorns.'

Rose cleaned the wound as quickly as she could. The

chorus of 'No thorns, no thorns, no thorns,' repeated until it suddenly stopped.

The patient had passed out from the pain. She finished cleaning the wound, using the soiled water to wipe the man's legs and bottom. She wished she could have used fresh water but she had to work quickly now, while he was unconscious, while he couldn't feel anything. She reached between his testicles and wiped his penis and lower belly. If anybody had told her a year ago she would be washing a man, she would have laughed in their face. But war, and time, change everybody.

She poured some fresh water out of the jug onto a clean cloth. She turned the patient over on to his back, careful to make sure the wound didn't touch the bottom sheet. She wiped the thin bony chest, ribs poking through the pale skin, and moved up to the neck and face.

She stopped.

The cloth fell from her fingers and her hand went to her mouth.

Beneath her, his head resting against the pillow, lay David Russell.

Chapter Twenty-Eight

No.11 General Hospital, Boulogne, France.
October 19, 1915.

David recovered quickly from his wounds. Soon, he and Rose were spending most afternoons sitting out on the lawn, basking in the warm rays of late summer.

'It isn't like that, you know,' David announced one afternoon after Rose had finished reading him the front page of the Times.

'What isn't?'

'War, the fighting.'

'I didn't think it was.'

'Those reporters spend their lives in Paris, filing their reports from some dining room in the Hotel de Crillon.'

'What is it like?'

He spoke softly. 'Dark and horrible, but strangely exciting. There's time where one forgets everything and everybody, plunging into the struggle without a thought of the past, present or the future.'

'Sometimes, I felt the same way when I was breaking windows for the WSPU. As if it were another person doing it, not me.'

David stared down at his hands lying in his lap. Rose wondered if his side were hurting him again. He still had shards of shrapnel buried beneath his skin. The doctors said it was pointless removing them all, just let the body get used to them.

'I did write, you know,' he said eventually.

She had been expecting this conversation for a long

time. Now, it had finally arrived, like a train slowly chugging into a station. 'Did you?'

'I was sent out with the BEF on one of the first ships to leave England. I wrote to you after our last meeting in Holloway, and again from France, before the fighting started.'

'I'd already been released by then. Asquith decided to let us go, after Mrs Pankhurst promised no more political action until after the war had finished. It seemed more important to win the war.'

'I wrote to your father's shop, after the first fighting at Mons. Glad to be alive, so many of the regulars died.'

Rose closed her eyes and bowed her head. 'He passed away in September. Couldn't understand the war, couldn't understand why people were fighting. He was German you know.'

David raised his head. 'But his name was Clarke.'

'He changed it when he came to England. Wanted to blend in more. His original name was Hans Schreiber. It amused him to be called Hans Clarke.'

'I'm sorry.'

'It was for the best. He had been lost since Mother died. She was his rock, his strength. Without her, he was just another little boy.' She took a deep breath. 'I moved to Worthing to be with one of my mother's sisters and then joined the VAD. They didn't seem to mind I'd been in prison.'

She stood up. 'Shall I push you around the garden? If Matron sees me sitting here, she'll think I'm bunking off.'

He released the brake on his wheelchair. 'When will I be able to walk again?'

It was time to break the news to him. 'Soon, I should imagine. The doctors say your hip is mending well. It's just a question of time, so they're sending you back to England to recuperate.'

They stopped in the middle of the path. 'I'm going home?'

'Well, not home exactly. To a place called Tylney Hall. A good place to rebuild your muscles, they tell me.'

'And what about us?'

'What about us?'

'I'm not letting you go this time, Rose. Not again.'

'I have to stay here in Boulogne. The army…'

'Then I'll stay too.'

'Your movement orders have already come through. You are to leave tomorrow.'

'So quick. How long have you known?'

'A couple of days.'

He bit his bottom lip. 'What are we going to do, Rose?'

'What we've always done. Make do and mend.'

'I don't want to do it any more. I want to marry you.'

'And what about your family?'

He laughed. 'They'll have to stand in line. I'm marrying you first.'

She didn't laugh. 'You know what I mean.'

He took her hand. 'One thing this war has taught me, Rose, is there are no second chances. This is the only life we have to live. And I would like to live mine with you.'

She withdrew her hand, running it down the side of her face and pushing a stray lock of hair into her cap. She knelt down in front of his wheelchair. 'David, this war has changed me too. There's no past, no future, just now, here together, me and you.'

'Let's get married, Rose?'

She nodded. 'I'd love to be your wife, for now and for ever.'

He leant forward and kissed her on the lips.

As he did, they heard the creak of the patio doors opening.

She stood up quickly. 'I'm being transferred back to England in February, let's arrange it all then. In the meantime, there is so much to do before you leave.' She began to push his wheelchair back towards the chateau.

He reached up behind his head and touched her hand. 'I'll write to you every day until we see each other again.'

Up ahead, at the patio doors, Rose could see Matron standing with her arms folded across her chest. 'I'd be much happier if you could think of a few words to say to the matron.'

He took his hand away. 'Don't worry, it's time for the famous Russell charm. An effect that can soothe even the most savage beast.'

'You don't know Matron.'

Chapter Twenty-Nine

Gretna Green, Scotland. March 31, 2016.

The drive was long from Manchester to Gretna Green, but the M6 was relatively free of traffic. Even more luckily there was just one lane closure, north of Lancaster. Jayne had picked up Mark from outside his home at eight in the morning. He was ready and waiting, standing outside the house. As he opened the car door, the curtains flickered and the shadow of his father appeared behind them.

He placed his overnight bag on the back seat and sat down next to her. 'We should leave pretty quickly.'

'Why?'

'My father asked to come at the last minute. Wanted to see for himself. I think he wants to gloat if we don't find anything.'

Jayne put the BMW in gear and pulled away from the house.

'Nice car,' said Mark.

'The reward to myself for a successful investigation a couple of months ago. A little treat...'

'More than a treat, I would say.' He looked around the car, admiring the comfort of the leather upholstery and the sleek German minimalism of the dashboard.

Jayne decided to find out more about him. 'You still live with your father?'

'I moved back two years ago when my marriage ended. She stayed in the house.'

'Any kids?'

'Two. Ten and eight, both girls.'

'Must be difficult.'

'It is. Even harder now her new man has moved in with them.'

'How are the kids handling it?'

He took a deep breath. 'On the surface, okay, but you never know what's happening beneath the obsession with Boy Bands and Barbies.'

She laughed. 'You see still see them?'

'Every day. They go to the school where I teach.'

'Isn't it awkward?'

'Not really. I can spend time with them after work when I'm Daddy again. In school, I'm Mr Russell. No kids yourself?'

Jayne swung the car onto the M60 before answering. 'No. I never felt grown up enough to have kids. What with the job and everything.'

'You were in the police?'

'Joined at 16 and worked my way up to Detective Inspector. Would never have risen any further though. Wasn't part of the club, so I took early retirement a few years ago.' She thought back to Dave again, his body lying in her arms, a hole in the middle of his chest. He'd been retired early too.

Should she tell Mark the truth? No, it was nobody's business but hers.

They lapsed into silence, the quiet roar of the engine the only sound as she raced northwards past Bolton.

Jayne thought of Paul. What was he doing now? Were they finally over? Done and dusted? Twelve years of marriage finished in just four minutes? She supposed she made her choice when she decided to go to Scotland.

Enough. Enough. Enough.

She'd had enough of thinking and worrying about her

marriage. Her job and this client were the most important things right now. This is what she needed to concentrate on.

Mark thought for a long while before asking his next question.

'Do you think we'll ever be able to prove the marriage?'

'Honestly, I don't know. The records in Gretna may tell us something. If not, we'll go to the Central Depository for Scottish Records in Edinburgh.'

'You're hoping the internet records missed something.'

'It's always better to check the original files. Sometimes, names get written incorrectly or misspelt. Or pages can be missed. Or pages may be so corrupted they can't transcribe them. And if they used an optical reader, then one never knows what can happen. Computer errors are often much worse than human error.'

'So there is a chance?'

'There's always a chance. There's always a record somewhere, it's just a question of finding it.'

'We only have four more days left. After then, the statute of limitations kicks in and it no longer matters what we discover, the crown gets everything.'

Once again, he lapsed into silence. Jayne wondered if his main concern was with his great grandmother's reputation or with the money. It didn't matter to her either way any more. She only cared about one thing; the person in the picture in Holloway Prison.

After a short stoppage for roadworks north of Lancaster, they raced through the hilly country of the North with the mountains of the Lake District a misty brown presence on their left. The road rolled up and down, with occasional farmhouses in dour grey stone, dotted through the rolling hills.

A large sign announced they were crossing the border

into Scotland. Jayne immediately exited the motorway, following the signs for the village. In just five minutes, they reached a T-junction and opposite them a sign proudly proclaimed 'Gretna Green. Famous Blacksmith's Shop.'

'So this is it then, where my great grandmother said she was married.'

'It's the place where thousands of young people, eager to get married, rushed over the border to commit themselves to each other over a blacksmith's anvil.'

'I wonder if my great grandmother was one of them, or whether it was all just one of her fantasies.'

'The only way to find out, is to ask.'

Chapter Thirty

Holton Hall, Derbyshire. April 24, 1916.

'You can't marry this shopgirl. I forbid it.' His mother's hand slapped the table shaking the china teacups.

'My mind is made up, Mother. I love Rose and she loves me.'

'Rose, is that her name? Sounds positively lower middle class. I suppose she has a sister called Daisy?'

'She's an only child. Her mother died some time ago, and her father died in 1914.'

His mother stood up. 'At least that is some relief, we won't have some lower class parents wandering around the rooms, picking up the china and asking how much it cost.'

'Mother, you go too far. Mr Clarke was a haberdasher not anything else.'

'Oh well, that is just perfect, we won't want for warm winter coats, will we?' she said with heavy irony.

'James, say something, tell your son what a fool he's being.'

David's father sat in his usual chair, a book resting on his lap. He obviously wanted to be back in the library where he belonged, nestled amongst his beloved butterflies, fungi and rhizomes. 'Marjory, he's old enough to do exactly as he pleases.'

'Old enough?' his mother shouted, 'he's still a boy.'

'Old enough to die for his country,' his father mumbled before returning to his book.

His mother strode over to the fireplace and pulled the cord. Walters, the butler, opened the doors immediately as if he had been listening outside. 'Yes, madam?'

'Fresh tea, this is cold.'

'Yes, madam.'

David needed something stronger. 'Bring me a whisky, Walters.'

'Yes, sir.'

'But it's only five o'clock, David. Is this what the army has taught you, how to drink?'

'And it's done a good job, Mother.'

His mother licked her lips. She walked over and sat down beside him, carefully smoothing the silk of her dress to avoid creases. She took his hand in hers. It was a soft hand, small and pink, a hand unused to doing anything except applying cream to a face.

'We do understand what you are going through, you know. War makes everything seem so urgent, so necessary. Only last week, Colonel Dawson in Matlock lost his son. I attended the service to commemorate the boy. There was the colonel in the front row, blubbering away, wishing he had told the boy he loved him. I tell you, David, I was quite shocked. What is the world coming to? What's happened to standards and decorum?'

'I knew the son, Mother. Ronnie was his name. Shall I tell you what happened to him? He was caught in a chlorine attack at Ypres. He wanted to get his gas helmet on but decided to tell his men to put on theirs first. He charged up and down the line, shouting to his men. Until the gas got him.'

'A canary in a coal mine.' David's brother, Toby, had spoken for the first time. He was leaning on the mantlepiece, dressed in an elegantly tailored lounge suit, smoking casually, without a care in the world.

Lady Lappiter sniffed haughtily. 'I do wish you

wouldn't practise such a disgusting habit in the house, Toby.'

'I'm not practising, Mother, I'm actually rather proficient.'

'Disgusting habit. Put it out.'

David's brother sighed but extinguished the cigarette in the ashtray by his elbow.

His mother took David's hand again, trying a different tack. 'You know, the Smythe girl...'

'Emily?'

'Cousin to Lord Ampleforth. You used to play with her as a child.'

'Mother, she came here to visit with her uncle. You used to force us together. I would have been much happier playing with my toy soldiers...'

'Look where it's got you.' His mother left the implication hanging in the air. 'Anyway, she was visiting over in Bakewell and I happened to hear she has come into a sizeable fortune from some uncle who manufactured ladies' underwear.' His mother sniffed as if something terrible had managed to work its way into her nose.

Walters returned with the tea and David's whisky. 'Shall I pour, madam?'

His mother waved him away as one would get rid of an annoying fly. 'What was I saying? Yes, that's it... anyway, she's in Bakewell at the moment staying with the Anstruthers. She would make a fine wife.'

'So now you are selling me off to the highest bidder.'

'Not at all, David.' His mother held out her arms in the picture of innocence. 'In the long term, she would make a far better choice.'

David slammed his whisky down onto the table. His father looked up from his book and then immediately returned to it. 'Mother. I'm going to marry Rose and there is nothing you or anybody else can do to stop me.' He stood up. 'And now, if you will excuse me, I have to get a train, Rose is waiting for me.'

He strode out of the room, followed by his mother and brother. The father looked up once more from his book, shook his head slightly, and continued reading.

His mother caught up with him in the hallway as Walters was helping him put on his army greatcoat. 'You must not marry this girl. I will not have it, do you understand? I will never be able to face my friends and tell them my son had married a shopgirl…'

'And I could never face myself unless I married Rose. Goodbye Mother, I'm sure you'll think of something to say to your friends. You were always a proficient liar.'

With those words, he pulled open the door and strode out to the car waiting to take him to the station.

'Toby,' his mother hissed, 'don't let your brother out of your sight. Don't let him do anything stupid.'

'But, Mother.'

'Follow him. Just do it.'

Toby sighed, took his coat, and joined his brother in the car. 'I've been sent to watch over you.'

'Don't get in my way, Toby, I will marry her.'

His younger brother took a cigarette out of his silver case, and lit it. 'I don't intend to, David. But tonight, I will do anything to be away from her.' He blew a long stream of smoke out of the window towards the house.

The driver put the car in gear and it moved off down the driveway. David looked back over his shoulder, seeing his mother framed in the stone arch of the Hall. She looked like she was made of the same stone as the rest of the building. Old, cold, pitted, stone.

Chapter Thirty-One

Gretna Green, Scotland. March 31, 2016.

'Our ancestor was married in Gretna Green, could we check the records?'

'Oh, how wonderful. I'll be happy to help you.' The woman's soft burr was typically lowland Scots. Her badge proclaimed her as a guide with the name of Annie. Jayne had approached her as soon as they entered the old blacksmith's shop.

'They were married in late April 1916.'

'Ooh, a war wedding. There were a lot of those, I'll tell you. Were they married here at the blacksmith's?'

'Does it matter?' asked Mark.

'Not really, but we do like to know. It was our cottage industry during those days. People were on leave and they wanted quick weddings. None of the living in sin we see these days. Now let me just get on one of the wee computer things and I'll check the records. Please follow me.'

She carried on talking as they walked over to the computer. 'Have you come far on this lovely day?'

'From Manchester,' replied Jayne.

'Ooh, so far.' The 'r' lasted almost as long as the rest of the sentence. She put on her reading glasses and entered her password into the computer. The machine whirred for a moment before a home page flashed up. 'What was the name of the groom?'

'David Russell,' answered Mark.

The woman typed the name into the field. 'And the bride?'

'Rose Clarke.'

'A lovely name Rose. It's my daughter's name. She's married with three kids now and lives in London. Don't know what she sees in the place, myself.' She typed in the name as she spoke and pressed return.

The machine clicked and whirred like an asthmatic alcoholic.

'No results, I'm afraid. What was the date, again?'

'Late April 1916. April 25, to be exact.'

Annie typed in the date. Again the machine whirred and clicked as it searched through its database.

'No results, I'm afraid. Are you sure they were married here?'

'Positive. My great grandmother remembered coming here clearly.'

'Well, the records start when the family took over in 1887. They are pretty good after 1920, but some are missing from the earlier period. It depended on the blacksmith preacher.'

'Blacksmith preacher?'

'Well, if they were married in the shop, then he would have entered a record in the book.'

'The book?' asked Jayne.

'Aye, the family kept all the original records from those days.'

'Could we see the book for the period?'

Annie frowned. 'Well, it's highly irregular, and all the records are in the database.'

'I am a genealogist.' Jayne handed over her card. 'I'm working with Mr Russell to discover his family tree. His great grandmother said she was married here in 1916.'

Annie stared at the card. 'Well, I suppose you are a genealogist and you have come a long way. Let me have a chat with my boss.'

'Thank you, Annie.'

The guide strolled over to enter a door into the back room.

'It's not looking good,' said Mark.

'Perhaps they missed a page or lost that particular record. But we won't know unless we see the original book.'

A few seconds later, Annie appeared carrying a large red volume. 'This is the original registry book.' She laid the volume down on the counter. 'Now you said the date was April 25, 1916, didn't you?'

She opened the volume. On each page a list of names, signatures, and names of witnesses was inscribed in a variety of handwriting styles.

'April 22, 1916.' Annie turned the page. 'April 23, April 24.' She turned the page once more. 'April 26.' She went back one page and looked again. 'Strange, April 25 isn't here. Maybe he didn't write down the records for the day? Or there weren't any marriages? Are you sure it was April 25?'

'My great grandmother always said it was that date.'

'Could I take a look?' asked Jayne.

Annie stepped back.

Jayne turned the pages carefully. April 22, four marriages, three were of soldiers; two privates and a corporal. April 23, one marriage, a civilian. April 24, two marriages, both private soldiers. April 26, four marriages. One was a captain in the Scots Guards, marrying an 18-year-old girl. She turned over all the pages until the end of the month.

Definitely no David Russell or Rose Clarke listed. She went back to April 24 and turned the page once again, examining it closely. 'Is it common for there to be no records on a day?'

'It happens. The blacksmith preacher may have gone to Dumfries or Edinburgh.' She shrugged her shoulders. 'Perhaps nobody wanted to get married.'

Jayne lifted up the book and examined it closely. Was there a small stub of page in the binding? She moved the book so it caught the light. There was a sharp edge hidden there as if the page had been cut out.

Annie held out her arms wanting the book returned. Jayne closed it and handed it back.

'You could try the Central Depositary of Records in Edinburgh. If someone was married in Scotland, a copy of the certificate was always sent there.'

'Thank you, Annie, you've been a great help. I think we will go to Edinburgh tomorrow and check the records.'

'I'm sorry we couldn't find what you were looking for. It's a shame really, I could have printed a lovely certificate for you for just ten pounds.'

When they were outside, Mark asked, 'What now? There were no records. Strange it should be the day my great grandmother said she married.'

'The page had been cut out.'

'What?'

'Somebody had cut the page from the record.'

'We need to go back inside...'

Jayne held his arm. 'The page was cut a long time ago, Mark, probably when your great grandmother married. The edge of the cut was the same faded yellow as the rest of the paper.'

'So what do we do now?'

'Well, it tells me something was going on in 1916 we know nothing about.'

'You think my great grandmother did get married here?'

'I don't know, Mark, but something smells funny, all my instincts tell me something is wrong, very wrong.'

'Let's go to Edinburgh and check there.'

Jayne shook her head. 'It's late and the registry office will be closed by the time we arrive. I think we should check into the hotel and have a glass of wine. Wine helps the brain solve problems. Little known fact, that.'

Chapter Thirty-Two

Didsbury, Manchester. March 31, 2016.

Herbert Small sat in his car outside the house. That morning, he had followed Mrs Sinclair as she had driven to Sale, picking up Mark Russell before driving north.

Well done, Mrs Sinclair, you're going to Gretna Green. Exactly what I would have done.

He followed them to the point where the M61 joined the M6, the main road heading to Scotland, before turning off and heading back to Manchester. He wasn't sure how long they would be away, but he was sure with such a long drive, she wouldn't make it back before late evening.

He took the next exit off the motorway and drove back to her house, waiting for that wonderful time when Manchester sits down to its dinner and the streets go quiet.

He checked her road once more.

Empty.

The gloves were lying next to him on the car seat. He put them on and stepped out of the car, picking up an official-looking notepad and folder. Just another researcher asking for people's opinions on washing machines or yogurt or political parties.

Walking confidently up the drive, he rapped on the door as he had done before.

He checked the street once again. Still empty. Taking out the jemmy from his pocket, he forced it into the gap between the lock and the door jamb, forcing the door open with a soft pop.

One more look down the street and he stepped into the

house, closing the door behind him.

'Mrs Sinclair, for an ex-policewoman your security is pretty lax. No alarm. Only one lock on the door. No security at all. You should be ashamed.'

He walked down the hall to the kitchen. There was a loud squeal on his left and he jumped back in fright. A black and white cat raced past him and up the stairs to the second floor.

He'd forgotten about the bloody cat.

The computer was still on the counter on one of those modern kitchen islands. He was hopeless with computers so there was no way he was going to be able to access her files, but on his last visit, he noticed Mrs Sinclair kept paper copies of her research in box files.

He found the file he was looking for and opened it. Inside were the fruits of her research so far. Not bad, Mrs Sinclair, you've come pretty far in just a couple of days.

He took the files and placed them with his notebook.

On the counter next to the computer, he noticed a clear acetate file with two envelopes inside. This had been lying next to her when he visited previously.

He glanced at the clock. Better get a move on. She might be back any time soon. He took the acetate file and slid it into his notebook. Plenty of time to see what's inside the envelopes later.

Now was the time for some fun. He picked up the laptop and threw it down to the floor as hard as he could. The screen smashed and stuck out at a strange angle. He stomped on it a few times, breaking the keyboard and completely shattering what was left of the screen.

Then he opened the fridge door and threw the food, wine, chocolate, butter, cheese, milk and eggs around the kitchen, making certain to cover the wall. He hadn't had so much fun since he was a kid torturing a cat with hot water.

He opened the cupboards, emptying all the crockery he could reach onto the floor. What a lovely sound it made as it smashed into the wooden parquet.

The clock ticked onto 7 p.m. No time like the present. He picked it off the wall and tossed it into the pile of crockery, food and computer parts on the floor.

What a mess you've got me into.

Time to go.

On his way out, he knocked the paintings off the wall in the hall. A friendly greeting for Mrs Sinclair when she returned.

Herbert Small took one last look at his handiwork, nodded in appreciation and left the house.

He was sure Mrs Sinclair would get the message. Nobody messes with Herbert Small.

Nobody.

Chapter Thirty-Three

**Gretna Manse Hotel, Gretna Green, Scotland.
March 31, 2016.**

They checked in to separate rooms at the Gretna Manse Hotel. Jayne immediately had a shower, luxuriating in the soothing heat of the water. Had she made the right choice coming here? Should she have stayed with Paul and gone to London with him? Should she work harder to rescue her marriage? After all, they had been together for nearly 12 years.

Too many questions, too few answers. As she dried herself off, she forced her mind to work on the case. The missing page from the registry still bothered her. Who had cut it out in 1916? And why? Was that page the missing record?

She quickly dressed in a casual top and jeans before she met Mark in the bar of the hotel for a drink. She thought about ringing him to cancel, but decided she needed to escape the four walls of her room.

A tartan waistcoated man approached them as they sat down. 'And what will you be having, madam?'

'A glass of wine, please; something red with a bit of a kick to it.'

'We have an Australian Shiraz?'

'Perfect.'

'And you, sir?'

'A whisky, please.'

The barman turned to the row upon row of bottles of Scotch behind him. 'I'll need a little more help, sir.'

Mark stared at the never-ending row of amber-coloured

bottles, light shining through the glass. 'I don't know, something peaty, I think.'

'A 12-year-old Caol Ila perhaps, from Islay.'

'Sounds good, but I'll never be able to pronounce it.'

'Not to worry, sir. I've been practising the Gaelic for years.'

'Not from here, then?'

'Noooo, not a lowlander, even though I've lived here for nigh on 20 years. A highlander, another outsider.' He poured out their drinks. 'But I married a lovely lass from these parts and here I am. Are you just married?'

Mark and Jayne looked at each other. 'Do we look like we're married?' laughed Jayne.

'Sorry, I just presumed. Not many people come here for the sunny weather.'

They laughed again. 'No, we're here to research Mark's great grandmother. Always said she was married in Gretna Green.'

'Did you find the record? I've heard they'll print out a certificate for you commemorating the marriage over the anvil. Have to pay though. Have to pay for everything these days.'

'There's no record, unfortunately.' Jayne sipped the Shiraz. It wasn't bad, a little oaky. The Australians tended to go overboard with the oak, but it had a lovely jammy taste of fruit with a nice hint of pepper at the end.

'What a shame, you've made a wasted journey. Seen Gretna Green though. Either a place of great happiness or sadness depending on your view of marriage,' he laughed.

'That's true. But my great grandmother was certain she had been married here.'

'Aye, she could have been.' The barman thought for a moment. 'You should check the register.'

'What register?'

'The hotel register. The family who owns the place have had it for at least four generations. Nothing gets thrown away.'

'You mean they still have the registers for 1916? Could we look at them?'

'Aye, they're all in the library. I can get the key from the missus if you'd like. Just give me a second.'

As good as his word, he came back a moment later with an old brass key dangling on a red ribbon. 'The library is on the second floor. The hotel registers are kept in an armoire on the facing wall.'

Jayne put down her drink. 'We'll be back.'

'Aye, didn't Arnold Schwarzenegger say the same thing?'

Jayne rushed out of the bar, turning left to climb the stairs.

Mark followed her. 'What good will this do, Jayne? It's a hotel register not a marriage register.'

'Bear with me, Mark, I have a hunch.'

The library was empty of people. In its centre was a table covered in old magazines extolling the virtues of 'Bonnie Scotland'. Against the far wall, just as the barman had described, stood a tall walnut armoire with a glass front.

Jayne inserted the brass key into the lock and opened the glass door. She scanned the tall, leather ledgers inside, spotting each had a year inscribed on the spine. After two minutes of fruitless searching, she eventually found 1916 between 1892 and 1912. Where else would it be?

She pulled it out and put it down on the desk. The title page stated clearly this was the hotel register of the Gretna Manse Hotel for 1916. On each page was a list of names, addresses, dates checked in and checked out, and room numbers assigned.

Jayne flicked through the pages until she found April 25, 1916.

A sharp breath of surprise escaped her lips as she saw the names written there.

Chapter Thirty-Four

Gretna Manse Hotel, Scotland. April 25, 1916.

Rose had been waiting for David for over seven hours. Why was he so late? She had travelled up on the train from Manchester, changing at Carlisle before finally arriving in Gretna. The train had been full of soldiers, and a kindly guard, seeing she was travelling alone, had moved her to an empty compartment in first class.

She had taken a horse-drawn buggy from the station, lugging her single bag up the steps to the hotel. The elderly receptionist had looked her up and down as one would regard cattle at a market, before sniffing and turning the register towards her.

'It'll be single room, will it?'

'For tonight,' Rose had answered as forcefully as she could.

'Breakfast is at eight to eight thirty. The room has to be empty before noon.' She handed over a large brass key, leaving Rose to find the room on her own.

The furniture inside was stark in the way of country hotels; a single bed, an old wooden dresser with a basin and water jug standing on it, and a copy of Gideon's Bible sitting on the bedside table. A shared bathroom was along the corridor. The lighting was a single gas lamp above the bed; electricity had not yet penetrated this far. There was no fire made in the hearth.

Where was David? He should have been here hours ago. She checked the watch hanging from her dress. 6.30. It was still light outside and the birds were active, harvesting the last insects before darkness descended.

She heard the sound of horses' hooves outside, rushed to the window and peered through the lace curtain.

He was here. But he was with someone else, someone she didn't recognise.

Heavy footsteps on the stairs, someone was running up. A light tap on the door. She rushed over and wrenched it open.

He stood there in his best uniform, a wry smile on his face. 'Come on, there's no time to waste.' He grabbed her hand.

'Why, what's the rush?'

'We're to be married, aren't we? Time to wake the black-smith preacher.'

'But… but… but, I haven't changed.'

'No need, you look beautiful as you are.'

They rushed down the stairs. At the bottom, the sour-faced receptionist and a tall, elegantly dressed man were waiting for them.

'This is my brother, Toby.'

The tall man smirked and held out his hand. 'Miss Clarke, I presume.'

'Come on, you can do the introductions later. The cab is waiting to take us to the village.'

'We're not to be married here?'

'Not at all. We're going to be married like thousands of other loving couples before us, in a blacksmith's forge, by the blacksmith preacher.'

Toby laughed. 'You never struck me as a romantic, brother.'

David hugged Rose tightly. 'This woman brings out a side of me I didn't know existed. Are you ready, Rose?'

She nodded.

'Let's be on our way, then.'

The cab took them to the centre of the village not far away. A few children were playing football in the street. For a moment, they stopped and waved at the passing cab, shouting 'God bless the bride,' and holding their hands up to the window. David gave them each sixpence, and they carried on shouting their greetings until the cab stopped outside the forge.

'The preacher is in his house at the back,' said the cabbie, 'and that will be three shillings, plus a shilling for the wait.'

David gave him a ten-shilling note and was rewarded with a raise of the hat and a blessing, 'May the good Lord give a long and fruitful life to you both. I'll wait to take you back to the hotel.'

'Thank you.'

They hurried around the side of the forge to get the preacher. The man was already putting on his coat. 'I heard the racket coming down the road. I thought for a moment there was a stramash, but I can see from the both of ye, you're here to be married.'

The man was old, but with a canny look to his face.

'Now, there are two questions I have to ask you before I can perform the marriage. Do you have the money?'

He held out his hand and David placed two pound notes in it.

'That's gud, excellent. My wife can act as the other witness but her fee is another pound.'

David opened his wallet and added a pound to the man's hand.

'Gud. Finally, have you lived in Scotland for 21 days or more?' He leant in conspiratorially and whispered, 'Always answer yes is my advice.'

David smiled. 'There's no need, I've been in Paisley for the last three months training the men.' He winked outrageously at the preacher.

'That's gud, very gud. We can begin.'

He ushered them through to the old forge. The walls were whitewashed and tools hung from hooks driven into the bricks. A desk stood on the corner and a large iron anvil occupied the centre of the room. A sign on the wall proclaimed this was the original blacksmith's forge.

'Thousands of couples like yourselves have been married in this room over the years. I have the normal declaration for both parties to say, if that is suitable for both of you.'

Rose coughed. 'Actually, we both agreed a different oath. We would like you to say these words.' She reached into her bag and handed a folded piece of paper to the preacher.

He read the words written on it. 'Well, they are unusual, missing out the commitment to obey the husband in all things, but they are not proscribed by law. Do you both agree to this form of the oath?'

David and Rose looked at each other, turning back to the preacher in unison to say, 'We do.'

The preacher nodded and began speaking. 'Please place your hands together over the anvil. Repeat after me, I...'

He nodded here at David.

'I, David Russell, join my life with yours. Wherever you go, I will go; whatever you face, I will face. For good or ill, in happiness or sadness, come riches or poverty. With deepest joy I receive you into my life that together we may be one. I promise you my love, my fullest devotion, my most tender care. I pledge to you my life as a loving and faithful husband.'

'You certainly know the oath, Captain Russell. And now it's your turn, Miss Clarke.'

Rose began without waiting for the preacher. 'I, Rose Clarke, join my life with yours. Wherever you go, I will go; whatever you face, I will face. For good or ill, in happiness or sadness, come riches or poverty. With deepest joy I receive you into my life that together we may be one. I promise you my love, my fullest devotion, my most tender care. I pledge to you my life as a loving and faithful wife.'

'It seems you no longer need me as you are both man and wife. You may kiss the bride.' David took Rose in his arms and kissed her lightly on her lips, conscious the old woman and his brother were watching him. Then, he looked into her eyes, saw the light of happiness in them, and kissed her again, deeply now, pouring his heart and soul into the kiss.

The preacher coughed. 'When you've finished, you'll need to sign the register on the table.' The old woman brought two chairs from the wall and placed them next to the table. Their names had already been written in the register by her.

Rose picked up the pen and her hand shook as she signed a wavering signature. *Rose A. Clarke.*

David was more composed, signing his name with a flourish. *Capt. David Russell. MC.*

The blacksmith preacher shook both of them by the hand. 'I'll send the certificate up to the Manse later, and I'll send a copy to the registrar in Edinburgh.'

'That's it?' asked Rose.

'That's it, you are now man and wife. Mr and Mrs David Russell.'

Toby came over to shake their hands. 'Congratulations, Brother, and Mrs Russell. Or perhaps I should call you sister now?'

'Just call me Rose, everyone else does.'

'Your carriage is waiting, dear.' David bowed in an exaggerated way.

Rose lengthened her posture and strode out with her arm linked in his. As they climbed into the cab, the driver lifted his hat and said, 'Congratulations, madam and sir.'

Rose leant over and whispered to David, 'I'm a Madam now, am I?'

'For now, and for the rest of time.'

Toby was behind them, patting his pockets. 'Damn, I've left my cigarette case inside, won't be a sec.' He ran back into the blacksmith's forge.

The horse snorted, eager to be on its way.

'I've booked the honeymoon suite for us.'

Rose let out a sigh of relief. 'Wonderful, I don't think I could have borne the first night of our wedding in that lonely room.'

'Sorry I was late - missed the train.'

Rose put her hand on top of his. 'Was the meeting with your parents difficult?'

He turned and smiled at her. 'No more difficult than normal. They will come to love you as much as I do, Rose, I'm sure they will.'

The horse snorted again.

'Where's Toby, he's taking his time…'

Just as David was about to jump down from the cab, Toby came running out of the blacksmith's forge, stuffing something into his pocket. 'Found it, finally.'

He jumped in the cab next to them and the driver clicked the horse forward.

After a glass of champagne to celebrate their marriage, Toby made his excuses and retired upstairs.

After waiting for ten minutes, looking at his watch three times, taking umpteen sips of champagne, David finally turned to Rose. 'I suppose we should go up then?'

Rose smiled. 'I suppose we should.'

Chapter Thirty-Five

Gretna Manse Hotel, Scotland. March 31, 2016.

Jayne touched the yellowing paper with her finger. Halfway down the page, written in a crabbed script, was an entry.

Rose Clarke. Wibbersley Hospital, Manchester. April 25, 1916. Room 27.

The entry had been ruled through neatly with red ink, twice. Beneath it was another entry.

Captain and Mrs Russell. Holton Hall, Derbyshire. April 25, 1916 - April 27, 1916. H.S.

Jayne took out her phone and snapped the cover of the hotel register, the April 25 page and the ones before and after it for her records.

'What does it mean, Jayne?'

'I'm not certain, Mark. At least we know a woman with the same name was staying in the hotel the day she was supposed to be married. And David Russell was staying here with his wife that evening.'

'But what do the two red lines mean?'

'And what's 'H.S'? Let's ask our friendly barman.'

They went downstairs and showed him the picture.

'Well, I don't know for sure why there are two red lines through the name, but I would guess the guest either moved room or checked out.'

'And the "H.S"?'

'That's easy. It's the honeymoon suite. It's still the same room if you would like to see it?'

Jayne and Mark looked at each other and both shook

their heads.

'Can I be getting you another round?'

'Please do. Just one more question. What are the ticks for next to the room number?'

'Oh, it means the guest has paid. If there was an X, it would mean bill later.'

'But there's nothing next to my great grandmother's name?'

The barman scratched his head. 'Sorry, I can't help you, but I can get another drink.' He went back to the bar.

'This must be my great grandmother, mustn't it?' Mark had a pleading note in his voice.

'I'm pretty sure it is. We know she was a VAD in France, perhaps she also served in Manchester. From what I know, they were moved around from hospital to hospital. The name and date are too much of a coincidence for it not to be her.'

'Perhaps she checked in first and they moved to the honeymoon suite when Captain Russell arrived,' said Mark, 'getting married in the blacksmith's shop.'

'That could be one solution. But we have no record of a marriage there.' She held up the picture on the phone. 'This hotel register doesn't prove they were married, only that they stayed in the same hotel on the evening your great grandmother said they were married. It's not proof in a court of law.'

'It must be her.'

'Unfortunately, we have no name for Mrs Russell. It could be your great grandmother or it might be another woman.'

'It must be my great grandmother, it's the only answer.'

'There is one other possibility…'

'What's that?'

'Your great grandmother followed Captain Russell and his new wife here.'

Mark's face fell. 'Like a stalker, you mean?'

Jayne nodded. 'But it doesn't fit with her character from what I know of her.'

Mark shook his head. 'I can't believe it. I don't believe it.'

'Neither do I. But it means we must find a record of the marriage.' She drained the last of the wine from her glass. 'I think we should make an early start for Edinburgh tomorrow. We need to find the certificate.'

Chapter Thirty-Six

Gretna Manse Hotel, Scotland. April 27, 1916.

Rose had never been so happy in her life. Forgotten were the dark days of her mother's death and nursing her father through his depression. Forgotten were the nights in Holloway, waiting for the turn of the key in the lock, the entry of the warders. Forgotten were the horrors of the ward; the men with no limbs, the stench of disinfectant and carbolic acid, the screams in the night from men who were about to die.

There was just her and David, alone, together.

She had been worried at first about the sex, but being a nurse had made the mysteries of the male body clear to her. And, for some reason, she and David just felt so right. The night and the following morning seemed to flow into each other, one eternal time of joy.

She had been ravenous at breakfast, helping herself to more toast and scrambled eggs. Her appetite had received knowing looks from the waiter but she couldn't care less. All that mattered was David was here with her.

His brother, Toby, had stopped by their breakfast table to wish them well. 'I've already checked out, David, I'm off to Edinburgh for a couple of days to see some old friends and then back home to Mother.'

'Give her my love,' said David.

'I will. And I'll also tell her what a beautiful daughter-in-law she now has.'

Rose touched his arm. 'Thank you, Toby, you're so kind. A true brother-in-law.'

'It's all you deserve, dearest Rose.'

He waved goodbye and walked out of the door.

The rest of the day was spent walking in the surrounding countryside. A beautiful area, with soft rolling fields and braes, dotted with the white painted cottages outlined in black, part of the landscape, as if they had been there since time immemorial. The weather had been kind; fleecy white clouds racing against a deep blue sky. At the top of a nearby hill, they stopped and rested for a moment.

Rose took his hand in hers. 'Tell me you will always love me.'

'I will always love you, darling Rose.'

'I wanted to hear the words.'

David put his arm around her shoulders. 'I will always remember this one moment when the only thing in our lives was each other.'

She looked up at the sky. 'One day, we will remember this time, you and me, sitting together on top of a Scottish hill, knowing all that mattered in the world was love.'

'Everybody should have a moment like this.'

They stayed just as they were for the next hour, not speaking, not saying anything, just holding each other close.

After a while the breeze blew stronger and the darkening clouds scurried across the sky.

David said, 'Shall we go back before the rains come?'

Rose was reluctant to leave the top of the hill, but finally nodded, gathering up her things, wishing the day would never end.

They returned to the hotel, missing dinner and staying together in their suite holding each other, as if the world was only them and nobody else existed.

Next morning, the sour-faced woman gave them their

certificate when they checked out. 'From the blacksmith preacher,' she announced, rolling her 'r's' like they would never end.

'Thank you. I'll keep this, Rose. The army may want it as proof of marriage.' He folded it precisely and placed it in his wallet. They took the same cab to the station as had driven them to their marriage.

'I hope you have a wonderful, long and happy life together,' said the cabby before clipping the horse into a trot.

Rose and David sat quietly in the back, holding each other's hand, not wanting to let go.

On arrival at the station, the cabby doffed his cap to them. 'You two walk through to the platform, I'll bring the suitcases.'

Rose and David walked arm in arm to wait for his train.

'Do you think his words will come true?'

'I'm sure they will, Rose. We will grow old disgracefully together.'

She laughed and reached into her bag. 'I have two presents for you. I hope the first will be useful in France.' She gave him a heavy black box.

'But I've given you nothing.'

'You've given me yourself, and it's the best present I could ever receive.'

David opened the box. Inside was a brand new wristlet watch.

'It's one of the new types, with luminous dials so you can see the time in the dark. I hope it's useful. I even had it inscribed on the back. See?'

'David turned it over. '*To David, April 25, 1916,*' he read out loud.

'The second is something to remember me by.' She gave him a square of paper folded into four.

He opened it out and there she was, or at least, there was her likeness. 'It's beautiful, Rose, it captures the glint in your eye and that hidden smile on your lips.'

'I drew it at the hospital. Something to remember your nurse by when you're at the Front.'

He kissed the picture once, folded it back into a square and placed it carefully into his wallet. Then, he reached out for Rose and pulled her to him, hugging her as tightly as he could.

They stayed there, two people standing t172ogether as one, until the train arrived in a flurry of smoke and opening doors.

The parting was quick, neither wanted to make that awful time last longer; a few words, a final kiss holding each other close, a last hug. There was a cheer from some soldiers as David ran to board the train just as it pulled away from the station. A wave and another kiss and the train hurried north to Glasgow in another cloud of steam.

And he was gone.

Rose stayed on the platform, watching him fade away into the distance, his face framed by the window of the train.

They say parting is always difficult. For Rose, it wasn't so much that he had gone, it was that she had been left behind, alone on that bleak station platform, waiting for her train south to Manchester.

Would she ever see him again?

Chapter Thirty-Seven

Edinburgh, Scotland. April 1, 2016.

Jayne and Mark left the hotel after an early breakfast and drove across Scotland to Edinburgh. Throughout the two hours of the journey, Mark was silent.

'I've booked a seat at the Scottish People's Research Centre in the Reid Room.'

Finally Mark spoke. 'This is a long shot, isn't it?'

Jayne realised it was the time to be honest with him. 'If the records are not online in either Find My Past or The Genealogist, they are unlikely to be available to the readers at the centre.'

'So why are we going then?'

'We have to be certain. Look, your great grandmother was definitely in Gretna Green on the night she says she was. I'm pretty certain the records had been cut from the register.'

'But who would want to do such a thing? They were just another couple enjoying a quick wedding during the war.'

'That's what we have to find out.'

Mark became silent again, before speaking once more. 'I can't help thinking about what you said.'

'And what did I say?'

'About my great grandmother being the World War One equivalent of a stalker. Could she have cut the records showing David Russell marrying another woman?'

'Why?'

'Jealousy. Envy. Possession.'

Jayne shook her head. 'From all I know about Rose

Clarke, I can't believe that. She was a proud, independent woman. I can't imagine her ever being so desperate as to follow another man all the way to Gretna Green on the night of his wedding. I think we must look for a more obvious solution.'

'Which is?'

'Rose Clarke and David Russell were married on April 25 in Gretna Green. We just have to prove it.'

Jayne parked the car around the corner from New Register House. It was a long time since she had visited Edinburgh and the only knowledge she had of the modern city came from Ian Rankin's Rebus novels. They seemed to concentrate on a darker, more alcoholic side of the city.

The building was made from the same honey-coloured stone as the rest of Edinburgh, and had the look and appearance of many of the government buildings of the time; solid, dependable, trustworthy.

The young receptionist was a woman of Chinese descent who spoke with the broadest Scots accent.

'How can I help you?'

'A seat reservation in the Reid Room for a Mrs Sinclair.' For a second, Jayne hesitated over the word 'Mrs'.

The woman checked her computer. 'I have it here. You'll have to get reader's tickets, I'm afraid. A strange local rule from the Scottish Parliament down the road.'

They passed over two driving licences.

The receptionist entered their details into the computer. 'And what would you like to see?'

'The marriage records for Gretna Green in 1916.'

'A wartime romance? No problem. Those records will be filed under Dumfries and Galloway.' She opened a metal filing cabinet and slid out the drawer, selecting two microfilms. 'Here you go.'

The young woman showed them to their seat in the Reid Room. 'Can you work the reader or would you like me to show you how to do it?'

'No, I'm fine. Just one other thing. If I understand correctly, each local registrar sent the records once a year to the Central Registry in Edinburgh?'

The young woman smiled at Jayne. 'That's correct.'

'These records were then collated and entered into the main register for Scotland.'

'Again, correct. Obviously, this was done by hand in those days, now, as with everything, it's all on a disc somewhere.'

'So if we wanted to look at the original records, how would we do that?'

'Well, it's most unusual as most of the records are held in the microfilms. The originals are not kept here but in a depository. You can order them but it will take at least five working days for them to get here.'

'If they exist…'

'That's right, if they exist.'

'Well, we'll take a look at these first and see if we need to check the originals.'

'No worries, give me a shout if you need me.'

Jayne threaded the microfilm though the reader and quickly whizzed through to the correct date and place: 'In 1916, there were four places where marriages were performed in Gretna Green.'

'You've been doing research.'

Jayne stopped at April 25. There were four weddings. None of them had the name Rose Clarke or David Russell. 'Look, the other venues sent their returns in but nothing from the blacksmith's shop.'

She moved the machine backwards two days and forwards two days. All four venues had returns for weddings, including the blacksmith's shop, but no Rose Clarke or David Russell.

Mark slumped down into his seat. 'What shall we do now?'

'I will request to see the originals sent by the blacksmith preacher and we can return to take a look at them. But to be honest, Mark, I would be surprised if we find anything.'

His shoulders seemed to sag even further. 'I suppose it's the end then. We'll never prove they were ever married.'

'But doesn't it strike you as strange we have a record for a Captain and Mrs David Russell staying in the honeymoon suite, but no record of their marriage?'

'They could have been married elsewhere?'

'Then why go to Gretna Green?' Jayne switched off the microfilm reader. 'It certainly seems bloody strange to me.'

Chapter Thirty-Eight

Didsbury, Manchester. April 1, 2016.

The long journey back to Manchester seemed to last much longer than driving up.

Before they left the building, Jayne had filled in a form to see the originals, more out of curiosity than anything else.

The Chinese lady behind the counter had helpfully suggested checking with the blacksmith's shop in Gretna Green itself, but Jayne had explained they had already performed a search. Even this lady's chirpiness seemed to be dampened by the news.

The woman examined the form carefully. 'You're looking for a marriage between a Rose Clarke and a David Russell in 1916?'

'Correct. We think it was in Gretna Green but it's not on the computer records.'

'That's strange. I had a similar request about three weeks ago from a man.'

Jayne's eyes widened. 'Is that so?'

'Was he another relative? A small, dapper man, wore a trilby.'

Jayne shook her head. 'Not a relative, I don't think. Did he find anything?'

'I don't know. He seemed to be in an awful hurry all the time. Impatient little man he was.'

'Could you ask them to find the documents as soon as possible? We are under a little time pressure.'

'No worries, I'll send the request into the depository and

stamp it express.' She leant forward and whispered to Rose. 'I'll also get them to send everything the rude little man found too. We should get it back in a couple of days. If you give me your number, I'll give you a call when it comes in.'

Jayne pulled out a business card from her wallet, writing her mobile number on the back.

'I'll also ask them to dig around for it, records often were misfiled during the war years.' She wrote a note at the bottom of the form. 'Thanks for coming. I hope we can find it for you.'

Mark had said nothing since leaving Edinburgh. It was only as they came off the M60 to go to his house he began to speak. 'My father will be gloating. I told you so. Waste of time.' He mimicked the whining voice of his father.

'You could show him the entry in the hotel reservations book. At least it proves both she and David Russell were there.'

'But not as man and wife.'

'It's not proof, I know, but...'

'I think we should give it up, Jayne. Mark shook his head. 'It's a wild goose chase, a waste of your time and mine. What can we do in three days?'

'Don't give up so easily. We must have missed something.'

'What, Jayne? You're the expert, you tell me what we missed.'

Jayne didn't have an answer.

Mark tapped the top of the dashboard.'Just take me home.'

Jayne dropped him outside his door. Once again, she saw the old man peeking out from behind the curtains. Mark didn't say goodbye as he left the car.

Men, why did they always act like boys? Not finding

anything was an obstacle in the investigation, but obstacles were there to be overcome. It was the same in the police force; grown men would be kicking the hell out of some poor defenceless locker just because a smart lawyer had thwarted them. Her advice was always work better, think smarter.

It still hadn't helped her with promotion though. She wasn't one of the boys.

She shrugged her shoulders and slotted an Oasis CD into the player. *Wonderwall* immediately boomed out from her speakers. She doubled the volume and put the car in gear, racing away from the problems of Mark Russell and his family. An American Cabernet was waiting for her in the wine fridge; she felt she deserved a decent drop tonight. And there was probably a meltingly smooth Valrhona hidden somewhere in the kitchen.

A part of her hoped that Paul would be at home so they could sort it all out. Another part of her hoped he wasn't.

While Liam Gallagher was belting out *Don't Look Back in Anger* in his Manchester whine, she realised how tired she was. It was a long drive back from Edinburgh. Even in the BMW, her back and shoulders were beginning to ache.

She cut off Liam in mid-snarl and parked the car. The house was quiet, no lights anywhere to be seen. At least Paul wasn't there. She wouldn't have to endure a long conversation about their marriage and why it had gone wrong.

Not tonight. She couldn't face it tonight.

She opened the front door. Immediately, the hairs on the back of her neck rose. There was a strange feeling about the place. Something was wrong. She switched on the light.

The pictures in the hall were lying on the floor. She ran into the kitchen. The computer lay smashed on the floor, a useless piece of junk. Pots and pans were scattered around the room. The Ikea clock was smashed. Milk and eggs and cheese were strewn everywhere. The stench of wine filled her nostrils as she crunched glassware and fragments of china beneath her feet.

The place had been trashed.

The cat? Where was Mr Smith?

A plaintive miaow answered her from beneath the island table. She reached down and hugged him to her.

Who had done this?

She ran upstairs, still carrying Mr Smith. The upstairs bedrooms were untouched, still as she had left them the day before.

Perhaps whoever did it was still in the house? She took an old cricket bat of Paul's and checked every room.

Nothing.

She ran back downstairs. The box files for all her cases lay strewn on the floor and there was no sign of the acetate folder. She searched high and low but it was gone.

Jayne picked up the stool and placed it next to the counter. She put her head in her hands. A terrible end to a terrible day. Who had done this to her beautiful home, the one place where she felt safe and secure?

Just as that thought was running through her head, the mobile rang. She picked it up expecting it to be Paul.

'Er, Mrs Sinclair, it's Richard Russell here. I won't beat about the bush. Mark and I have decided to dispense with your services. We won't be needing you any more.'

Chapter Thirty-Nine

Buxton, near Manchester. April 2, 2016.

It was Bono who accompanied her on the long drive out to Buxton. His plaintive croak on *I still haven't found what I'm looking* for seemed to be the perfect description of how she felt that morning.

Of course, she had called the police. Immediately they realised they were dealing with an ex-cop and sent two young bobbies round to the house, with a couple of detectives following half an hour later.

The young coppers were wonderfully supportive, checking she was okay and making sure nothing was touched before the detectives arrived. They looked so young both of them, perhaps the force was hiring babies these days.

The detectives were a different matter. She knew both of them vaguely from her time on the force. When she was a Detective Sergeant, they were just nameless plods, given the thankless task of patrolling the city centre on a Saturday night. It was known as the graveyard shift in the force, as it was where they buried the thugs and the no-hopers. For some reason, these two had escaped, but to her they were still zombies.

Their questions were routine, straight out of the police manual.

'Has anybody threatened you recently?'

'No.'

'Have you annoyed anybody at your workplace?'

'I work alone. And anyway, why would this be my

fault?' She pointed out the mess in the kitchen.

'Have you annoyed any of the neighbourhood gangs or kids?'

Jayne rolled her eyes to the ceiling. 'Noooo. And kids round here wouldn't do this.'

One of them just coughed. The other continued anyway. 'You said you were away last night…?'

'I was in Scotland. I spent the night in Gretna Green. The Gretna Green Manse, if you'd like to check with them.'

'A runaway marriage?' One of them laughed, but immediately stopped when he saw Jayne's face.

'No. Work.'

The other one coughed again. 'And what work do you do, Ms Sinclair?'

They obviously knew Jayne had once been in the force. 'I'm a genealogical investigator. I track down family mysteries.'

'Is this a dangerous line of work?'

'Not normally, no. Occasionally, one comes up against people who don't want their secrets to be revealed.'

'Could this be the case here?' The one who kept coughing at least had the beginnings of a police brain. Could this be to do with the case?

She thought immediately of Herbert Small and his visit the other night. That slimeball must be responsible. Only he would take the acetate folder with the drawing and the medallion.

If he was the one who did this to her, she wasn't going to tell the police, she was more than capable of handling him. 'To be honest, I don't know,' she answered, realising that starting a sentence with 'to be honest' was a giveaway to any copper.

The smart one wrote in his notebook.

The joker carried on regardless, going through his usual list of questions. 'To your knowledge, is anything missing?'

'No,' she lied.

'Have you checked?'

'Of course I've bloody checked. The place has been trashed. Nothing has been stolen.'

That stumped them. They were used to dealing with robberies and burglaries, not this.

'Who do you think could have done this?'

Should she tell them about Herbert Small?

No, these bozos would only screw it up and then she would never get the Russells' items back. 'If I knew, I would have told you the second you walked through the door,' she lied once again, hoping they wouldn't notice.

They didn't.

In the middle of the interview, she heard Paul let himself in. She had called him before calling the police.

'And this is your husband?'

'Yes.'

'You weren't at home tonight, sir?'

'No, he wasn't,' she answered for Paul as he looked around at the mess that was the kitchen.

'Are you okay, Jayne?' he said ignoring the police.

'Fine, Paul, I came home to this.'

He came across and gave her a hug. 'It's okay, don't worry, it will be okay.'

For a moment, hearing his words, Jayne felt a flood of emotion surge through her chest.

The detective joker repeated his question. 'You weren't at home last night, Mr Sinclair?'

'My surname is Jones. We wife kept our own names when we were married. And no, I wasn't at home, I was staying in a hotel.'

The smart detective stared pointedly at the joker. 'And why was that, sir?'

Jayne interrupted. 'Because, detectives, myself and my husband have recently split up. Is that enough personal information for you both?'

The smart one held his hands up. 'Jayne, you know the job, we have to ask the questions to cover our arses. You know what the forms are like.'

'It's not a domestic, okay? Paul would never do this.'

'They think... I...' Paul spluttered as he looked around the trashed kitchen.

It was Jayne's turn to calm him. 'It's standard procedure. Incidents like this are usually the work of an angry husband or lover.' She turned back to the detectives. 'Any more questions?'

They looked at each other. 'No, I think we're done here. We'll get the fingerprint boys to come over just as soon as they can. We've got a murder in Withington at the moment.'

'Don't bother.'

'We have to, Jayne. You've called it in, we have to follow up. In the meantime, I would get that fixed if I were you.' The smart detective pointed to the smashed lock on the front door. 'It suggests a break-in for reasons unknown. Your husband has a key, I presume.'

Jayne nodded.

'See, we're not as stupid as we look.' He pointed to the other detective. 'We'll follow up, Jayne. You know the drill. If you think of anything that could help, let me know immediately.' He handed over his card. 'We look after our own, Jayne, even when they are no longer one of us. I'll make sure the street lads come down here more often over the next few days.'

The fingerprint team finally came over, dusting the

place down and finding nothing.

With Paul's help, she tidied the place up just enough to make it habitable.

He spent the night in the spare bedroom. She was glad to have him around, even though she knew if there were trouble, she would be the one who sorted it out.

When he had gone to bed, she checked the box files. All her notes on the Russell case were missing. Even worse, she couldn't find the acetate file with the envelopes anywhere.

She didn't sleep a wink, wondering who had done this and why? Was Herbert Small responsible? Was it linked to the Russell case? Was he giving her a warning? Telling her to stay away?

It had to be him, nobody else had any interest in the case. But they had found nothing yet. Why would he destroy her home? The more she thought about it, the more she became convinced that only Herbert Small would do this to her. When she met him, she would give him such a kicking he would remember it for the rest of his life.

Eventually, she fell asleep to be woken by a loud banging. The locksmith had arrived on the dot at 8.30.

After he had gone and Paul had left for work, she couldn't bear to be in the house on her own. Even as she tidied up the mess, she knew she had to get out. There was only one person she wanted to see right now.

Her father was sat in his usual place facing the window, the Guardian open at the crossword. His head was back and his mouth open, a gentle snore the only sound.

She touched him on the shoulder and he awoke instantly.

'Hello, lass, good to see you.'

'You were napping?'

'I prefer to call it thinking with my eyes closed. Napping is for old people.'

'And you, a stripling of 72.'

He flexed his muscles. 'Plenty of life in the old dog yet.'

'Are you still terrorising the staff?'

'Not this week. I'll give 'em a break. Time off for good behaviour. How's the case?'

Jayne's face fell. 'Not good. No records in Scotland, but a hotel register in Gretna Green with Rose Clarke's name in it for the exact date she said she was there.'

'So what's the problem?'

'There's also an entry for a Captain and Mrs David Russell.'

'Could be her. She checked in first and he checked in later.'

'But why is there no record of their marriage?'

'You checked the original records in Edinburgh?'

'I checked the microfilms. No records. I've ordered the originals.'

He sucked in his breath through his teeth. 'If they are not on microfilm, it's unlikely they would be in the original records.'

'My feeling too. And there are a few other things…'

'Like?'

'I've just been sacked by my clients. Paul and I have broken up. And my house was broken into last night. Just a normal screwed-up evening for Jayne Sinclair.'

He put his arms up to give her a hug. She bent down and felt his thin arms wrap around her.

'The clients don't deserve you, lass.'

'Probably true.'

'You and Paul have been heading for a cliff for a long time.'

'Probably true.'

'And you'll find whoever broke into your house.'

Jayne thought for a moment. 'Definitely true.'

Her father pulled out of the hug and stared at her for a long time. 'I recognise the set of your jaw. I used to watch you as a kid when you couldn't do something; you'd grit your teeth and keep going till you made it. You're not giving up on this case, are you?'

Jayne smiled. Her father knew her so well, but until that moment, she hadn't even admitted it to herself. 'We're so close. There's something I'm missing. You know the feeling, when there's something you've forgotten but can't remember what it is.'

Her father stared out of the window.

Jayne kicked herself. How thoughtless could she be? 'I didn't mean it in that way, Dad.'

He smiled. 'I know you didn't, lass. But it's happening more and more often now. Some days I wake up and I just don't know where I am. It's even worse when I can't remember who I am, like my name is on the tip of my tongue and I can't quite remember it.'

She reached forward and gave him a hug. 'I'll always be here to remind you.'

He pushed her away. 'Don't go all soppy on me. What are your next steps?'

'I don't know. For once I'm stumped, Dad.'

'I've been thinking. I do it occasionally when I get tired of listening to the old biddies over there.' He turned and waved at three women watching TV. They waved back at him. 'Gagging for it, all three of them.'

'Dad, you can't say things like that.'

'Well, it's true. Drop their knickers in a shot that lot would. Anyway, what was I saying?'

'You've been thinking,' she reminded him.

'That was it. You told me Rose Clarke ended up in an asylum like this place, didn't she?'

'It's not that bad, Dad.'

'I know, there's always the Golden Girls over there.' He waved again and they waved back. 'Well, I remember you said it was in Hatherton. The village isn't far from here, near Bakewell. And I checked on Google, Holton Hall, the Russell's old residence, is just a couple of miles further on.'

'You checked on Google?'

'Somebody has to do some thinking around here. Perhaps they have records of her time there. It's a long shot, but as I see it, you've nowt else at the moment.'

'I'll go this afternoon as long as you promise me one thing.'

'Of course, anything for you, lass.'

'You'll leave the Golden Girls, and their knickers, alone.'

Her father just smiled.

Chapter Forty

Holton Hall, Derbyshire. April 28, 1916.

'He married her?' Lady Lappiter screamed at the top of her voice. 'After I expressly told him such a union was forbidden.'

Toby nodded his head.

Sir James Russell, David's father, looked up from his entomology book. 'Well, that's it then. Nothing to be done. We'll welcome the gal.'

'Welcome her? We'll do no such thing.' Lady Lappiter's voice rose the angrier it became. 'I'm having no gold-digging strumpet in my house.'

'Don't worry, Mother, I've made sure you won't have to welcome her.'

The book closed with a loud bang. 'What have you done?' The watery blue eyes of his father stared straight at him; the face was beginning to redden, the nostrils flaring.

Toby looked to his mother for help. 'I removed the record from the register.' He pulled out a page from the marriage registry in the Gretna Green blacksmith's shop. He gave a childish giggle. 'It was pretty easy, nobody was looking. I also arranged for the record in Edinburgh to vanish when it arrives. It was surprisingly inexpensive.'

'Good, so when David comes to his senses and realises what a ridiculous fool he has been, there will be no record of any marriage.' She smiled like a Derbyshire cat. 'For once, you haven't disappointed me, Toby.'

His father threw the book across the room, narrowly missing his son. 'You stupid, stupid, boy. What will you do when David finds out?'

His father struggled to get up from the chair, his face red and his moustache bristling with fury. 'What will you do then?'

Toby looked across at his mother.

'We will cross that bridge when we come to it, James. Do be quiet and go back to your ants and bees and spiders. You've let me run this family and this household for the last 30 years, why break the habit of a lifetime?'

Sir James Russell slammed his fist down on the table, rattling the bone china cups. 'Because you have gone too far this time, Marjory. I'm going to write to David telling him what you've done.' Sir James took two steps forward and collapsed over the table, the cups and saucers crashing onto the floor.

Lady Marjory was beside her husband in a second, loosening his tie. 'Toby, call Walters now, your father's having a heart attack.'

Toby just sat in his chair, staring at his father struggling for breath, his face redder and redder.

'TOBY!' Lady Lappiter screamed.

The door opened wide and Walters the butler rushed in, took one look at Sir James lying on the floor and rushed out again.

Toby just sat there, watching his father struggle for breath on the floor, his mouth opening and closing like a goldfish out of water.

'Help me!' his mother screamed at him once more.

He just sat in his chair, gripping the armrests tightly with his fingers.

By the time the doctor arrived from the village, Sir James Russell, Lord Lappiter, was already in a coma. The doctor ordered an ambulance to take him to the hospital in

Bakewell.

Lady Lappiter collapsed and was carried upstairs to her room, where the doctor administered a strong sedative.

Afterwards, the doctor spoke quietly to Toby. 'Between the two of us, I don't hold out much hope of a recovery, I'm afraid. The heart attack was massive. We'll do our best of course, but, if he recovers, and I doubt he will, the shock to the system was so great...' The doctor tailed off.

Toby just stood there, barely comprehending what the doctor was saying.

'You need to write to your brother. In Scotland, isn't he?'

Toby nodded, 'I think so.'

'I would warn him what's happened. He'll have to come back and sort out the estate. Would you like me to ask the lawyer to come?'

Toby snapped out of his inertia. He had to take control now. 'Please ask him to come tomorrow.'

'Would you like anything for the shock? Seeing your father so ill...'

Toby shook his head. 'It's not necessary, Doctor.' He walked towards the door and the doctor naturally followed him. 'Thank you for your time. I'm sure you did the best you could for my father. There will be no criticism of your treatment.'

The doctor stood up straighter. 'Your father had a long history of heart problems, it was only a matter of time...'

'Yes, yes, as I said there will be no criticism of your treatment. I'm sure I can trust you to keep news of my father's illness quiet for the moment. We wouldn't like people to be distressed, would we?' His eyes looked up towards the upper rooms where his mother was resting.

'Of course, you can rely on me.'

'Thank you, I don't want my mother more upset than

necessary. I'll contact my brother in due course. As you know, he's doing important war work at the moment. Walters will see you out.'

The doctor put on his hat. 'Good day to you, Mr Russell.'

'And to you, Dr McBride.'

Toby closed the door and leant against it. A smile crossed his face. He wouldn't write to his brother yet, not yet, let David go back to France and his fighting.

First, he had to make sure of his ground. Father might recover, and then again, he might not.

Chapter Forty-One

Holton Hall, Derbyshire. April 2, 2016.

Jayne took the A6 out of Buxton, turning left two miles after Bakewell on to a long tree-lined lane. She checked her satnav again; Holton Hall was another two hundred yards on the right.

She drove slowly, taking an unkempt turn-off and parking the car beneath a large sycamore just coming into leaf. In front of her, two padlocked iron gates guarded a short gravel driveway leading to an old stone hall. The windows were boarded up with metal shutters. The roof had three tall plants growing from one of the chimney stacks, while pale blue paint was peeling from the door in sharp, pointed flakes.

So this is where David Russell grew up. It certainly was a privileged life, different from a haberdasher's in Shoreditch.

She stood in front of the gates and for a moment, felt the past come to life. A Rolls Royce gliding down the driveway, young women in long dresses swishing elegantly through the grounds, the sound of a tennis ball being stroked on a court, the clink of glasses and ice in frosted jugs. And at the edge, hidden in the shadows, an immense and fragile sadness waiting to step out into the open air.

They didn't come often, these 'moments' as she liked to call them. But ever since she was a child, they had visited her at the strangest times, usually brought on by a smell or a sound or the taste in her mouth. It was like the past had come alive and she was surrounded by it.

Her father used to tease her about it. 'Your "moments" are nowt but a bit of imagination, lass. You have to stop reading all those history books.' But she knew it was more than that. It was as if she had tapped into a memory buried in the stones themselves, like a recording etched into the vinyl of an album. Somehow, she was the needle that brought it back to life.

She shook her head and was returned to the present. To a dull, dilapidated, desperate present.

Above her head, at the join where the two iron gates met, a small notice was displayed.

Holton Hall. To be sold by public auction on the 15 April, 2016. For further enquiries, contact Johnson Brothers Property Valuers and Auctioneers, Bakewell.

And, all at once, a wave of immense sadness washed over her, filling her with fear.

This was not a happy place. It had never been a happy place.

Chapter Forty-Two

Hatherton, Derbyshire. April 2, 2016.

After her dispiriting visit to Holton Hall, she travelled back towards Buxton to find the small village of Hatherton.

It was a beautiful part of England; rolling hills penetrated by deep dales and sharp-edged granite rocks. She remembered coming here with her father as a child, walking through Lathkill Dale listening to the sound of the water flowing down the shallow river and exploring the shafts of the old lead mines lining the sides of the valley.

Happy days, away from her mother. Just she and her father together, not talking much, except when she spotted something interesting like the dippers digging for grubs in the fast-flowing river. Her father was a fount of information, a man who seemed to know the name of every flower, every rock and every bird.

She parked the car in the centre of the village next to a war memorial. 'In remembrance' was carved at the top of the stone pillar, followed by the names of six men, all privates, who had died in the First World War. Beneath these names, in a different style of carving, were two others, casualties of the Second World War.

Around her, the robins sang as they fought for territory. A village shop-cum-post office-cum-cafe had a Walls Ice Cream sign posted outside the door. Inside, an old woman was arranging a plate of home-made scones on the counter.

As Jayne opened the door, a bell rang loudly and the woman looked up. 'I'm sorry to bother you, but I'm looking for Hatherton Hospital. I believe it's around here.'

'The old asylum?'

Jayne nodded.

'Nothing left of the place, dear. Closed 20 years ago it did. Village nearly closed with it. No jobs any more.'

'So it's not there?'

'Gone, like everything else. They put up a whole lot of maisonettes, townhouses and detached residences in its place. Or so they described them. Look more like boxes with windows, if you ask me. Some people drive as far as Sheffield every day. More fool them is what I think. Still, it kept the village alive, but why you would want to see the place beats me. You had a relative there, did you?'

'Yes, an aunt,' Jayne lied.

'Wasn't a very nice place. Oh, it were pretty enough, the old building, and they kept the grounds beautiful. Well, they had free workers with the residents, didn't they? But not a happy place. Wouldn't want to live in the new estate myself, too many memories, I think. It stands to reason, don't it?'

'I suppose it does.'

'Now, Mrs Atkins, she worked there for years and the stories she tells. Well, the hair on the back of your arms stands up at the thought, it does. Not a nice place, you couldn't pay me to live there.'

'Thank you.' Jayne was about to go, but then turned back. 'This Mrs Atkins, does she live nearby?'

'She's down at the end of the village, lived here all her life, and intends to die here, or so she says. Me, I think she has the secret of eternal life that one.'

Jayne pointed left. 'This way?'

'That's right, my love. Green door, you can't miss it. If you're going there, could you be a dear and take her milk for her. Save me doin' it later.'

'No problem. And could I have four of your scones, they look delicious.'

'She loves a scone, does Amy, she don't get many visitors and she loves to chat about the old days.'

Chapter Forty-Three

Hatherton, Derbyshire. April 2, 2016.

Jayne was sat in a small living room, balancing a cup of tea on one knee and a plate with a freshly buttered scone on the other.

She had knocked on the door and Mrs Atkins had greeted her like a long-lost friend, inviting her in immediately. So different from the big city where people were afraid of strangers, treating everybody with suspicion.

Mrs Atkins was a small woman with a back bent like a branch of hawthorn and a trace of white stubble around her jaw. Her eyes were the clearest shade of eggshell blue and probably still as sharp as the day she was born 83 years ago. Her one problem was her hearing.

'You'll have to speak up, dear, I'm as deaf as last Sunday.' She cupped her hand over her right ear, turning her head so it faced Jayne.

'I said lovely to meet you. The lady in the post office said…' Jayne shouted.

'I'm deaf dear, not stupid. You don't need to shout, just speak slowly and clearly.'

The old woman still had the ability to put people in their place. 'Sorry, Mrs Atkins. I just came to visit the old asylum,' Jayne enunciated as clearly as she could.

'Not there any more, dear, knocked it down years ago.'

'Did you work there?'

'I did. Started there when I was 16 and they had to throw me out when they were pulling the walls down. I were sad to see the place go, but the world changes. Care in the Community is what they called it. Just saving money it was. Dumping people who had nowhere else to go onto the streets. You know some of them had lived in the hospital all their lives, didn't know anything else. One man had been in Hatherton since he were five years old. Mr Sanderson, we called him. He was placed in the asylum in the 1920s and they shoved him out into a half-way house when he was in his 60s. I heard he couldn't manage. Wasn't used to looking after himself, see. Died, he did. Or so they said.' She touched the side of her nose. 'But we know better, don't we?'

Jayne decided to let the old woman talk. 'That's why I'm here, Mrs Atkins.'

'What, speak up woman, don't mumble.'

'I said that's why I'm visiting you. I wonder if you remember an old woman by the name of Clarke, Rose Clarke.'

The old woman spent some time with her head cocked to one side, before lifting up her cup with both hands and loudly slurping a large mouthful. Jayne saw the fingers were arthritic, knuckles swollen and wrists bending inwards. A hard life working in a mental hospital for all those years.

Shakily she put the cup back onto the saucer. 'Don't remember no Rose Clarke. We only had one Rose in those days. A lovely old woman she was, always polite and beautifully groomed, every day, making sure her hair was combed and her clothes were immaculate. Not like some of the others, I'll tell you. Some of them just let themselves go, but not Rose. Loved to draw too. Sat out in the garden sometimes, drawing the old building. I have one of her drawings somewhere. Now where was it?'

The old woman took a bite of a scone and washed it

down with a long slurp of tea, forgetting that she was supposed to be looking for the drawing. 'Every day, when I was working, she came and helped me serve the food. She was good at it too. Knew exactly where everything went. Shame about her though. She passed away in the 70s. She'd been there for years, nobody knew why, but there was nowhere else for her to go, so she stayed at the hospital. Told me once, her early days in the hospital had been hard, but she became used to it. Well, they all did, didn't they? Nowhere else to go.'

'Can you remember Rose's surname?'

Again, there was a long pause as the old woman dredged through her memories. 'I think she called herself Rose Russell. Quite a common name, Russell, especially round these parts. Had a London accent did Rose, not Derbyshire at all. At times, she acted like it was still 1916 and she was waiting for her husband to come home from war. I suppose that's what sent her round the bend.' Here, Mrs Atkins made a spiral with her index finger against her temple. 'Always talked of her son too, as if one day he would come and take her home. He never did, of course. Nobody ever left that place.'

So Rose had been in the asylum, the Russells had been telling the truth. Quietly, Jayne asked her next question. 'Do you remember when she passed away?'

'It must have been around 1974, I think. No, I tell a lie, it was after the miners' strike. You know, we had a generator and I had to get it started every evening when the power cuts came. Had to have light and heat, didn't we? But it were a right bugger that generator. Local miners used to send someone round to help me they did. Didn't want the patients to suffer, they said.' She stopped and slurped from her teacup. 'Now where was I?'

'You were telling me when Mrs Rose Russell passed away.'

'It must have been 1975 or 1976, somewhere round then.'

'What happened?'

'Well, she was cremated. Most of them were, you know. Cost too much to bury them and one of her relatives came for her things.'

'Her things?'

'An old case. She loved looking in it, carried it with her all the time. Almost as if she were going on holiday or about to leave the hospital. But it wasn't a large case, more like a vanity case, you know, for make-up and such like.'

Jayne took a deep breath. 'A relative came for the case?'

'A young man he was, in his thirties, had a London accent too. Quite handsome, with a quiff of dark hair. Looked like Elvis he did.'

Chapter Forty-Four

Northern Quarter, Manchester. April 2, 2016.

Herbert Small relaxed in his office. He liked to separate his work from his home, and coming here every day gave his life a regularity which he enjoyed.

He sipped his warm milk, revelling in the gentle warmth it delivered to his upset stomach. It seemed to be a family trait, a gippy tummy. His grandmother had suffered, and his mother, and now him.

Other people bestowed money and wealth and riches on their offspring, his family had given him an irritable bowel.

He checked his computer once more. After his activities of two nights ago, he was expecting a message from Mrs Sinclair, contrite and apologetic.

Nothing yet.

He laughed to himself. And then laughed again.

He hadn't had this much fun since he had strung up that cat from a tree by its hind legs. It had struggled and struggled, scratching with its unsheathed claws at an unknown enemy. He had watched it, wriggling and shaking and striking out until finally it had given up and just hung there, unmoving.

Slowly, he approached it and prodded the black chest with a stick. Instantly, it had come to life again, snarling and scratching and screeching.

He laughed again at the memory. Such fun he had as a child. Shame it wasn't with other children, but he always knew he was different, not like the rest.

And now he played with them like he played with that

cat. Mrs Sinclair was smart, but she would never find the birth certificate in time. It took him three weeks of diligent work to dig it up. By the time he had found the truth, the Russells had decided to sack him.

The little scrap of paper proved everything once and for all. What the Russells would give to take a look at it. But he wouldn't let them, not after the way they treated him. He had placed the certificate back in the same place he found it. There it would remain for another hundred years. Or until hell froze over. Whichever happened first.

He took another sip of warm milk. His stomach felt better as the warm liquid eased the queasiness that had bothered him all day. Dunphy had been easy to deal with too; 5000 pounds now bolstered Small's account simply for telling him what he could have found out with a single phone call; the Russells were still trying to prove their claim to the Lappiter estate. Another 5000 pounds would be paid after April 4, when they failed in their search. He had assured Dunphy that they would never succeed.

Perhaps, he should set himself up as an assurance company? It was certainly far more lucrative than trolling through the bottom of the Bona Vacantia list looking for pearls in beds of old oysters.

He picked up the silver medallion from his desk with its small bows of purple, white and green. Quite a pretty little thing and worth a bob or two, he guessed. Shame about the picture of the old harridan inside. Perhaps he should take it out and replace it with one of his mother?

One nagging doubt remained though. Mrs Sinclair. She was the wild card in his little game. Or was she a joker? He wasn't sure, but it was her presence that had made him uneasy.

He took another sip of milk to calm his stomach.

There were only a couple of days to go, no time for her to discover the truth. Shame about the Russells; if they had just been nicer to him, he would be telling them where to find the birth certificate instead of concealing it from them.

But that was the game, wasn't it. Fortune favours the brave.

Sure, he would lose some money from the legacy, but it wasn't much. Eamon Dunphy had more than compensated him for hiding the information.

All in all, it had been a satisfactory couple of days.

Herbert took another sip of milk and began to laugh. If only he could see the faces of the Russells now, particularly the old bastard.

'Have they realised yet they'll never find the truth?' And he began to laugh again, spilling the milk down his blue V-neck jumper.

Chapter Forty-Five

Sale, Manchester. April 2, 2016.

Jayne drove the 35 miles back to Manchester as quickly as she could, parking outside the Russell house in the suburb of Sale just as the sun was going down. She had stopped off for a short time at Bakewell Library on the way back to check out the local studies department.

As she walked up the path, the curtain at the window twitched again.

When she pressed the bell, Mark answered the door. 'Mrs Sinclair, I presume you want to return the envelopes?' He held out his hand.

'I think I've discovered something you need to hear, Mark.'

The father appeared at Mark's elbow. 'She's just after your money. They're all the same these bloody genealogists.'

'I thought I made it clear we didn't need your services any more,' Mark said.

'You did make it clear. But there's something you should know. Are you going to invite me in, or am I going to stand on the step with the neighbours watching all day long?'

Almost reluctantly Mark stepped aside and showed Jayne into the front room. The decor was a throwback to the early 70s, complete with a flock of geese climbing the wall and a picture of Tretchikoff's Green Lady hanging over the mantlepiece.

They sat down on a couch that had seen better days. The father remained stood next to the old, unused fireplace.

There was no offer of tea or biscuits.

'I made a trip to Hatherton today. You'll remember it well, Mr Russell?'

'It's where my grandmother was in hospital, what of it?'

'Well, I met an interesting old lady who used to work at the hospital. I always wondered, Mark, why you had just a suffragette medallion and an old drawing. Are they all your great grandmother left behind when she died?'

He looked at his father. 'It's all we have of her. If there was anything else we would have given it to you. It was hard enough getting my father to give you those two things.'

'Well, the old lady who worked at the hospital remembered your great grandmother. Said she always carried a small case, a vanity case, with her all the time. It was her prized possession, staying by her side wherever she went.'

Mark looked again at his father, who flicked up his quiff of hair with his fingers. 'And?'

'And when she died, the case was given to a young man with a solid black quiff.' She stared at the father. 'A man who looked like Elvis.'

The old man suddenly became nervous, fumbling with his matches to light a cigarette.

Mark stood up, looming over his father. 'Dad, is this true?'

'What of it? When she died, I went to pick up her stuff. Your grandfather had already passed away and I was living in Manchester with you and your mother. We hadn't split up yet, or more accurately, she hadn't left me yet. I made the long traipse out to Derbyshire. I hated her and I hated that place.'

Mark's voice was quiet, but menacing. 'What happened to the case, Dad?'

The old man looked like a trapped ferret. 'I don't know, lost it somewhere.'

Mark took a step towards his father. The old man shrank backwards. 'I'd had enough of it all. Never should have shown you the picture or the medallion. I thought if I just gave you those things it would keep you quiet, but you carried on.'

'What was in the case?' The voice had a hint of violence now. Jayne tensed herself, ready to spring forward if Mark attacked his father.

The old man sat down in an armchair. It was as if all the air had been let out of his body and he had become smaller. 'It destroyed her and my father. He always had to live with the stigma of a mother in a mental home. He couldn't ever escape it. And I just had enough. I didn't want you to go through it the same way I did. Not after all this time. I wanted to forget the past.'

'Dad, where's the case?'

The old man's shoulders sagged even further. The answer when it came was a whisper. 'Upstairs. Under my bed.'

Mark jumped up. Jayne heard feet running up the stairs and across the ceiling.

The father stared at her with undisguised malevolence. 'See what you've done, you interfering bitch.'

Then, the feet raced down the stairs and Mark rushed into the room with a small grey vanity case, placing it on the coffee table by the couch.

'Mark, don't open it. It's not worth it, not now,' the father pleaded.

Mark clicked the old latches and they snapped open. He lifted the lid and looked inside.

Chapter Forty-Six

Sale, Manchester. April 2, 2016.

Beneath a pile of drawings of the old asylum building, Mark found a studio photograph of Rose holding a small bunch of flowers, lying on top of some letters bound in a purple ribbon. She was dressed in a neat white uniform with a dark cross imprinted in the centre of her apron and a small white hat perched on her head. On the top right of the photograph was embossed a name. Mark tilted it in the light to read it.

'I think it says, John Thomas and Sons, Oxford Road.'

'Probably the name of the studio,' said Jayne.

'It must be her photograph, looks like she's wearing a nurse's uniform. What was she doing in Manchester?' He looked at his father, who was staring at a spot on the old carpet. 'Dad, why did you hide these from me?'

'You'll see. It'll do no use. Destroyed my grandmother, it did, chasing after fantasies. Chasing after the Russells all her life. And my father? What sort of life was it, a mother in a mental hospital and him trying to make the best of life with a great aunt in Worthing? He spent his whole life living down the shame. It destroyed him, I didn't want it to destroy you too.'

Mark reached into the case and pulled out the bundle of five yellowing envelopes, again tied with purple ribbon. The first envelope bore the stamp of the British Army and a postmark from France. The address on the cover was written in faded blue ink and a clear, confident hand.

Rose Clarke,
c/o Wibbersley Hospital,
Flixton,
Manchester.

'That's just down the road from here.' Mark carefully pulled out a yellowing letter, written on lined army notepaper. He unfolded it and began to read.

Jayne saw his lips move as his eyes scanned the page. 'Don't keep us waiting, Mark. What does it say?'

Mark coughed once and began to read out loud.

'My darling Rose,

Obviously, I can't tell you where I am but if you were to imagine where you were working recently you wouldn't be far wrong.

The men of my new regiment are in fine spirit and even if I do say so myself, they are one of the finest companies in the British Army, fit, strong and spirited. They will make a good show against the Boche.

Thank you for your letter, the parcel and the photograph. Both finally caught up with me in our camp over here. The socks were a godsend as were the whisky and the lighter. How clever of you to engrave it with my name. I'd forgotten how much time you had spent with the men who had been here. Of course, you know what we need.

And thank you for the wonderful picture. Sometimes, I forget how beautiful you are and how lucky I am.

I miss you so much, Rose. Those few days we spent together in Scotland will stay with me for the rest of my life. A time of joy and happiness and love which I will never forget.'

Mark turned the page and continued reading.

'You are my soul, my centre, my love, my life. My one and only, Rose. I long for the day when this war is over and we can be together for ever and ever and ever.

I love you with all my heart,

David.

There was silence in the living room when Mark had finished reading.

'It's a beautiful letter,' said Jayne, 'he obviously loved her very much.'

Mark pinched his top lip with his index finger and thumb. 'He doesn't say he was married, does he? Just that they spent time together in Scotland.'

'The hotel register said Captain and Mrs Russell.'

The father lifted his head and spoke. 'That's what they had to say in those days. Not like today when you can just go and stay at any hotel without a by-your-leave. Those days, they had standards. Unmarried couples couldn't spend the night together in a room.'

'So they had to say they were married.' Jayne frowned. 'I don't believe David Russell and Rose just spent a night together. It's not like her. Or him.'

'It was war. Lots goes on in wartime. And there's still no proof, is there?'

Jayne was beginning to dislike this bitter old man intensely. 'Mark, please read the next letter. Perhaps it will help.'

Chapter Forty-Seven

Wibbersley Hospital, Flixton, Manchester.
June 20, 1916.

The stub of Captain Arnold's leg was suppurating again. Rose removed the dressing and gently cleaned the sticky white, green and red mess from the end of what had been his thigh. The Captain lay back in his bed holding the metal rails above his head and gritting his teeth. Rose had pulled the screens around the bed before she had begun to redress the wound. Some of the men cried during this procedure, tears flowing from their eyes as they begged her to stop.

But she had to carry on. Sister was watching and waiting for an error, hovering like the Angel of Death, not a supporter of life. This particular nurse, a woman from Yorkshire, loved her rules. Those who could walk were to be up and out of their beds by 6.30 in the morning. The ones who couldn't had to be woken anyway. Breakfast was at 7 a.m. sharp and woe betide any VAD who delivered her trays a few minutes late.

This hospital was under military regulations and would be run with strict discipline, enforced with sharp words and written comments on the ward book.

The men hated her with a passion, each one in their own way rebelling against her rule. But she broke the most rebellious easily; a dressing changed twice a day instead of twice a week. A hot water bath where the water was a little too hot. Letters from home forgotten or misplaced. A thousand petty rules enforced more than rigorously. For the most part, they shut up and accepted their fate like cattle in a byre.

It was Rose who suffered the most:

'Miss Clarke, you were three minutes late this morning.'

'Miss Clarke, redress this wound.'

'Miss Clarke, this toilet is filthy, clean it immediately.'

Rose bore it all, thinking of David and the baby growing inside her. She told nobody of her marriage, wanting to avoid the bitter jealousy of the sister and the jokes of the other VADs.

She wrapped the final bandage over the stump of the leg and fastened it with a safety pin, making sure it lay along the leg at 90 degrees. Captain Arnold was sweating profusely but still managed a whispered thank you.

Rose checked her watch. Time to prepare the trays for lunch and, after it was finished at 1.25, she had 30 minutes to herself. She was supposed to eat, but usually just threw herself on the bunk and napped. Today, though, she would write to David.

She rushed through the preparation of the trays, making sure everything was precisely positioned and ordered. Luckily, cook was on time and she managed to get out onto the wards exactly at 12.30. Sister was standing there, waiting, staring at the watch fastened to her uniform. She checked the first tray Rose delivered to Lieutenant Davies, looking over it like a beagle eyeing a morsel of food.

'And how are you today, Lieutenant?' asked Rose.

The sister was a stickler for the correct forms of address. No first names or nicknames, just ranks. Davies was known by the other men as Taffy for obvious reasons.

'Better than yesterday, and worse than tomorrow, Rose,' the Lieutenant answered cheerfully.

'Lieutenant Davies, you will address Miss Clarke by her surname. We have no time for frivolous informality in this ward.'

'No, Sister. I mean yes, Sister,' stammered the Lieutenant.

Sister Colman signalled Rose was to move on to the next bed.

'Would you like some more bread and butter?' Rose asked the Lieutenant.

'Yes, please, Rose. I mean Miss Clarke.'

'Here you are. Anything else I can get for you?'

The sister's small beady eyes stared at Rose.

'I'm fine thank you, Nurse.' Lieutenant Davies looked at the sister, daring her to rebuke him. The use of 'Nurse' for an uncertified VAD was a crime punishable by death in the sister's eyes.

Rose pushed the cart to the next bed. The sister joined her, whispering in her ear. 'If you talk to every patient, Miss Clarke, you will not be able to complete the trays on schedule at 1 p.m.'

'But, Sister, they like me to talk to them otherwise…'

'Otherwise, the men in the next ward will receive cold food. I do wish you would think of them, Miss Clarke.'

Rose knew it was useless to argue but carried on regardless. 'Sometimes, I'm the only person they talk to.'

'Miss Clarke, the men in this ward are here to get better, they are not here for your amusement. Would you like me to report you to the VAD coordinator?'

'No, Sister.'

'Well, perform your duties with alacrity, Miss Clarke. With alacrity, do I make myself clear?'

'Yes, Sister.'

'I will be checking you finish precisely at 1 p.m.'

'Yes, Sister.'

The sister walked back to her office at the end of the

ward. Rose carried on delivering the trays and talking to the men, finishing on time. Sister was waiting as she had promised, watch in hand and sneer on her face.

'Just in time, Miss Clarke. Now collect the trays, if you please.'

'Some of the men haven't finished, Sister.'

'Just do as you are told, Miss Clarke.'

Rose collected the trays, allowing the men who hadn't finished their food time to eat.

At the end of the service, she rushed back to her bunk, kicked off her shoes and wriggled her tired toes. She picked up the letter she had received that morning and read it through once again. He was in France, he couldn't tell her where, but she could guess. He was going up to the line in the next few days. She hoped he would be safe wherever he was sent. She didn't know what she would do if something happened to him.

Time to write to David and tell him the news. One of the more friendly doctors had confirmed the results when he examined her earlier.

She picked up the pen and wrote.

Darling,

I have some wonderful news for you. At least, I think it is wonderful and I hope you do too. I'm going to have your baby...

Chapter Forty-Eight

Sale, Manchester. April 2, 2016.

Mark unwrapped the second letter from the bundle. It was written on the same army notepaper in a neat, precise, hand.

Darling Rose,

I'm to be a father? You wouldn't believe how happy I was to hear your news. Are you suffering terribly? Is it painful? Are you feeling sick?

I wish I could be there with you, Rose, to hold your hand and wipe your brow if you are not feeling well.

You must make sure you eat properly. Remember you're eating for two now. When will you stop work? I worry about you walking those long corridors, carrying and cleaning all day long. You mustn't tire yourself out. Would you like me to write to the hospital asking them to give you light duties? I'm sure they would help if I asked. I know how you feel about such things, Rose, but please let me know if you want me to write the letter. You should think of yourself and the baby now.

As for me, I've been transferred to an Irish regiment because there's a shortage of officers with combat experience. The men are the salt of the earth, and the subalterns rule them with an iron fist. I haven't learnt much about them yet, only having arrived at the training camp in you-know-where yesterday, but I'll soon whip them into shape.

Talk of the next push is getting stronger at the moment.

But don't worry, the men will look after me.

I told my sergeant, Flaherty is his name, you were pregnant and all he could say was 'I've seven myself, I only have to look at the wife and she drops another one.'

I can hear Flaherty calling for me now, Rose. Please look after yourself and the baby.

Remember I love you more than life itself.

Always yours,

David

Mark finished reading the letter. For a moment, all three of them were silent. It was Jayne who spoke first.

'The child must have been your grandfather. He was born in February 1917 and David Russell's name is on the birth certificate.'

'Perhaps he wasn't the father.' Mr Russell lit a cigarette with his lighter. 'The dates are very close. Married at the end of April and the baby born at the beginning of February. Smells funny to me.' He inhaled and blew out a long stream of blue smoke.

'Why do you always have to sneer about Rose, Dad? She was your grandmother.'

'You never met her. You never saw the pain she put my father through with her fantasies and her lies. You never saw how much my father hated going to see her. But he went anyway, from London to Derbyshire, because that's what a son did in those days.'

'In those days…' sneered Mark. 'In those days, women were locked up for life for no reason.'

The father stayed quiet.

'Let's read the next letter,' said Jayne, stopping their

bickering.

Mark unwrapped the next letter from the bundle and began reading. The tone was immediately darker than the others, less joyful.

My darling,

How are you feeling? Is the baby causing you too much discomfort? I wish I could be there with you, Rose.

As I write this, I can hear the boom of an 18-pounder in the field behind the farmhouse where we are billeted. The battery fires every two minutes, I can almost time them. Three loud crashes ring out and then silence. It's like waiting for a shoe to drop. I'm sitting at the kitchen table. I don't know where the owners of the farm are living, perhaps they ran away at the beginning of the war, or are hiding somewhere close. I will never know.

A cat lives here. Lieutenant Crawford gave him our leftovers, not that there was much left over. He just smelt it, turned his nose up and walked away, tail waving like a flag in a breeze. Obviously, farmyard rats taste much better than our tinned bully beef.

The guns are firing again, one after the other. Every time, the farmhouse shakes and tiles fall from the roof, crashing down to the ground. If they carry on for much longer there will be nothing left of this house save a heap of bricks with a cat sitting on top licking his paws.

I miss you so much, Rose. I miss holding you tight in the middle of the night, hearing the sigh of your breathing and touching the softness of your breast. (Don't worry, a friend is being posted back to London tomorrow, so this letter can avoid the army censors.)

Mark stopped reading and picked up the envelope. 'It's

postmarked London and there seems to be no censor's stamp.'

'Please carry on reading, Mark,' said Jayne.

Mark's eyes scanned the page and found his place. '*I was sorry to read in your last letter that the morning sickness has started. It seems to be a bit early, not that I know anything about being pregnant. Can you ask one of the doctors to look after you? Is it safe to carry on working in your condition?*

Please look after yourself, Rose, you're all I have. You're all that matters, now more than ever. There's going to be a big push soon. Everybody seems to think it will be a walk in the park, but I'm not so sure. It seems I'm not sure of anything any more.

Except for one thing. I love you.

You're not to worry though, I'll keep myself safe and sound, no heroics from me.

I desperately want to hold you and our baby in my arms, Rose. It's all that keeps me alive and keeps me going through the mud and the slime and the stupidity.'

Mark stopped reading. 'There's a different pen, now.' He searched for his place again. '*I have to go, we're moving forward and I have to give this to Lieutenant Rimmer. I love you, Rose, I'll always love you. Your David.*'

'What's the date on the letter?'

'28 June, 1916,' read Mark.

Jayne thought for a moment. 'Three days before the Battle of the Somme. Three days before he dies along with 19,000 other men on that dreadful first day.'

Mark didn't answer and, for once, the father kept silent too.

'Please read the next letter, Mark.'

'There are two more.' He picked up the next letter.

Jayne could see it wasn't as long as the others and the neat, confident handwriting had been replaced by something more rushed; a nervous scrawl as if somebody had written it in a hurry.

'My darling Rose,' Mark began to read out loud.

Chapter Forty-Nine

Hawthorn Ridge, the Somme. July 1, 1916.

Perhaps, three hours from now, he would be dead.

Captain David Russell shook his head to banish the morbid thoughts from his mind. He had so much to live for, too much to live for.

Outside, the shells still rained down on the forward trenches of the Germans. The solid crump of the 9.2s, the whine of the 18-pounders, and whoosh of the trench mortars, were accompanied by the occasional boom of the Howitzers. A whole orchestra of murder.

Next to him, Crawford lay curled up in a bunk far too short for him, snoring gently through an open mouth, his diary lying on his chest. The man would win gold in an Olympic sleeping contest. He should confiscate the diary as they were forbidden by the High Command, but he didn't have the heart. Writing in it was the one thing keeping Crawford sane and focussed.

He felt something bite his wrist. They had only been in the line for six hours and already the lice were inside his clothes, burrowing into his skin. Never mind, he would soon get used to them. A man could get used to anything.

A German shell from a counter battery exploded somewhere behind the line. The candle flickered in a Fry's Chocolate tin that served as a sconce, and a fine line of chalk dribbled from the ceiling above his head.

He looked down at the letter to his parents lying on the orange crate. His mother wouldn't be happy when she read it, but he didn't care. His father would carry out his wishes to the letter.

He picked up the pen and wrote the last two paragraphs quickly, signing his name with a flourish. He had made it as clear as possible, there could be no misunderstanding.

Sealing the letter in one of the army's thin envelopes, he placed it next to the letter to Rose he had written earlier. If they were to reach England, he would have to send both of them back to Division before the attack.

He licked his index finger and thumb, and extinguished the flame of the candle. The dugout was plunged into darkness with just the occasional flashes of red from the shrapnel shells slipping round the army blanket covering the entrance.

He sat in the darkness for a moment with the smell of the extinguished candle for company. Crawford in his bunk snored on. A German flare illuminated the curtain with an intense white light for a few seconds before softening to a glow. The artillery kept on firing steadily, each gun making a different sound, distinguishable from the others.

Standing up quickly, he felt his legs give way beneath him. 'Set an example to the men, Russell. Show them how to behave.' He heard the voice of his old training sergeant. The man had died at Mons, his throat slashed by a piece of hot shrapnel. The old soldier would never speak again, but still the grating voice lived on in David's head.

He pushed through the curtain and stepped outside into the thin slime of mud lining the bottom of the reserve trench. Sergeant Flaherty was leaning against the hastily built parapet smoking a Sweet Afton, the smoke forming a white cloud around his head. As soon as he saw Captain Russell, he stood to attention, throwing the cigarette away.

'At ease, Sergeant. The men are comfortable?' He knew it was a ridiculous question before the words had even left his mouth. What did comfort matter at a time like this?

The sergeant answered anyway. 'They are, sir.' It was a mellow accent from the midland counties of Ireland, soft, slow, like the voice of a cow who had been grazing in rich fields for a long hot summer. 'They've had their smokes and a tot of rum.' Three men behind Flaherty nodded their heads in unison, the new steel helmets falling over their eyes.

'Good.' There was nothing else David could say. He didn't know these men, couldn't even address them by their surname. He had been transferred to join the fourth battalion of the Fusiliers just two weeks ago from his own regular battalion. Apparently, they were lacking battle-hardened officers for the big push.

Over to the East, the sun was lightening the sky above the German trenches. He could see the shells landing now, throwing up plumes of earth of all shapes and sizes.

'Nothing could live through the barrage, sir. We're going to walk right in and collect the prisoners like rounding up cattle from the fields.'

Russell looked again. A shrapnel shell exploded in the air above the German lines, throwing red sparks like a giant Catherine wheel into the air. A firework display to kill rather than amuse. 'I suppose so, Sergeant.'

He checked the watch Rose had given him in Scotland; it seemed so long ago now since he had held her in his arms. Just the two of them, the world forgotten.

'Who's the youngest man in the company, Sergeant?'

Flaherty thought for a moment. 'McCrossan, sir. Says he's 18 but I don't think he's much over 16, meself.'

David looked at the letters to Rose and his parents. 'Give him these and tell him to take them to the P.O. in Division.'

'Yes, sir.'

'Make sure he takes his time, Sergeant.'

Flaherty understood exactly what David was doing. 'I will, sir, he won't be back until well after noon.'

'What time are we going over the top, sir?' asked one of the men.

'7.35, Private…?'

'Sheehan, sir.'

'It'll come quickly enough, Private Sheehan.'

'I suppose it will,' agreed the soldier, 'and it's a lovely morning for it, sir.'

The sky was clearing rapidly. A few lazy clouds drifted over their heads uncertain whether to watch the drama unfolding beneath them or continue on in their merry way. 'At least it's not raining.'

The private held up his finger to the air. 'No chance of that, sir. It will be as blue as a daisy's arse. Begging your pardon, sir.' The private touched his curled finger to the side of his helmet.

'Sergeant, make sure the men eat before 6.30.'

'No food, sir.'

'Send a couple of men back for some hot tea at least. And make sure they have another measure of rum with the tea.'

The sergeant made the same curled finger salute to the side of his helmet. 'Yes, sir.'

David turned on his heels and returned back inside the small dugout, hearing his sergeant calling McCrossan's name loudly.

Crawford was sitting on the bunk, swigging from a flask. He offered it to Russell.

The Captain shook his head. 'Later, maybe.'

'Not long to go.'

Russell looked at his watch again. The minute hand had hardly moved. Was time getting slower? '6 a.m. now. Just 90 minutes before it starts.'

Crawford stood up, bending over to avoid hitting his head on the low roof. 'I should check my platoon, make sure they are in position.'

'Get the sergeant to check the men's feet. It will give him, and them, something to do.'

Crawford rubbed his nose. He had been an accountant in civilian life and always complained the trenches were bad for his sinuses. 'Will do.' He handed over the flask. 'You take it, but make sure you leave some for me. I'm going to need it later.'

Russell took the flask but had no intention of drinking any of the whisky inside. He thought about the letter he had just written to Rose and realised it didn't tell her how he felt. Or how much he missed her. Or how he loved her.

He pulled a piece of paper from his knapsack, placing its pristine whiteness on the stained wood of the orange crate.

As he did, another German shell landed nearby, rattling the dugout and splitting one of the planks holding up the ceiling. More chalk spilled onto the floor in a steady rain.

Outside, he could hear someone screaming for a stretcher bearer in a communication trench in the rear. He thanked God none of his men had been killed or injured yet.

He had another letter to write. A longer letter this time, to the woman he loved. He wanted to tell her what he felt for her and the hope he had for their future together.

Picking up the pen, he began writing as another shell landed near his trench and more white chalk dribbled down from a gap between the boards above his head.

Chapter Fifty

Sale, Manchester. April 2, 2016.

Mark coughed twice, clearing his throat.

'My darling Rose,' he began again. 'Well, the big push is on. I can't tell you where I am but I'm sure you will be reading about it in the papers soon. The men are spirited and willing and there's talk about us being in Berlin before Christmas.'

'What's the date at the top of the letter?' interrupted Jayne.

Mark stopped reading and scanned the letter, finally finding the date. 'July 1, 1916.'

'The first day of the Somme. He must have been in one of the early waves going over the top.' Then her voice lowered a register. 'The records show he was killed later that day.'

The only sound was the ticking of a clock on the mantlepiece. One of those fake French carriage clocks bought in Argos. Jayne wished the bloody thing would be quiet.

Mark began reading again.

'I'm not so confident any more. We have been pounding the enemy for a week now. They say nobody could survive the artillery, but they've said the same before and been proven wrong.

Whatever happens I intend to do my duty, Rose. No stu-

pid heroics though; I want, I need, to come back to you and our baby. It's all that matters. I will come back to you.'

Here, Mark stopped for a moment and caught his breath.

'I love you and miss you. It is only thoughts of you that keep me going. I will come back to you my darling Rose.'

Mark let the letter drop back in the case. 'He just signed it, David.'

Chapter Fifty-One

Hawthorn Ridge, the Somme. July 1, 1916.

The artillery fire from the 9.2s and the 18-pounders surged into a hurricane of noise, drowning out the sound of the German batteries. David Russell looked through the viewfinder up the gradual slope to the German lines on the ridge.

He could see the outline of the forward trench cut into the chalk. Plumes of dirt and dust were thrown into the air as the shells struck home. All above the trench, shrapnel exploded at 15 metres throwing down its red hot lumps of metal on the defenders below.

'Poor buggers,' muttered Sergeant Flaherty beside him. 'I wouldn't put my worst enemy tru' dat.'

'He is your worst enemy, Sergeant, and he would do the same to you given half the chance.'

'I suppose he would, sir, but I wouldn't give him half a chance.'

Captain Russell frowned. 'Issue another tot of rum to the men at 7 a.m. and give them all the cigarettes we have left.'

'Yes, sir. They'll think it's Christmas.'

'And those are the illuminations are they?' He pointed to the noise and clamour across at the German trenches. A white star shell fired from the German trenches, rose and flared in the sky above their heads.

'At least someone is still alive.'

Russell stepped down from the firing step and was immediately jostled by a tall thin man carrying a large wooden box on the end of three legs. From instinct, Russell checked out the badges on the shoulder of the man's uniform, but there weren't any.

'Terribly sorry, old chap. Need to set up over there.' The man pointed to an exposed position on a firing step.

'Are you sure? Jerry's guns are pretty accurate.'

He patted the box. 'Have to give her a clear line of sight when the big bang happens.'

Russell frowned again, not understanding what the man was talking about.

'It's a camera, Captain. We're going to film the big bang and your chaps as they advance on the German lines. You are going to be famous. Oh, it's Malins by the way.' He put the legs of the box down into the mud and slime at the bottom of the trench and stuck out his hand.

Russell shook it. 'You're going to film us?'

'That's the idea. Have to get the big show on film.'

One of Malins' assistants brushed past them. 'If we don't get it set up soon, sir, we'll be too late.'

Malins checked his watch. 'Right you are, Corporal. It's set to go off at 7.20. Over there, we're told.'

'What's set to go off?'

'You mean you don't know?'

'Don't know what?'

'The big bang.'

Russell shook his head.

'Sometimes this army astounds me.' Malins pointed over to the left. 'The sappers have planted a couple of tons of explosive over there on Hawthorn Ridge.' He checked his watch again. 'In 38 minutes, they're going to let it off. Should be quite a show. Make Guy Fawkes look like a boy with a banger. Anyway, I need to go and set up.' He leant in and whispered in Russell's ear. 'Good luck, and keep your head down.'

With a wave, he followed his men down to the front of the reserve trench and around a bend, vanishing from sight.

Above the captain's head, a plane flew towards the German lines, wiggling its wings as if drunk with the joy of flight. The sky around it was a lovely eggshell blue with just traces of fine cloud drifting across it on the wind.

A perfect day.

His mind raced back to another perfect day just six weeks ago, lying on his back in the freshly mown grass, staring up at another perfect sky. But this time, Rose had been by his side, her body warm against his. He remembered picking up her hand and kissing the soft skin on the inside of her wrist. So smooth, so fragile, with just a faint line of blue showing though the pale whiteness.

'Sir.' It was Sergeant Flaherty again. 'The men have been given their rum and cigarettes.'

'Thank you, Sergeant. Tell them to keep their heads down. We are going over the top in the second wave at 7.35.'

'Yes, sir.' Flaherty saluted theatrically and returned to the men, telling them to squat down on the firing steps and keep their heads down. A few were smoking, others staring into mid-air, a few more chatting unconcernedly as if they were waiting for a country bus which hadn't arrived yet.

David Russell lifted the blanket at the entrance to the cramped dugout. Crawford was already there, lying on the bunk smoking and writing in his diary.

He sat down in front of the orange crate, the piece of paper, no longer white, stared back at him. The heading was still at the top of the page, My darling Rose, but the rest was blank. What was he going to say? He could tell her the truth and say how scared he was and how he might die in the next hour, but he knew he wouldn't. What could she do? And how would she feel reading such a letter?

Instead, he pushed the noise of the artillery from his mind, and concentrated on her face. The smile that touched the corner of her lips, as if she knew something he could only guess at. The way her blonde hair curled down over one eye, to be pushed back casually by her long, slender fingers. The softness of her nipple against the whiteness of her breast.

He pulled the paper towards him and began to tell her how much he loved her, and how he longed to touch her swelling belly.

It was everything he wanted to say when he was with her but never could.

Chapter Fifty-Two

Sale, Manchester. April 2, 2016.

Mark reached forward into the case. 'This is the final letter to Rose.' He opened the envelope and pulled out a single sheet of army notepaper, coughing once to clear his throat. 'It's also dated July 1, 1916. He must have written it after the previous one before he went over the top.' He coughed once more and began reading.

'My Darling Rose,

In my last letter, I didn't tell you how much I love you. It's not easy for me to express my feelings. In my family and at school, we were taught to keep them inside, never show them. The British stiff upper lip and all that.

But I don't care any more.

If I am to die in this desperate war, I want you to know how much I love you. To me, you are life itself; pure, honest, sweet life. And the life growing in you will imbibe your purity as only babies can.

I can't imagine living without you, my Rose. You make me happy and joyous just by my being near you, inhaling the same air as you breathe. One night, after our wedding, I lay awake watching you as you slept. Your face so peaceful, your mouth so red, your skin so soft. And, in that moment, I knew I had found the woman with whom I wanted to spend the rest of my years.

We will grow old together, Rose, age shall not weary us, nor time corrode your beauty. For me, you will be beautiful for ever.

You are my life, my love, my everything, my darling Rose. I love the way your smile kisses the edge of your lips. The way your eyes shine with a brightness only God could create. The way your hair curls to cover your eye. The way your skin trembles beneath my fingers.

I love each and every inch of your body and soul.

My one and only, Rose.

Whatever happens, remember I love you. In your darkest hours, always remember I love you.

Your David.'

Jayne couldn't say anything. Mark coughed nervously. For once the old man just sat there, quietly puffing on his cigarette, staring into mid-air.

Chapter Fifty-Three

Hawthorn Ridge, the Somme. July 1, 1916.

He blew his whistle, hearing it echo down the ragged line of the trench. Men began to climb out of the trench on the ladders, led by Sergeant Flaherty.

The dust and dirt from the explosion on Hawthorn Ridge had died down to be replaced by the soft light of a July morning.

Corporal Doyle passed him a rifle. 'You might need this, sir.'

'I hope I don't, Corporal.'

His men were assembling into a line, being chivvied along by Sergeant Flaherty. A few German shells were shrieking over their heads, landing in the communication trenches behind them. A shout of 'stretcher bearer' came from somewhere in the distance.

He peered out up the ridge into the smoke. The acrid smell of lyddite was everywhere, filling his nostrils with its bitter tang. Where was the first wave? Was it already in the first line and advancing on the second? He hoped not. Their battalion commander had drilled into them all the importance of timing. Everything was to be done to a timetable. They were to go through to the third German trench in the first ten minutes and wait for support. That's why the men were carrying ladders, sandbags, wire and other kit; to block the captured trenches in case of a German counter attack.

He joined the end of the line. Blew his whistle once more and the men began to move off, advancing uphill towards the German trenches. One of the corporals, not from his platoon, luckily, began shouting and waving his arms. 'Get 'em, lads. Get 'em,' encouraging the men forward.

Before he could shout anything, Sergeant Flaherty had bellowed, 'Steady, lads. Walk, don't run.'

Far in front of him, he could see the red explosions still landing in the white chalk. A flash of bright red against the green and white. A cloud of cordite and then nothing.

The men were still walking forward, rifles at the slope arms, a long ragged line. Suddenly, a gap appeared to his left. A German shell had exploded in mid-air, showering shrapnel down, tearing a hole in their ranks.

The sergeant again, his voice cutting through the shell-fire. 'Close up on the left. Steady lads.'

A noise.

A sound like someone rapping at a door with the sharp edge of a knife. Why did anyone want to come here into this hellhole?

The noise again. Louder now, more insistent.

A man fell in front of him. Just stopped moving forward and fell face first into the grass.

Then another, and another.

He looked behind him. The third wave hadn't left the trenches yet. They were behind time, somebody would get a rocket.

He glanced at his watch. Just four minutes had gone since he had blown his whistle. An age and half a lifetime.

To his left and right, there were just a few men left, grouping together to protect themselves from the machine guns, seeking safety in numbers. They mustn't bunch together. He must get across and warn them.

He stumbled, nearly falling. At his feet lay a body, face staring at the sky, a few spots of mud splashed artfully on the cheeks. Sheehan. The man who had been drinking rum and laughing and smoking in the trench just half an hour before.

Dead eyes staring up at the blue sky.

More German whizz-bangs roaring over his head. The constant chatter of the machine guns. The stench of cordite.

A hare raced past him, the eyes bulging with fear from its round head, running towards the German wire and slipping beneath it.

The wire. It was still there. Uncut. Undamaged.

He saw a gap, a hole where the wire wasn't as thick as elsewhere. He began to run towards it. As he raced closer, he saw a hedge of khaki bodies in front of him, the flashes on their shoulders proudly shouting out the name of his regiment.

The first wave.

A force like a blast of heat from an oven threw him onto his back, tumbling down into a still-smoking shell hole. His leg was drenched in hot water. Why were the Germans firing hot water?

He looked down at his khaki trousers. They were wet, the green turning a dark shade of mauve. Was he hit? But there was no pain. He couldn't feel anything.

Sergeant Flaherty jumped into the shell hole, landing next to him, followed by three other men. They huddled down into the safety of the bottom, curling like children in a bed too small for them.

The sergeant shouted in his ear. 'Their first trench is just 20 yards away, sir. Shall we rush it?'

'Where's the rest of the men?'

'Back there, sir.' The sergeant pointed backwards to No Man's Land.

Another shell exploded above them, showering red hot

metal down onto their heads.

'We can't stay here, sir.'

Machine gun bullets splattered the grass around them, throwing up little spurts of Flanders into the air as they buried themselves into the soil.

'The third wave?'

'Dunno, sir.'

Captain Russell popped his head over the edge of the shell hole and looked back towards their trench. The ground behind him was empty save for a scattering of bodies, stretched out on the ground as if they were enjoying a sunny day in the park.

He checked his watch. 'They should be behind us.'

The sergeant popped his head up. 'Nothing, sir.'

'We can't stay here. Have to go forward, Sergeant.'

'Yes, sir.' He roused the three men with a kick of his boot. 'You heard the officer.'

Captain Russell grabbed his rifle and pushed off with his leg against the muddy bottom. He felt a pain shoot up through his hip and he collapsed against the dirt.

The sergeant scrambled out of the shell hole with the men, standing upright for a second before collapsing backwards, a bullet in his face.

David stared at his sergeant, blood and bone lay splattered where a nose had once been. It was the face of a man who wouldn't smile. Or joke. Or laugh. Or frown, any more.

Where were the others?

He scrambled up out of the shell hole, ignoring the pain in his leg. The three men who had been with him lay face down on the ground in front of the wire.

He staggered forward.

There were other men in front of him. Men he vaguely

recognised, firing at the Germans.

A sharp blow to the side of his head, throwing him forwards. The earth rose up to meet him, wrapping him in its musty arms.

The darkness.

Blessed darkness.

Chapter Fifty-Four

Sale, Manchester. April 2, 2016.

Mark let the letter slip from his hands and fall back into the case.

Nobody said a word until old Mr Russell finally sighed, 'Look at the envelope.'

Mark sorted through the sheets of paper in the case and found the envelope. The same hand had written Rose's address on the cover, but this envelope was more creased and dirty than the others with a large brown stain in the corner.

'Turn it over,' said Mark's father.

Mark looked at the reverse side. 'There's something written there. It's faint and faded.' He held the envelope up to the light. 'I think it's German.'

'Give it to me,' said Jayne.

As if from memory, Mark's father raised his head and spoke. 'It says 'Gefunden auf einem Britischen Offizier. Feldlazarett 27.' I had it translated by a German friend. It simply means 'Found on a British Officer at Feldlazarett 27.' Look at the stamp and the postmark.'

Mark turned the envelope back to the front. The stamp on the cover was German. A light blue stamp with a Teutonic woman looking to the left. In the top corner, a large '20' appeared, but printed across the bottom were the words '25 cents'. Beneath the image, 'Deutsche Reich' was etched in bold capitals. The postmark was in the same Teutonic typeface; 'Le Cateau. 11 July'.

'But that's ten days after he was supposed to have died. How could a dead man post a letter?'

Chapter Fifty-Five

Behind the German lines, the Somme. July 1, 1916.

David awoke. Above him the sky was a deep blue with clouds racing across it, chasing each other like lambs in a field. He was aware of an ache on the side of his head as if his helmet were on too tight and pressing down on the top of his ear. He tried to move his hand to adjust the helmet but his hand wouldn't move. He tried again but still the hand stayed where it was, the pain in his head increasing. Was he tied down?

A jolt beneath him lifted his body up in the air and dropped it down again. He was still staring up at the sky.

'Lie still there, old chap, not long now.'

Something blocked the light. A black shadow of a man, sharply rounded head showing he was still wearing his tin helmet. He tried to lift his shoulders up towards the man.

A hand pushed him down again, forcing him into the wood.

'Lie still, old man. We don't want Jerry to get excited, do we?'

The light changed behind the man's face. A cloud crossed the sun. The sky was white, too bright. He closed his eyes. The pain in his head, someone was inside his hat, pounding away with a shovel. He wanted to shout take the man out of my head, take him out. But he couldn't. He opened his eyes. Too bright. Too much light. Close them again. Keep them shut. Make the pain go away. Please make the pain go away.

The light was blocked again as the man with the tin hat

leant forward to speak to him. 'You're behind their lines. The Germans found you wandering through their second trench, it's a wonder they didn't kill you.'

David tried to lift himself up again, but the hand pushed him down.

'Lie still, old chap. You've been hit. I'm taking you to a German casualty station. They'll look after you.'

David's body melted into the hard wood beneath him. The pain surged through his head again.

Make it stop. Make the pain stop.

Rose flashed through his mind; her smile just touching the edge of her lips. The softness of her mouth against his. The taste of her breath.

Make the pain go away. Please make the pain go away. His head felt like it was going to explode. A shell going off in his forehead.

Bang.

He passed out.

Chapter Fifty-Six

**Behind the German lines, Feldlazarett 27.
July 2, 1916.**

Hauptmann Redel scanned the men lying in the bunks from the entrance to the hut. There were 12 soldiers waiting for an operation. He had neither the time nor the resources to save all of them. Once again, he faced a decision he hated; which of these men would he try to save, condemning the rest to die in the warm embrace of Mother Morphine.

For him, there was just one simple criterion; who had the best chance of survival.

Unlike most doctors, he didn't care if the patient lying in the bed wore khaki or field grey. If a man wasn't going to survive, there was no point in operating on him.

His corporal had already performed a preliminary triage, placing the most hopeless cases closest to the door so they would be easier to remove once they died.

He glanced across at the four bunks on his right. All except one were still and unmoving, their chests rising slightly as they clung onto life. The one in the corner was moaning, 'Mutti, Mutti,' in a thick Bavarian accent. Hauptmann Redel leant over his bunk and saw the white matter of the brain exposed through a broken and bloody skull.

The man would not live much longer. Hauptmann Redel wished he would at least go quietly. He gestured to his corporal to give the man more morphine. At least then, he might dream himself into the warmth of his mother's arms.

The Hauptmann closed his eyes. Two years of this. Two years of deciding who would live and who would die. How long could he continue?

He looked across at the next two bunks in the row. One was occupied by an English soldier. His corporal lifted the bloodstained blanket to reveal a smashed leg, the tibia hanging on, attached by a thick strand of skin. He could amputate but, looking at the man's face, he wouldn't survive the shock of the operation.

Redel reached into the man's top right pocket and took out his paybook. He opened it and saw the man's name and rank. Private Edward Hughes, a private in the Inniskilling Fusiliers. An Ulsterman it seemed. Well, this one certainly wouldn't be fighting for the unity of that woebegone country any more. He passed the paybook back to the corporal who added it to the pile in the box.

It had been Redel's concession to humanity, his one attempt to bring some common decency to this war. He collected the paybooks of the enlisted men and the notebooks of the officers, separating them into those who lived and those who died. When the fighting died down, he would send the documents back with one of the walking wounded. At least then the relatives and sweethearts would know what happened to their loved ones.

Redel recognised the futility of his action in the middle of a war where thousands were buried beneath the chalk of Flanders. Or blown to smithereens by a mine. Or mown down with the industrial efficiency of a machine gun. But he did it anyway. Twice he had been reprimanded by his commanding officers. He carried on regardless.

He would not become less human even though he was surrounded by endless hours of inhumanity. A futile gesture, but one he insisted on carrying out.

The corporal touched his arm. Looking down at the wounded man's leg, Redel shook his head and the corporal threw the blanket over the body. The man moaned in response, a deep, dark moan from the bottom of some vast pit of pain.

'More morphine,' Redel instructed his corporal.

The German in the bed next to him was in slightly better shape; at least his eyes were open as he watched the doctor check his hand. A few mumbled words made little sense.

Redel ordered the corporal to prepare the man for amputation. At least it was the left arm, so the man wouldn't have to learn to write again. Unless, of course, he was left-handed.

Redel moved on to the next bed. An English officer, shivering despite the warmth of the Feldlazarett.

'Nicht bewegung,' he said gently, 'don't move.'

Redel pulled the blanket up over the man's shoulders, examining his face at the same time. A shell had blown off most of the left ear, exposing the skull beneath. The face and left eye had been pockmarked by shrapnel. He would never see again out of that particular eye.

The corporal drew his attention to another wound on the leg. Here, the man was lucky, the bullet had gone straight through the flesh without touching an artery.

But the face? The man had once been handsome, but now only extensive plastic surgery could return him to something similar to a human being.

He would have to remove the shrapnel piece by piece. There was no certainty the man would survive the operation. His persistent shivering meant shock had already set in.

Hauptmann Redel opened the top right flap of his uniform, removing the notebook, giving it to his corporal. He shook his head and ordered more morphine for this officer.

He stood up, ready to move onto the next bed. As he did, the officer grabbed him by the wrist and said, 'Rose? I miss you, Rose.'

Redel removed the hand and placed it back on the bunk. 'You are in a German Feldlazarett. You have been wounded. Just lie here and do not move. The corporal will give you something to ease the pain.'

The man grabbed his arm again. 'Tell Rose I love her.'

The man was obviously feverish, dreaming of some woman back in England he had once loved.

Hauptmann Redel tried to release the grip on his arm, but the man held on tight. The officer was gabbling now, the words making no sense. Redel tried to remove the man's arm, but still he clung on. He nodded at the corporal, who ran to get more morphine.

Redel sat down on the bunk next to the man, waiting for the corporal to return. The officer seemed to relax a little, becoming less agitated and reaching with his right arm into the inside pocket of his jacket.

In his hand he held a cheap brown envelope, obviously issued by the British Army. The officer's hand was shaking as he passed the envelope over to the Hauptmann. On it was an address;

Rose Clarke,
Ward 5,
Wibbersley Hospital,
Flixton,
Manchester.

Was this the man's wife? From his time in England, Redel didn't recognise the name of the hospital, but he knew Manchester well enough; a grimy northern town where soot and smoke and dirt filled the air.

The corporal came back with a syrette of morphine, ready to inject the man.

Redel stopped him. 'I've changed my mind, prepare this man for operation.'

'But Hauptmann, his injuries…?'

'You have your orders, Corporal'

The officer watched as Redel placed the letter in his pocket. 'Tell Rose, I love her,' he mumbled again, before his head fell backwards onto the blood-soaked pillow.

The man would probably not survive the operation, but Redel would try. Perhaps this woman would keep him alive.

Even in the midst of war, there has to be hope. We all need hope.

'Let's move on, Corporal, we have a lot of men to see today.'

'Yes, sir.'

'And make sure those documents are returned to the British.'

'Yes, sir.'

Redel recognised the reluctance in the corporal's voice. It was a waste of time, but the corporal would do as he had been instructed.

Another shell landed in the field next to the hospital, rattling the sides of the Feldlazarett.

'It seems the British would prefer us not to save their men.'

'I hoped they would stop shelling us, sir. We have the Red Cross on the roof.'

As he waited for the next shell to explode, Redel had just one hope; the killing would stop soon.

He had seen enough death.

Chapter Fifty-Seven

Behind the German lines, Feldlazarett 27.
July 3, 1916.

When he awoke, there were voices in his head but he couldn't understand what they were saying. The sounds were sharp and guttural and long, as if they would never end. He was lifted up and dumped on a low bench. The light was gone, a browner, softer glow now.

A hand patting his arm. 'They'll look after you. I have to go now, old chap. Boche are taking me away. Look after yourself.'

The voice faded away. Did he know him? Where was he? What was he doing here?

The khaki was rough beneath his fingers, covered in mud and dirt and still damp from the blood. He felt his fingers slide along his leg. He could move. He could feel.

His hand lifted as if by magic and he saw it and the five fingers wriggling in the brown light. They were caressing the light, stroking it to make it brighter.

A harsh voice. 'Nicht bewegen.' Another hand came in and forced his down to his side. 'Nicht bewegen,' the harsh voice repeated. 'Listen, English, you in Feldlazarett, you understand. Doctor see you soon. Don't move.' The voice was German. Why was the voice German?

And then he remembered what he had been told in his dream. Was he really behind German lines?

David listened to the sounds around him. A harsh cough. A groan on his left. Farther away, the soft crump of shells exploding. Closer, somebody whispering words beneath his breath. David strained to hear. 'Mutti, Mutti, Mutti,' over and over again.

A figure standing in front of him, black against the soft light. Was it Rose? He grabbed her hand.

'You are in a German Feldlazeratt.' A voice, a cultured voice. 'You have been wounded.'

Hands moving towards his head. A sharp pain lancing into his eye. A breath of cold wind over his head. Why was his head so cold? Another stab of pain. Why was the man hurting him? He tried to scream but no sounds came from his mouth.

Stop it. Stop it. Stop it.

Stop the pain.

The man sat up again, his face shadowed in the light. David could see the uniform, bluish grey, not English, not Khaki.

Another stab of pain through his eye.

'You have been shot through the head, Captain. We will operate soon. The Feldwebel will collect your belongings. Your notebook will be sent back when we exchange prisoners.'

A shell landed nearby, rattling the roof. David could see motes of dust floating in the air, trapped in the glare of a beam of light.

The cultured voice continued, 'I do wish you British would not shell a hospital. It is against the rules of war. In the meantime, lie still, until we are ready to remove the fragments from your head.'

David felt a pair of hands come in and search the inside of his jacket. Don't take my notebook. Take the letter. Send it to Rose.

'Nicht bewegen.' The harsh voice again.

And then he was alone, with only the groans and the

moans and the man on the stretcher next to him muttering 'Mutti, Mutti, Mutti,' over and over again.

A plane flew over. At least, he thought it was a plane. The sound was a single engine, the pitch of the motor rising and falling, followed by the soft crump of artillery shells landing in the distance.

He closed his eyes.

When he opened them again, it was dark. The man on the stretcher next to him was silent now. No more muttered words. On the other side, somebody was moaning with pain, a constant drone-like sound.

Shut up. Shut up. Shut up.

David wanted to shout out, order the man to be quiet, but his mouth was dry, the tongue swollen and solid, sticking to the roof of his mouth. Water, please give me water.

Another man was crying in the far corner like the sobs of a child who has lost his favourite toy.

Shut up. Shut up.

And there was Rose, floating between the beds, offering cups of water to the injured. His father was standing next to her. Why was his father standing next to her? Was he helping Rose?

The sobs of the man grew louder and more plaintive.

Stop crying, stop crying.

He closed his eyes.

When he opened them again, Rose was gone and his father was no longer there.

The pain stabbed between his eyes and he felt cold. So cold. Why is it so cold? Give me a blanket. Cover me over. I have to stay warm for Rose and the baby. I have to see her again. Hold her in my arms. Feel the weight of her body against mine.

And then the smell of her hair wafted across him.

She was here.

It was her smell, the fresh just-washed smell of her blonde hair. He loved the aroma. Like a morning in early spring when all was well with the world, the birds were singing and life was pushing its way through the cruel soil.

He inhaled again. But the smell of her hair was gone.

His head was so cold, so cold.

What was that above his head? The sound of another plane? But they didn't fly at night. Was it night? The room was dark. He couldn't see anybody or anything any more.

Have they covered my head?

Why have they covered my head?

Chapter Fifty-Eight

Le Cateau, behind the German lines. July 11, 1916.

Hauptmann Redel hated the war. So many broken bodies, twisted and maimed beyond recognition. For what? To advance 20 yards further, gaining a small slice of somebody else's cake?

He finished the glass of wine, grimacing as he did so. Far too acid. The bottle was empty again. Had he drunk it so quickly? His hand shot up into the air. A waiter appeared almost immediately.

'Encore du vin,' he ordered.

The waiter bowed and scuttled away to bring him another bottle. He was sat outside a dirty old estaminet in Le Cateau, or what was left of the town. Wagons rumbled past loaded with supplies for the front. Soldiers ambled along the street looking for the nearest brothel. Two officers sat down at the next table, ignoring him, recognising the flashes of the Medical Corps and leaving him to drink alone.

It was how he wanted it. Alone, drinking, his hand shaking as he gripped the glass.

The only time it didn't shake was when he held a scalpel or a saw in his hands. One to slice, the other to chop. Legs, heads, arms, feet, toes, brains, fingers, hips, knees. He had cut them all.

'To the bits of the human body,' he said out loud.

The other officers stared at him, finally turning their bodies away.

One day I may slice your injured nose from your face, he thought as the lieutenant shifted his chair, then you won't be able to look down it at me.

So many had died recently, English as well as German. And they were still in the same place now as they were the day the attacks began.

'To moving forward.' He lifted his glass and toasted the officers at the table next to him. They ignored him. 'No, well here's to standing still.' He rose from his table and finished the glass of wine in one gulp.

The officers answered him by picking up their glasses and moving inside the estaminet.

He slumped back on his chair. 'Fuck you, too,' he mumbled under his breath.

Then he remembered why he had come into town in the first place. He pulled five letters from the inside of his soiled jacket. His orderly had given them to him, asking what he should do.

'You have taken the notebooks and sent them back to the British?'

'Yes, Hauptmann Redel, exactly as you ordered. Two separate bundles. One for those who survived and another for those who died.'

At least the British will know what happened to their men.

Redel had taken the letters, shoving them in his overall pocket, only finding them later at the end of the night. Now here he was, on his enforced leave, sitting in a dirty cafe in an ugly town, looking at the last words of some British soldiers.

He spread the letters out in front of him. Five different hands, but always the same standard envelope; the cheap British army paper that crumpled like soft tissue.

He had a fondness for the British, developed in the arms of a woman from Brixton when he had been studying at St

Mary's in London. A strange people, so insular and convinced of their superiority, yet inferior in almost everything, from their beer, to their food, to the way they lived and to their health.

He had lived in London for two years; enjoying the opera and Covent Garden, even becoming fond of the strange brown liquid the English called beer. Thank God, the French made all their wine for them.

He picked up his glass. It was empty again. The waiter came running with another bottle, leaving it on the table and scurrying back into his cafe.

Hauptmann Redel poured himself another glass, spilling some on one of the letters. He wiped the spillage off, only spreading it even more across the envelope. The address was slightly smudged. A Rose Clarke, at a hospital near Manchester.

He remembered Manchester. A black, dirty city with a big German population, and smoke pouring from a myriad of factory chimneys. Cottonopolis they called it. He wondered how his old German friends from the city were faring now. Were they in jail? Or something worse? You never knew with the British.

He looked at the envelope again. Was this woman a wife? A mother? A sister? A lover?

He would never know.

He put his hand up in the air. The waiter shuffled out to serve him. 'Avez-vous timbres pour envoyer ces lettres en Angleterre?' he asked the waiter in his heavily accented French.

'Angleterre?'

Redel sighed, he had been through this before. 'Bien sûr, Angleterre.'

The waiter scratched his head and wandered inside, returning five minutes later with a book of stamps. 'Timbres,' he announced proudly.

Redel placed the stamp at the top left-hand corner, writing in German on the back of each letter. He had decided not to write in English. The family who received the letter had to know it was a German who sent it. That one man had done them a kindness in the middle of this rotten war.

The post box was opposite the estaminet. Redel lurched up from his seat and tottered over to it, putting each letter one by one into the gaping mouth.

He staggered back to his seat at the table, poured himself another glass of wine. A tear ran down his face. When would this war ever end?

Chapter Fifty-Nine

Holton Hall, Derbyshire. July 18, 1916.

Lady Lappiter chose a black silk dress and matched it with a grey hat from her wardrobe.

'Jennings, whatever happened to the black felt hat I used to have?' She searched through the wardrobe but it wasn't there.

'You gave it to charity two years ago, ma'am. Said you wouldn't be needing it any more,' her lady's maid answered.

'Bother.' She put the grey hat on again. 'I can't wear this again. I wore it yesterday. And anyway, the grey is fighting with the deep black of the silk.'

'No, ma'am.'

'Have we time to go to Marchant's?'

'The funeral is at 3 p.m., ma'am.'

She made a quick decision. 'Ask Silcock to bring the car around, we'll have to go. And telephone Marchant's to tell them I'm on my way.'

'Yes, ma'am.'

Lady Lappiter looked at herself in the mirror. Not bad for somebody in her fifties. She would cut a fine figure at the funeral for her husband this afternoon. All the good and great of Derbyshire would be there, of course, even the Duke of Devonshire. She had been invited to tea with the Duchess next week to commiserate her on her losses; her husband to a heart attack and her son on the fields of Flanders. What would she wear? A trip to Manchester would be needed again. She couldn't wear something old and tattered to tea with the Duchess, even if it did have to be black.

Such a fetching colour on her, she thought.

Her son bustled into the room, followed by the maid. For some reason he was agitated, holding a piece of paper in his hand and waving it about.

'Mother, Mother, it's from David...'

'Don't be stupid, Toby, David is dead. We received a telegram three days ago from the War Office.'

'It's a letter from him, he must have...'

She held up her hand and stopped him in mid-sentence. There were certain things one never talked about in front of the servants. 'Jennings, you can leave us. Make sure the car is at the front and waiting. I want to leave in precisely eight minutes.'

'Yes, ma'am.'

As soon as her maid had closed the door, Lady Lappiter spoke to her son in a low voice. 'Take three breaths, Toby, and then quietly tell me what has you so troubled.' She turned back to face the mirror. Perhaps this dress was a little too tight.

Toby did as he was told and took three breaths before sitting down. As calmly as possible, he said, 'You don't realise, Mother, he's left everything to the trollop.'

Lady Lappiter's eyebrow rose a fraction. 'I will not have that sort of language in this house, Toby. Explain yourself.'

'I was going through Father's mail, the letters he has received since passing away. I recognised David's handwriting and the yellow army notepaper. Here, read it for yourself.'

He passed over the letter to his mother, before retreating back to his seat well out of reach. She ignored him for a while, searching for her pince-nez on the dressing table before placing it on her nose and reading.

Dear Father,

I am writing this to you on the eve of the big push. By the time you read it, we will probably be advancing on Germany with the Kaiser's armies in full retreat. The men are in good spirits and I couldn't have asked for a finer bunch of chaps to command.

I remember you telling me of your time in India with the regiment. The excitement you felt before battle. I never understood what you meant but now I do. A sense of not knowing what the future holds gives one a strange sense of elation, of almost god-like understanding of everything and everybody.

That is why I am writing this letter to you as I know you will carry out my wishes without fear or favour.

Father, I married Rose in Gretna Green last month. I know this was against Mother's wishes. But you have to understand I love her with all my heart and wish to spend the rest of my life with her.

I know you didn't marry Mother for love. As you explained to me, it was a matter of expediency, the estate had to be protected. But I am different, the world is different from your time. I love Rose and when you meet her, you will love her as much as I do.

Rose and I are expecting a baby. I hope it is a boy to carry on the family line. Whatever happens to me in thie war, this child is your grandchild and my heir. I know I can rely on you to follow my wishes.

I've just been called by my sergeant, we are assembling the men before the attack. Wish me luck Father. I know, whatever happens, I won't let you or the men down.

Your loving son, David.

Lady Lappiter threw the letter onto her dressing table. 'The bitch, she's given him a child.'

'What are we going to do, Mother?'

She checked the letter once more, reading it quickly. 'Has anybody else seen this?'

Toby shook his head. 'I don't think so. It was lying with a pile of other letters on Father's desk, Walters must have put them there.'

Lady Lappiter's mind was racing. Her son's fleshy lips were making an unappealing sucking sound.

'You're sure nobody else has seen this?'

Toby nodded.

She took the Dunhill lighter, a present from her late husband, off the dresser. She pressed down on the gold lever and a small bright blue flame shot from its mouth. 'You must tell nobody about this. You are Lord Lappiter now and will remain so, is that clear?'

Toby nodded again, his cheeks wobbling and his hair falling across the high forehead.

She brought the small blue flame up to the bottom edge of the letter. Immediately, the paper began to blacken and burn. As the flame began to shoot up to her long elegant fingers, she dropped the burning fragments into the onyx ashtray.

Toby was leaning over her, the flame reflected in his eyes, burning brightly.

'You are Lord Lappiter. That trollop and her child will receive nothing, do you understand me, Toby?'

He watched as the last of the flames died away, leaving just blackened ashes, where writing could be vaguely seen.

'Now wash the ashes down the sink before Jennings returns. We don't want anybody finding them, do we?'

'No, Mother.'

Chapter Sixty

Wibbersley Hospital, Flixton, Manchester.
July 20, 1916.

'And summer's lease hath all too short a fate.' Rose didn't know why this suddenly popped into her head as she was preparing the trays for lunch. It was wrong anyway. Wasn't the line from Shakespeare 'And summer's lease hath all too short a date'? She would have to look it up later in the copy of the Sonnets in the hospital's library.

She had lost count of the number of trays she had prepared. She returned to her trolley and counted; 48. Still another 36 to make up.

Only five minutes to go before she was due to start. Sister Colman was on duty today and Rose would receive a telling-off and a note in the ward diary if she were just ten seconds late.

Where had all the time gone? She knew exactly where. In the toilet being sick again. God, she hated this feeling. All she had to do was look at food and her throat would fill up with bile. It was worse in the morning when the smell of bacon frying and the sight of eggs swimming in fat combined to bring vomit racing up her throat.

The cook was no help, delighting in seeing her suffer. 'Had six myself. First one's always the worst. Should've kept your legs shut. That's what I always tell my girls. Keep your legs shut and the buggers can't get in to do the dirty. Mind you, two of my daughters have already had kids with their men in France, so nobody listens to me, do they. Here, where you goin', your bacon and eggs is goin' cold.'

Rose tried to stay in the toilet for as short a time as possible, particularly if Sister Colman was working. She'd already received two warnings from her. A third would mean a visit to the matron.

As she was coughing what remained of yesterday evening's dinner into the white porcelain, she thought of David. Why hadn't she heard anything yet? Was he wounded? Had his letters been sent to the right place? She had checked the list of casualties every evening in the newspapers and his name hadn't appeared at all. There were other officers from his regiment in the obituaries but not him.

No news was good news, wasn't it? Perhaps the letters from the front were sent to the wrong place. Or held up waiting to be put on a boat across the channel?

She stood up and wiped her mouth. Please let him be alive.

The clock ticked over to 12.25. She had to stop daydreaming or she would get nothing done. Perhaps this was another symptom of being pregnant. Dash and bugger it.

Quickly she put the last glasses on the trays and placed them on the trolley. She pushed it down the kitchen to where the cook was ready and waiting with the plates of food and their aluminium cloches. Today was Wednesday so it was Irish stew. Most of the men liked their stew, said it reminded them of the trenches; all brown and soggy. The cook was in a good mood and loaded the plates quickly.

Rose pushed the full trolley down the corridor to the first ward. Only a few seconds late, if she ran, she would just make it. She broke into a trot, stopping only when she reached the ward door, entering at exactly 12.30.

Sister was stood behind it, watch in hand. 'Good to see you finally, Miss Clarke. Do get a move on, won't you?'

'Yes, Sister.'

She pushed the trolley to the first bed. Captain Harris, both legs amputated above the knee. He was always a little morose so Rose put on her best it's-a-wonderful-day smile. 'Good afternoon, Captain Harris. And how are we today?'

'We are fine but still sitting in here, waiting to go home. When am I going home, Miss Clarke?'

The sister was listening so Rose became the perfect nurse. 'When the doctors think you are well enough, Captain Harris. Now, set a good example to the rest of the men and eat all your lunch. You need to build up your strength for when you leave, don't you?'

'I suppose so.'

As she adjusted his pillow, she leant in and whispered, 'They're coming round this afternoon. I think you're going soon.'

A broad grin crossed Captain Harris' face. 'This afternoon?'

'Eat all your stew. It does build you up.'

The sister turned away and padded back to her desk at the head of the ward.

'That's what I've heard but don't quote me. And start smiling. You know they like to see a happy patient.'

'I don't know what we would do without you, Rose. Old Buggerlugs over there hasn't smiled since hell froze over. Right old sourpuss, she is.'

'Shhhh, and eat your food. They are coming at 2.30.'

The Captain sat up a little straighter. 'Right you are, Rose. Happy as a lamb, me, now I know I'm going home.'

The rest of the lunchtime passed quickly and without incident. Rose was just about to go back to her room for a lie-down when Sister came with a letter. An army letter.

'You're supposed to receive these before 9 a.m., Miss Clarke. For some reason, somebody put it on my desk.'

It must be from David. She snatched it from the sister's hands and tore it open.

It was from David. But it was dated before the attack. He must have sent it before then. She quickly read it through. He told her he loved her and said he had sorted everything out with his parents. At least he had managed to convince them. But where were his other letters? This was two weeks old. What had happened since then?

The sister was still standing in front of her holding another envelope, a frown creasing the space between her eyes. Rose snatched it from her. The stamp was German. Had David been captured? Was he a prisoner of war? There was German writing on the envelope; a crabbed Teutonic hand. What did it mean?

For the first time, Rose noticed Sister Colman looking at her. There was a sadness, a sorrow in her eyes.

'The writing... it's in German. Is he a prisoner?' Rose stammered.

Sister Colman touched Rose's hand. In a soft voice, she said, 'The words mean found on a British officer in a casualty clearing station.'

For what seemed like a long time, Rose didn't understand. She tried to ask a question but her mouth just opened and closed like a goldfish breathing air.

And then she finally understood.

A keening scream came from deep within her body.

Was that her? Was it her making the sound?

And then she was on the floor and the sister was holding her head on her lap and stroking her forehead.

She felt a surge of pain in the depths of her stomach and screamed out loud at the world.

Her baby, what would happen to her baby?

Chapter Sixty-One

Sale, Manchester. April 2, 2016.

'I don't understand, what's going on?' Mark passed the envelope across to Jayne.

She took it and examined the postmark. 'It appears to have been posted on July 11 in Le Cateau. That town wasn't captured by the British until late in the war.' She turned over the envelope. 'In an occupied town and with a German postage stamp. Somebody must have found the letter and sent it on.'

'Very strange. Perhaps he didn't die on July 1 after all?'

'Or somebody found this on his body and decided to post it for some reason.'

'A German, obviously, but why?'

'Why? Why? Why? It doesn't matter why.' The father lit another cigarette. Jayne noticed his hands were trembling.

'The letters tell us a lot, Dad. Rose Clarke and David Russell were together in Gretna Green. They were expecting a child together. And he called her "my darling".'

'Still useless.' The old man took a long drag on his cigarette, holding it between two fingers with the cigarette facing his palm. It reminded Jayne of pictures she had seen of Elvis fans in the 1950s, a throwback to an earlier age. His quiff shivered as he expelled the smoke out through his lips.

'But Dad, they show they were in a relationship.'

'In a relationship, my arse. What's a relationship?' he sneered. 'All that matters is whether they were married or not. And there's no proof.'

'But Mr Russell, Mark is right. These letters prove they were together.'

'They prove nothing,' the old man shouted back at Jayne, stabbing the air between them with his lit cigarette. 'Look at what's left in the case and you'll see.'

Mark checked inside the case once more. At the bottom, he found two newspaper articles. One, from the Daily Mail of 22 June 1922, bellowed in a bold black headline;

GOLD DIGGER CLAIMS PEER'S FORTUNE.

Proceedings began today at the Court of Chancery into claims by an unemployed shopgirl, Miss Rose Clarke, that her five-year-old son is the rightful heir to the Lappiter fortune and title.

Sir Toby Russell, the present heir, speaking before the trial, was careful to deny the claim. 'Miss Clarke is just a gold digger who, since the war, has made repeated claims against my late brother. We are happy finally to have our day in court to deny all these spurious allegations.'

Sir Toby inherited the title in 1916 on the death of his elder brother, Captain David Russell. He is a well-known 'man about town' having escorted famous celebrities from the world of stage and screen to a variety of night clubs.

The trial is expected to last three days.'

Mark finished reading abruptly.

'She took him to court, a brave thing to do,' said Jayne.

'Brave? It was stupid. How was she ever going to win?' The old man finished the cigarette, throwing the end in the empty fireplace.

Chapter Sixty-Two

The Court of Chancery, London. May 11, 1923.

Rose inhaled three times, composing herself. A clerk, wearing a white wig and gown, approached her holding a bible. She held out her hand and placed it lightly on the book, glad to have something to stop the hand from shaking.

'Do you, Rose Clarke...' began the clerk

'My name is Rose Russell.'

'That is not what is written in our records, Miss Clarke. You must swear by your given name.' The Judge interjected.

'But I was married to David Russell, Your Honour. As a married woman...'

'That is precisely what we have gathered in this courtroom to ascertain, is it not, Miss Clarke?' Lord Justice Rampton looked at Rose over the top of his spectacles. 'You will swear as instructed by the clerk of the court.'

'Yes, Your Honour.'

The clerk began again. 'Do you, Rose Clarke, swear you will tell the truth, the whole truth and nothing but the truth?'

'I do.'

After waiting for five years since the end of the war, the time for justice had finally arrived. Yesterday, the court had spent a painful time establishing the details of David's death. She had to live through his last moments again. An officer, Lieutenant Crawford, a former comrade, testified he had seen him in a German casualty clearing station on

July 3rd, lying on a stretcher. But afterwards, David had vanished, presumed dead, buried in some mass grave somewhere.

Another unknown soldier, known only to God.

Rose had sat through the testimony, glancing occasionally across at David's brother and his mother, sitting behind their barrister. Toby, even more of a dandy than she remembered, had smiled at her once or twice. Not a nice smile, more like that of a hyena. The old woman never looked her way, never acknowledged her presence.

Her son, called David after his father, was staying with his auntie in Worthing. She couldn't bring him to a place like this, couldn't let him hear what they would say about her or his father.

As the barrister rose to face her, Rose rubbed her hands against the frayed linen of her best dress. She had spent every penny she had, and borrowed the rest, to bring this case to trial. Her solicitor had advised her against it. The barrister had said the chances of winning were slim. But she had to try. For David's sake she had to try.

'Good morning, Miss Clarke, may I call you Rose?' her barrister began. His face was florid beneath the white hair of the wig. She couldn't help noticing it was slightly askew. If Sister had seen her cap like this, she would have been on a report.

'Good morning, Mr Hampson. Of course you may.'

'Thank you, Rose. When did you first meet David Russell?'

'It was on April 25th, 1913.'

'You remember the date exactly.'

'Of course, I do. Doesn't every woman remember the date when she met her husband?'

The judge stared at her. 'Miss Clarke, you are here to

275

answer questions, not to ask them. I would leave such inter-locution to your advocate, if I were you.'

The journalists tittered and scribbled the judge's words in their notepads.

'Please continue, Mr Hampson.'

'Thank you, My Lord. And you began a relationship with him from that time?'

'On that date, we chatted on a tram journey back to my home.'

The judge coughed. 'Miss Clarke, is it normal for you, an unaccompanied female, to chat with a stranger on a tram?'

Again, the press laughed, louder this time.

'No, it isn't My Lord, but Mr Russell had insisted on escorting me to the terminus.'

The judge wrote in his case book and mouthed the words out loud, 'insisted on escorting me to the terminus,' before laying down his pen. 'Is it normal these days for a gentleman to escort a lady only as far as the terminus, rather than to her home? It sounds most strange to me.'

'I refused to let him see me home.'

'You refused to let him. How strong-willed of you, Miss Clarke.' The judge looked up, expecting the laughs which he dutifully received.

'I didn't want him to know where I lived.'

The judge wrote and mouthed the words in his case book, 'Didn't want him to know.'

'But he did know, didn't he, Rose. Didn't he turn up at your father's shop the following week?' Her barrister was trying to keep the questioning on track.

'He did, Mr Hampson. He came to my shop the follow-ing week.'

'And he kept coming back.'

'Yes, he did.'

'And eventually, you both formed a relationship.'

'We began to see each other regularly.'

The judge held up his hand. 'Let me understand this correctly, Miss Clarke. Mr Russell came to your shop?'

'My father's shop. We lived above it.'

The judge smiled. 'But Miss Clarke, how did he know where it was if you didn't allow him to take you home?'

'He must have heard me tell the taxi driver the address.'

The judge's lips formed an upside down 'U'. 'Resourceful chaps, these soldiers when they are chasing a lady.'

Once again, the court erupted in laughter. The judge seemed to bask in the glory of his witticism. Her barrister tried to bring the court back to his line of questioning.

'You formed a liaison.'

'We became good friends.'

'But this friendship ended?'

'I broke it off. I could see no future in it.'

'When was this?'

'In 1914.'

The judge raised his pen once again. 'This line of questioning raises two questions which I would rather ask the witness now, if it is agreeable to you, Mr Hampson?'

'As Your Lordship pleases.'

He turned to Rose standing alone in the witness stand. 'Miss Clarke, when you broke off your...' he searched for the right word, '...relationship with Mr Russell, did you know he was the heir to Lord Lappiter? That he would, in fact, become the next Lord Lappiter on the death of his father?'

'I did, My Lord. It was one of the reasons I broke it off.'

'There were others?'

'Yes, My Lord. I felt we didn't have a future, we were

two different people from different backgrounds.'

The judge wrote a note in his book. 'And now for my second question; when exactly did this break in your relationship occur?'

'On the 23rd July, 1914, Your Honour.'

'Let me understand this correctly, Miss Clarke, you discontinued a relationship with a serving officer in His Majesty's army in the week before war was declared?'

A murmur ran around the court.

'But the war had nothing to do with it, Your Honour. Our relationship ended for other reasons, nothing to do with the war. We were two different people from different backgrounds. I couldn't see a future for us.'

The judge wrote in his book and, without looking up said, 'You may continue, Mr Hampson.'

'Thank you, My Lord. Rose, at the start of the war you volunteered to nurse our wounded?'

'I became a VAD, if that's what you mean?'

'And served in England and in France in that capacity.'

'I did, Mr Hampson.'

'And how did you meet Mr Russell again?'

'It was the autumn of 1915, I was working in a hospital in Boulogne. He was one of the wounded at the Battle of Loos.'

'And you nursed him back to health?'

'I helped to nurse him, there were others…'

Her barrister interrupted her. 'Your relationship was re-ignited?'

'We became good friends again.'

'Did you become lovers?' the judge asked bluntly.

'No, My Lord, we did not at that time. We did not become lovers until our wedding night on April 25th, 1916.'

'Let's get to that now, if we may, Rose. David Russell

asked you to marry him and you agreed.'

'He did. I was working in a hospital in Manchester. We decided to get married in Gretna Green as it was closer to his camp and it could be done more quickly.'

'Tell the court what happened.'

For a moment, tears formed in Rose's eye as she remembered that wonderful day in 1916. She saw the judge staring at her with his beaked nose and waiting pen. She wasn't going to let them see her cry. These bastards were not going to see her in tears. She breathed in and stood erect. 'We both travelled up to Gretna separately. David had gone to see his parents in Derbyshire to tell them.'

'That's a lie,' shouted Toby Russell. Immediately, a buzz surged around the gallery. A few watchers stood up to get a better look at the man who had interrupted the witness.

The judge hammered his gavel onto his desk. 'Mr Russell, you will please keep your interruptions to a minimum. You will be allowed to give evidence later.'

The noise in the courtroom gradually subsided.

'So, Rose, you arrived in Gretna Green first?'

'David arrived later with his brother...'

'Another lie. The woman is a patent liar...' shouted Toby from his seat. His mother instantly patted his shoulder to calm him.

The judge banged his gavel down hard. 'If you make another interruption in my courtroom, Lord Lappiter, you will be escorted from here and charged with contempt. Do I make myself clear?'

Toby Russell just nodded and leant into his mother.

'Please continue, Mr Hampson.'

'Where were you married?'

'That evening in the blacksmith's shop.'

'By a registered preacher?'

'Yes, by the preacher Duncan Gillespie.'

He twisted his body towards the judge. 'Unfortunately Mr Gillespie is dead My Lord, and can't give testimony here today.'

'Not many dead men can, Mr Hampson.'

'No, My Lord. Quite correct, My Lord.' He turned back to Rose. 'But there is no record of your wedding, either in the blacksmith's shop or the Central Registry in Edinburgh. How do you explain that?'

'I can't, Mr Hampson. Perhaps the record was mislaid.'

'The record was mislaid...' The judge spoke out loud as he wrote the note in his book.

Mr Hampson carried on regardless. 'And what happened to your copy of the marriage certificate? The one given to you by the preacher?'

'David took it. He needed the records to show the army so his salary would be given to me when he was at the front.'

'Does the army have these records, Mr Hampson? It would save us an awful lot of time and expense if they produced them.'

'I'm sorry, My Lord, the army has been unable to produce any records for Captain Russell's regiment. Apparently, they have been lost.'

'More mislaid records.' The judge shook his head. 'Please continue, Mr Hampson.'

'So, Rose, you gave birth to Mr Russell's child nine months after the wedding.'

For the first time, the opposing council rose lazily to his feet. He looked like a cadaver who had just been woken from a long death. 'I object, My Lord. There is no evidence of marriage, and without such evidence, the child cannot be that of David Russell, the then Lord Lappiter.'

'I agree, Mr Anderson. This court will decide if a marriage took place. You will call the boy by his mother's name until we have made our judgement.'

Rose's interrupted the interchange. 'But My Lord, the child has been registered as David Russell not David Clarke.'

'I have made my judgement, Mr Hampson, please proceed.'

'As Your Lordship pleases.' He turned back to his client. 'Rose, just a few more questions. You have brought this prosecution with no expectation of monetary gain?'

'None at all. I want to see my marriage to David recognised and my son accepted as his rightful heir. Nothing else. It's for David's memory I do this, no other reason. It's what he would have wanted.'

'Thank you, Rose. That is the end of the questions I have for this witness, My Lord.'

'Good, well timed, Mr Hampson. We will now retire for luncheon. The court will resume at two o'clock in the afternoon.'

Chapter Sixty-Three

Sale, Manchester. April 2, 2016.

Mark stopped reading. 'That's the end of this newspaper report.'

'Must have had a deadline. Nothing else in there?' asked Jayne.

Mark searched through the case. 'Nothing. Just some old suffragette pamphlets.'

The old man snorted. 'Stupid woman, taking them on. What did she hope to gain? The toffs will always stick together, always.'

Jayne felt her fists clenching and unclenching. 'Your grandmother was not a 'stupid woman', Mr Russell. She was principled and brave and honest.'

'And she was mad. Ended up spending the rest of her life in an asylum, she did. My dad never got over the shame. Used to tell people she was dead. Well, she was to him.'

Jayne felt like squeezing his scrawny neck until it could croak no more. Instead, she spoke through gritted teeth. 'I don't say this often to clients, or even ex-clients. But you are a stupid, stupid man who doesn't deserve such a grandmother.'

The old man shrank back, shocked by the vehemence of her attack.

Mark spoke quickly. 'What happened in the trial?'

Jayne stopped clenching and unclenching her fists. Men like him were not worth the trouble of a skinned knuckle.

'Is there anything online?'

Jayne stopped staring at the old man. What a sad, bitter life he had led. 'If you have a laptop, I'll check,' she eventually said.

Mark went into the back room and returned with an old IBM ThinkPad. It would have to do. Jayne googled the year and Rose's name. 'Well, no trial transcript is available. We'll probably have to go to the National Archives in Kew and search there, but, hello, there's something in the British Newspaper Archive. An article from the Daily Sketch.'

'Let's hope it's better than the Daily Mail.'

'Nothing could be worse than the Daily Mail.'

Mark's father looked at her out of the corner of his eye. He was about to say something, but instead kept silent.

A newspaper page popped up on the screen with one long article in five densely packed columns. Jayne began reading the headline.

CLAIM AGAINST LORD LAPPITER.
WOMAN'S ACCUSATIONS.

Chapter Sixty-Four

The Court of Chancery, London. May 11, 1923.

'All rise.' The clerk called in a clear voice as the judge strolled in after his luncheon. He sat down behind his large imposing desk, elevated above the court. Rose remained standing in the dock as everybody else sat down.

Over a cup of tea during the break, her barrister told her it had gone well that morning, she had come across as a believable witness. All she had to do was answer the questions this afternoon as directly as she could, without arguing with the judge.

She looked across at the judge with his beaked nose and eyebrows like an overgrown hedge. He had obviously dined well; a red flush suffused his jowls.

'Let us begin, Mr Anderson. I would like to complete the testimony of this witness before the end of the day.'

The barrister for the Russell family was tall and ascetic, the white hair of the wig ageing him prematurely. The cheeks were hollow, with the yellow skin stretched tightly across the skull. The overall impression was that a living corpse had risen to speak. 'It should be no problem, My Lord,' he enunciated slowly.

'Good, I knew I could rely on you, Mr Anderson. Please proceed.'

'As you please, My Lord.' The barrister scrutinised a sheet of paper in front of him, then turned his body to face Rose. 'Good afternoon, Miss Clarke. Just a few details for the court, Miss Clarke, if you please.'

'Of course, Mr Anderson.' She rubbed her hands against

her skirt again. She hoped he wouldn't see. The court was hot and dark, lit only by a weak bulb and a few table lamps.

The judge sat above her to her left. On her right, the viewing seats were packed with reporters eager to tell their readers all the juicy details. In front of her, Mr Anderson held on to his gown with his left hand as if it were about to fall off.

'You are Miss Rose Clarke, of Curtain Road, Shoreditch?'

'It's where I was born, but I now live with my aunt and my son at Queen's Road in Worthing.'

'Miss Clarke, I know a lady doesn't like to give her age but you were born in 1892, is that correct?' The question drew titters from the assembled male members of the press.

'That is correct. 23 July, 1892.'

'Miss Clarke, your father was an immigrant to this country, was he not?'

Why does he keep calling me Miss Clarke? Rose thought. 'I don't see what my father has to do with this case.'

Once again, the judge peered over the top of his spectacles. 'That is for me to decide, Miss Clarke. Just answer the question.'

'But...'

'Just answer the question, Miss Clarke.'

Why did they both keep calling her Miss Clarke? She was Mrs Russell. She breathed in again and asked, 'What was the question?'

The barrister sighed, a dramatic sigh as if to say who was this idiot he was dealing with. The press lapped up the theatrics, scribbling furiously in their notepads. 'Your father, Miss Clarke, was an immigrant to this country, was he not?'

'He was. He came here in 1886 with my mother to make a better life. He worked hard and set up his own haberdashery in 1890, just before I was born.'

'Yes, yes…' The barrister waved his hand dismissively. 'But where did he come from?'

'I don't see what this has to do with…'

'Where did he come from, Miss Clarke?'

'He came from Germany.'

A sharp intake of breath from the journalists. The judge made a note in his case book.

'And was his original name, Schreiber?'

'It was. Just as the royal family's original name was Hohenzollern until they changed it to Windsor in 1917.'

'May I remind you, Miss Clarke, the royal family is not on trial here.'

'And may I remind you, Mr Anderson, neither am I.'

The press scribbled furiously. The judge just stared at her. Inwardly, Rose felt better. She enjoyed knocking the wind out of the barrister's sails.

Mr Anderson checked his notes and picked up a piece of paper. 'I believe you have been to prison, Miss Clarke.'

Her barrister finally rose to his feet. 'I object, m'lud, Miss Clarke's prison record has no relevance to whether or not she was married to Mr Russell.'

'My Lord, it has every relevance to her character which, I am trying to establish, is not one to be trusted by this court.'

'I will allow this line of questioning, Mr Hampson. Your client has placed herself in the dock. She will answer Mr Anderson's questions.'

Her barrister simply nodded his head and sat down again.

'Miss Clarke…'

Why did they keep calling her Miss?

'…Is it true you were arrested twice by the police?'

'Who else would I be arrested by?'

The barrister looked at the judge.

Once again he peered over his spectacles. 'Please answer Mr Anderson's questions, Miss Clarke. He asks them, not you, is that clear?'

Rose coughed.

The judge repeated, 'Is that clear?'

'Yes, Your Honour. I was arrested twice. By the police,' she added.

'And what were you charged with on the first occasion?'

'I was charged with malicious damage, because…'

'And on the second occasion?'

'I was a suffragette, a member of the WSPA…'

The judge slammed his hand down on the table. 'I will not tell you again, Miss Clarke. Answer Mr Anderson's questions and only his questions.'

'But, My Lord…'

'But me no buts, Miss Clarke. Answer the question.'

A buzz travelled around the courtroom as the journalists all began speaking at once. For the first time, Rose saw David's mother smile before the mask returned to her face.

'And the second occasion, Miss Clarke?' the barrister repeated.

'On the second occasion I was arrested for obstruction.'

'When was this?'

'1914.'

'And where was this?'

Rose's hands reached forward and grabbed the rail of the Witness stand. 'Outside Buckingham Palace.'

'Our nation was about to go to war and you were demonstrating outside the home of the King?'

The barrister was playing to the gallery, Rose could see it clearly. 'Demonstrations against unjust laws have always been allowed in Britain, even if the demonstration occurs on Buckingham Palace Road.'

The barrister glanced across at the judge and raised his eyebrow before continuing with his questioning. 'And did you not remain in jail until you were released by the Grace of His Majesty on August 10, 1914, after the outbreak of war?'

Rose nodded.

'I didn't hear your answer, Miss Clarke.'

She held her head up. 'Yes, I did.'

'Now, let us come to your supposed relationship with Mr Russell.'

'My husband...'

'That is for the court, and his Lordship, to decide, Miss Clarke.' The barrister nodded in the direction of the judge who smiled in return. The secret little glances between the two annoyed Rose even more.

'Now, you say you met Mr Russell in 1913. Where exactly did you meet him?'

'I don't remember the exact name of the street.'

'You don't? Why is that?'

'We had been demonstrating against the Cat and Mouse Act.'

'By we, I presume you mean the other members of the Women's Social and Political Union, rather than Mr Russell?' The members of the press thought this was extremely witty.

'Yes, the women of the WSPU who were fighting for votes for women.'

'And you were one of them.'

'I was.'

'And where was Mr Russell?'

'I don't know where exactly, but I had been arrested by a policeman and pushed against a wall. David came to my rescue...'

'Your rescue? Why would you need rescuing from the police, Miss Clarke?'

Rose realised she was being led into a trap but she couldn't see any way out without telling the truth. 'The policeman assaulted me, David stopped him.'

'A policeman assaulted you, did he? And how did Mr Russell stop him exactly?'

Rose took a deep breath. 'He pushed him to the ground.'

Mr Anderson's mouth opened wide and he was once again looking around the court theatrically. 'Are you asking us to believe the son of a peer of the realm assaulted a policeman to rescue a damsel in distress?' The gallery laughed.

'That's what happened.'

'And so Mr Russell has assaulted a policeman to save you, Miss Clarke. What happened next?'

'We jumped on a tram to get away and headed to Clapham.'

'An escape by electric tram. It does make a change from a knight in shining armour mounted on his steed.' The gallery and the journalists laughed again.

Rose felt her face becoming redder and redder.

'Isn't it more likely, Miss Clarke, that Mr Russell met you on a tram, engaged you in conversation and you gave him your address asking him to come around at the weekend? He was a gentleman and, coming from a lower social class, you looked forward to making his acquaintance. Or something more.'

'That's not true, I resisted David. I didn't even want to

see him again.'

'You see, Miss Clarke, we do not deny you knew Mr Russell. We don't even deny you may have had a "relationship" with him.' Here he held his fingers up and made quotation marks. The gallery understood the sexual reference immediately. Mr Anderson carried on in a quieter voice once the laughter had died down. 'We simply deny you were ever married to Mr Russell. Miss Clarke, I put it that you are nothing but a gold digger who is using her friendship with a man who died in the service of his country to profit from that death.'

'That's not true. I loved David and he loved me. We were married in Gretna Green!' Rose shouted from the witness box. Why didn't he believe her? Why did nobody believe her?

Muttering ran around the court which was silenced by the banging of the judge's gavel. 'Pray continue, Mr Anderson.'

'Certainly, My Lord. Let us concern ourselves with your so-called marriage, now, shall we?' He smiled at her, tobacco-stained teeth as large as tombstones. 'Of course, we sent someone to Gretna and the hotel where you stayed. Nobody remembers you.'

'I was there. I was there.'

'You were there, Miss Clarke. We saw the register. You checked in under your maiden name…'

'I checked in first, David followed with his brother later.'

Mr Anderson ignored the outburst, carrying on as if nothing had happened. 'Captain Russell did check in later with a woman whom he called his wife. But as we all know, these things happen during wartime.' He shrugged his shoulders as if to say boys will be boys.

'But Toby was there, he was the witness to our marriage.'

'May it please the court, the present Lord Lappiter will testify later he was at home in Derbyshire during the period mentioned. His presence at the family home has been confirmed under oath by his mother, the Dowager Lady Lappiter.'

'He's lying. They are both lying. He was there!' Rose screamed at the top of her voice, collapsing across the front of the dock.

The judge took off his glasses. 'Mr Hampson, you will please control your client. Such outbursts will not be tolerated in my court.'

'Of course, My Lord.'

Rose straightened her back and wiped her tears. She wouldn't let these men beat her down, not now, not today, not ever.

'Are you ready to carry on Miss Clarke?' Mr Anderson asked in a voice dripping in fake sincerity.

Rose just nodded in reply.

'Finally, we come to the letters. We do not doubt Captain Russell was enamoured of you Miss Clarke, one might almost say he was infatuated...'

'We loved each other.'

Mr Anderson ignored her response. 'He may also have accepted your child as his baby, but in the absence of prima facie evidence of a marriage, your son can only be termed a bastard, if he were Captain Russell's son, and as such has no claim to the estate or the title.'

'He is not a bastard. He was born after our wedding on April 25th, 1916,' Rose said.

'Unfortunately, Miss Clarke, there is no proof. And I'm certain His Lordship will agree with me when I say, without proof your claim is unfounded. I will go on to state that it is malicious and spiteful, traducing the honour of Lord Lappiter and his mother.'

With those final words, he sat down.

Rose was left gripping the rail of the dock. A court official came forward and tapped her on the shoulder. 'You've finished giving evidence, Miss.'

But Rose found her hands continued to grip the rail, she couldn't leave, she had to say something. 'I just want to say…'

'Mr Anderson has finished with you, Miss Clarke…' the judge spoke from his chair.

'But…'

'And as it's the afternoon, we will retire for the day. Tomorrow, we will begin at 9.30… if that is necessary,' he added, staring at Rose's barrister.

He stood up and left the court.

Rose was left gripping the rail of the dock as if she no longer existed.

Chapter Sixty-Five

Sale, Manchester. April 2, 2016.

Mark finished reading the detailed description of the trial in the article. 'He destroyed her. That bastard destroyed my great grandmother.' He shook his head.

'She deserved it. You can't take them on and win. She should have just got on with life, found another feller and settled down. Lots of other women did.'

Jayne began to detest the little man with the ridiculous quiff sitting in front of her, smoking another cigarette. 'Your grandmother was a brave woman, Mr Russell. You should be proud of her.'

'Proud? I'm ashamed. My dad spent his whole life with a mother locked away in an asylum. He was always worried that one day he would end up like her, living his life in a fantasy. He hated her with all his heart. He just wanted to be normal, have a mother who stayed at home and made him lunch and washed his clothes, just like all the other kids. The title, the money, he didn't care at all. I don't care at all.' He turned to his son. 'Please Mark, for my sake, give it all up. I don't want you to end up like her.'

'I will, Dad, I promise. Let me ask Mrs Sinclair one more question and I promise I'll stop. No more, okay?'

'Just give it up, Mark, there's no point. She had her day in court and she was told she was a liar. What more do you want to know?'

'I want to know what happened to her after the trial. Mrs Sinclair, did you find out why she was put into the asylum?'

Jayne pulled out a photocopy of the Derbyshire register

for 23rd September, 1923, she had found in Bakewell library. 'This is from a local newspaper. It's dated four months after the end of the trial.'

Mark took the paper and read the headline:

WOMAN ARRESTED OUTSIDE PEER'S HOME.

Chapter Sixty-Six

Holton Hall, Derbyshire. September 21, 1923.

Rose stood outside the wrought iron gates of Holton Hall. The rain continued to drift down in a soft drizzle, soaking her head. She pushed a lock of hair behind her ear. David was holding her hand tightly. She could feel a slight trembling in the tiny fingers.

'It's wet, Mummy. What are we doing here?'

After thinking about it for the last week, Rose had finally taken the train to Manchester and another to Bakewell. They had walked the two miles from the station in the rain. David hadn't cried once, hadn't said a thing until they had arrived outside the gate.

'It's a beautiful house, Mummy. Are we going to live here?'

'You are going to live here, David. It's where your father grew up.'

It was the right decision. After the court case, Rose had nothing. No reputation. No money. No future. David needed more than she could give him. He needed a home and warmth and a roof over his head. She had none of those, not any more. A row with her aunt had seen to that.

'You should never have gone to court,' her aunt had shouted at her one evening.

'It was my only chance to prove them wrong.'

'Your solicitor and your barrister told you not to go. How stupid, how stubborn can you be? Didn't you think of the boy?'

She always thought of the boy. He looked exactly like

his father. The same open smile. The same gentle temper. The same love of activity, pouring his heart into everything he did. She loved the way his tongue peeped out between his lips when he concentrated, just like his father.

He was his father's son.

Light shone from every room in the house and the sounds of jazz drifted across the lawns and down the driveway. There seemed to be some sort of party going on. She took a deep breath and rang the bell.

'Can I ring next time, Mother?' David asked.

Nobody answered the ring. Nobody came down the driveway. 'Why don't you ring it now?'

David reached up on tip toes and pressed the button. Again, they heard no sound.

On the long journey, Rose had thought about what she was going to say. They had to accept him, he was Toby's brother's son. She would explain she wanted nothing, just to see him looked after and well educated. If they accepted him, she would vanish forever, never seeing or troubling them again.

But what if they said no? Of course, she had considered the possibility. The weight in her bag was the answer if it happened. She wasn't leaving here until they accepted him as one of them, as David's son.

There was still nobody coming out from the house.

'Maybe it's not working,' said David, as if reading her thoughts.

'Ring it again.'

David reached up and pressed the button. As he did so, a voice from the door of the house shouted, 'Coming, coming, hold your horses.'

Rose could hear the sound of feet on gravel coming down the drive, accompanied by muttering. 'People coming here on a night like this.'

A man appeared wearing a black morning coat and carrying an even blacker umbrella. 'What do you want? The tradesman's entrance is round the back.'

Rose took a deep breath. 'I want to see Lord Lappiter.'

'His Lordship is indisposed at the moment.'

The sounds of laughter and music came from the house.

'I want to see Toby.'

The man sighed. 'As I told you, His Lordship is indispose...' He stopped halfway through his sentence, and leant forward. 'You're that woman, aren't you?'

The rain teemed down now. Rose pushed a wet curl away from her eyes. 'My name is Rose Russell. I am here to see Lord Lappiter.'

The man in the morning coat stared at David closely. 'He certainly looks like the young master.'

Rose put her arm across David's shoulder. 'I want to see Lord Lappiter,' she repeated.

Another loud guffaw erupted from the house. The butler hesitated, looked over his shoulder and looked back at David. 'I will fetch him. Please stay here.'

The man hurried away, his steps beating a retreat on the sodden gravel.

'Is my uncle coming?'

Rose smiled down at her son. 'He's coming, don't worry.'

They stood outside the gates, listening to the sounds of the party in the house. The rain still swept across the open road, covering the wrought iron with a sheen of water. The gates looked almost silver in the light of the lantern.

After ten minutes, she heard the sound of footsteps on the wet gravel. Two pairs of footsteps. Silhouetted against the light from the house, the tall figure of Toby advanced towards her, and next to him, the shorter figure of the butler holding an umbrella over his head.

'I do think you have some cheek coming here on a night like this. Don't you know I have guests?'

Even from behind the gate, Rose could smell alcohol on his breath. The champagne glass in his hand was empty.

'I've come to see you about David.' She patted her son's head. He smiled up at her.

'What about the little bastard?'

Rose gripped her son's shoulder, pulling him to her. 'You shouldn't talk about your brother's son like that.'

'He's not my brother's son.'

'He is.'

'Prove it.'

'You were there Toby, the night we were married in Gretna Green. You were a witness.'

Toby Russell swayed slightly on his feet. 'Prove it.'

'You saw our marriage in the blacksmith's shop with your own eyes.'

He smashed the empty champagne glass onto the gravel. 'Listen, you little trollop, my brother may have fucked you for the fun of it, but you can't prove you were married to him, or that this thing is his son. You could have fucked half the soldiers in the British Army for all I know.'

Rose pulled David closer to her. 'You need to look after him. You have to take care of him, he's your brother's son.'

'I have to do nothing.' Toby Russell turned away and began to walk up the drive, the butler chasing after him with the black umbrella.

'I'll go away. You'll never see me again. You can bring David up exactly how you want.'

He stopped for a moment. Then, he turned, smiled and walked back toward her. 'Listen, you dirty slag, I want nothing to do with this boy. I will be marrying the Honourable Agatha Lyne next month. We don't want your boy hanging around this house, stinking the place with his rotten clothes and cheap stench. Now, be off, before I call the police.'

Rose reached into her bag. 'We're never leaving here, Toby.' She brought out the heavy pair of handcuffs and snapped one end on her wrist and the other on the wrought iron gate.

'Mother, what are you doing?'

'We're staying here until this man accepts you as his brother's son.'

Toby Russell smiled. 'Once a suffragette, always a suffragette, Rose. Walters, call the police and get me the chief constable on the phone.'

He walked away from the gates, his feet crunching on the gravel. Half way down the drive he began to laugh; a laugh which became louder and louder the nearer he walked to the house.

Chapter Sixty-Seven

Sale, Manchester. April 2, 2016.

'My father talked to me about that night.' Mr Russell lit another cigarette, taking a long drag before he continued speaking. 'He was six and all he remembered was feeling cold and lonely. The police came and cut his mother away from the gate. He remembered trying to hold on to her as she was screaming his name, but the police dragged her away from him.'

The old man had tears in his eyes. 'He told me this when the cancer had spread to his liver and he was lying in the hospice waiting to die. It was as if he had buried it so deeply only the prospect of death had brought it back to him.'

'What happened, Dad?'

'The policemen pulled his mother away. Another woman took him and he spent the night locked up in a room in some home or other. He remembered crying all night, curling up on a rough blanket and screaming for his mother.

'Nobody came to see him. There was just a single window high up in the wall which the wind and rain battered against the whole night long. He lay there alone, crying for his mother.

In the morning, two men and a woman came for him. They took him to another home where there were lots of other boys. He told me he asked for his mother but they said she wasn't coming.'

'What did he do?'

'He didn't tell me. But it can't have been easy. He was six years old and all alone in the world. He didn't know how long he was in the home, but one day his great aunt came for him and he was taken by her to live in Worthing. She was an old woman, set in her ways, but kind to him, he said.'

'When did he see his mother again?'

'He told me he was 25 before he saw her again. He knew where she was, but his aunt didn't want him to see her, and besides, it was a long way to go.'

'What made him change his mind?'

'The war. The Second World War. He was training in Sheffield. He had a weekend off, so he took a train to the hospital in Derbyshire. He told me he walked in to the asylum and she recognised him immediately, as if he had only visited yesterday. She had been inside for nearly 20 years by then. Already an old woman, but she recognised him. They sat and talked. She never mentioned that night, perhaps she had buried it deep in her memories. She still thought she was married to David and he would come back one day from the war to take her home. She showed him the case and the letters. He never forgot the letters.'

The father took another drag from the cigarette, letting the smoke slide out from his mouth and rise to the ceiling. 'He died in 1973, before she did. I tried to tell her, but I don't think she understood. She was still living in 1916 I think, still waiting for David to come home from war.'

Mark left the couch and knelt down in front of his father. 'I'm sorry you had to live through this again, Dad.'

The eyes of Mr Russell were glazed with tears. 'My grandmother's obsession destroyed my father, it affected me. I can't let it you become obsessed by it, Mark. That's why I hid the case and the letters. I can't let the past destroy you too.'

'It won't, Dad. But we have to get rid of this demon that's haunted our family. If we don't solve it now, it will only haunt the next generation.'

The old man nodded.

Mark reached forward and hugged his father, the two of them rocking gently together.

As quietly as she could, Jayne walked out of the room, taking one last look at Mark and his father before she closed the door. They were still there, neither speaking to each other, just holding each other so the world could no longer pull them apart.

Chapter Sixty-Eight

Didsbury, Manchester. April 2, 2016.

Jayne parked the car and opened the door to her home, expecting to be greeted by the mess she had left behind. Instead, a new laptop sat in the kitchen, the pictures were back on the walls and the place was spotlessly clean and tidy.

On the new computer, a Post-it note was stuck to the monitor. 'It's the least I could do.' It was signed Paul.

She opened the fridge. Two bottles of a New Zealand Sauvignon Blanc from Saint Clair lay on the top shelf next to a bottle of Dead Arm Shiraz.

She took out the Shiraz and opened it, letting it breathe for a few moments. Beside the sink, four new Riedel glasses were upside down drying. She poured a generous helping of the Dead Arm and inhaled the sticky jamminess of the wine.

Paul was a good man, she knew that. It was a shame it hadn't worked out between the two of them. They just didn't love each other any more. Jayne had finally come to terms with it, and, with the realisation, had come a strange kind of peace. She would do everything in her power to ensure they remained good friends. For twelve years they had been lovers, there was no point in now being enemies.

She switched on the new computer. After the requisite whirrs and swooshes, her homepage, brighter than before, smiled back at her. 'Finally, your computer skills have come in useful, Paul Jones. And here's to you.' She raised her glass to the ceiling and took a generous mouthful, rolling it around to coat her teeth and tongue. The blackcurrant and pepper lasted long after she had swallowed, filling her mouth with a jammy aftertaste.

'Not bad, Mr Jones. You know how to choose a decent drop or three.'

What should she do next? The investigation had reached a dead end. Without a wedding certificate, they would never be able to prove the marriage had existed. And with the last Lord Lappiter having died, a DNA test to prove a link between Mark and the family was no longer an option. Even then, all it would prove was that Mark was a descendent of David Russell, not that he was the rightful heir to the title and the estate.

Only two days left before the crown officially sequestered the estate. No doubt it would be used to pay off the national debt, but whatever the size of the inheritance, it would only have the impact of a raindrop on the deserts of the Sahara.

Her mobile rang.

She was tempted to ignore it. It rang again, louder this time, rattling the edge of the counter where she had put it. She drank another mouthful from her glass. The wine was beginning to open up nicely.

It rang once more, and shivered its way to the edge of the counter, dropping like an electronic lemming.

She caught it and pressed the answer button. 'Thanks for all you did. And thanks especially for the wine.'

'Mrs Sinclair?'

It was Mark's voice. 'Hello, Mark… I thought you were somebody else.'

'Mrs Sinclair. I've spoken with my father and we've decided to…'

Here it was again. This was the second time she was

going to be removed from this case. She took a deep breath, bracing herself for the bad news.

'We've decided we want to stop. For good, this time.'

There it was, the news she had been expecting ever since she had left their house in Sale.

Mark continued. 'It's no use dragging up the past, Mrs Sinclair, sometimes it just wants to stay buried.'

'But you wanted to know, Mark, you needed to know.'

'That was before I realised how much it upset my dad. The past is dead and buried, Mrs Sinclair, let's leave it that way.'

'But it isn't. We drag our pasts round with us all the time. For some people, it's a joy, a remembrance of wonderful times or marvellous people. For others it's a terrible burden, dragging a terrible albatross of misfortune through life, a weight they can neither discard nor abandon. Only the truth can set you free, Mr Russell, only the truth.'

'My father has carried the weight for his whole life, Mrs Sinclair, I can't ask him to continue any more. I must share it with him, don't you understand. We'll never find the truth. He knows that, he's always known it.'

'But, Mr Russell…'

'We've decided, Mrs Sinclair. My father thanks you for all your efforts on his behalf, but we have gone far enough now. It's time to stop. We will, of course, abide by our agreement and pay all your expenses so far for the investigation, my father insists. Thank you once again, and goodbye.'

The phone went dead. Jayne slammed it down in frustration. There had to be an answer, the truth was always out there, just waiting to be found. All she had to do was discover what rock it was hidden under.

And then a voice in her head said, 'Give this one a rest,

Jayne, you can't win all of them.' It was her old sergeant counselling her as he always did when she was frustrated with a case going nowhere.

For once, she would listen to the voice.

She picked up her wine and finished it off in one gulp, pouring herself another generous helping. Perhaps Paul had also left her some chocolate?

Chapter Sixty-Nine

Buxton, near Manchester. April 3, 2016.

Her father wasn't in his usual chair in front of the picture window. For a moment Jayne panicked. Where was he? Had he gone missing again?

She found an attendant and asked to know where he was.

The woman looked in the usual spot and then pointed out of the window to two people sitting on a bench enjoying the early spring sunshine.

Jayne looked closer. It was her father, sitting next to a woman with carefully coiffured hair. Her father was laughing, pointing to something in the newspaper lying between them.

Her father was laughing.

Jayne's wine headache vanished in a second. Happiness was a much better analgesic than any tablet.

Out of the corner of his eye, her father caught sight of Jayne and waved for her to join them. She walked out through the open doors onto the patio. She saw the woman face-to-face now. A lovely, warm, open face, a shock of white hair, carefully coordinated clothes, and long, elegant fingers. So unlike her own mother.

'This is Mrs Thompson, Jayne.' He turned to the woman. 'And this is Jayne, my daughter.'

They both said, 'pleased to meet you' at the same time, followed by an awkward silence and laughter.

'After nearly a year in this den of iniquity, I've finally met somebody who can do the Guardian crossword quicker than me.'

'Don't exaggerate, Robert, you did get five down.' Jayne noticed an elegantly manicured hand rested gently on her father's. For a moment, an absurd wave of jealousy flowed up through her body, and then she dismissed it. 'That's great, Dad. Have you been here for long, Mrs Thompson?'

'Call me, Vera, love, your father is so old-fashioned sometimes.' There was a hint of Lancashire in the voice. A warmth in tone at odds with the carefully cultivated image the woman presented.

'I'm Jayne.'

'Me, Tarzan,' her father joked, looking for a reaction from Vera. She obliged with a big, warm-hearted laugh and gentle dig in his ribs.

'Have you been here long, Vera?'

'Just arrived. Met your father a couple of days ago.'

Her father laughed. 'I found somebody had finished the crossword yesterday before I'd even looked at it. Well, I was so annoyed and then I found out the culprit was Vera, and we hit it off straight away.'

This was the happiest she had seen her father in the last year. The joy in his eyes made her so happy. 'That's great, Dad.'

'Problem is, the crossword used to last me all day, but between the two of us, we finish it off before the elevenses come around.'

'Do you want me to bring the book of Guardian crosswords next time I come? Vera and you can work your way through it.'

Her father looked across at Vera, who nodded. 'That would be champion, lass.'

'Great, I'll bring two next time I come.'

'You must meet my daughter, Sharon. She doesn't come

as often as you, lives too far away, in Birmingham.'

Jayne saw a sadness behind the smiling eyes of the old woman.

'Lass, it's a lovely day, why don't you take a shot of us sitting on the bench?'

Vera became coy, dabbing at her hair like a 13-year-old. 'I couldn't, Robert, I'm not ready.'

'You look grand, lass. Go on, Jayne.'

Jayne noticed her father had changed. Gone was the old shirt with its frayed collar and the tea-stained cardigan. He was now wearing a fresh shirt and tie, with the V-necked merino wool jumper Jayne had given him at Christmas. He even had sharp creases in the centre of his trousers.

She brought up her phone and found the camera app. He leant into Vera and they both smiled. She clicked the button and said, 'One more, for luck.'

'We all need a bit of luck, don't we?' said her father adjusting his position on the bench to lean in closer to Vera.

She pressed the button again, stepping forward to show them both the result.

'Will you look at my hair? Seems like something the cat's dragged in.'

'Get away with you, lass. You look stunning. Now, let me take a picture of you with our Jayne. Two roses sitting in a garden.'

'Your father always says the sweetest things.'

Jayne handed the phone to her father. She saw how old his fingers were. Creased and long, with misshapen nails from a lifetime of hard work. Why should she be jealous of his moments of happiness with this woman? She put her arm around Vera's shoulder and held her close.

'You look like sisters,' her father said.

Vera blushed. 'Enough with the sweet talk, Robert.'

Her father fiddled with the phone, trying to find the right button to press. 'Which one is it, lass, these new-fangled lemons are so fiddly?'

'It's an Apple, Dad.'

'I know, lass,' said her father archly, 'but it could be a Cox's pippin for all the use I can make of it. There's a picture stuck to the screen.'

He handed the phone back to her. Somehow, he had entered the gallery of shots and found the pictures of the old hotel register in Gretna Green. She looked for the line with the words 'Captain and Mrs Russell' written on it, but it wasn't there. This must be one of the other pages she had shot with her phone.

And then she saw it, staring right at her, jumping out from the page onto the screen.

'Dad, I have to go, something's come up.'

Her father's face fell. 'Of course, lass, come back soon.'

Jayne ran through the patio doors, turned and ran back. 'Nice to meet you, Vera,' she shouted, before rushing off again without waiting for a response.

Chapter Seventy

Sale, Manchester. April 3, 2016.

Once again, the curtain flickered as she walked up the short pathway to the front door. She pressed the doorbell and the door opened almost immediately as if Mark had been waiting for her.

'Mark, I…'

'I told you, Mrs Sinclair. It's over, we no longer want to continue the investigation.'

'But please, Mark, I've discovered something new.'

'Mrs Sinclair, we can't keep doing this. My father is an old man, he's had enough.'

Mark began to close the door, Jayne put her foot in the gap to stop him, a trick she'd used many times in the police.

'Please take your foot away or I will call the police.'

'Mark, just two minutes of your time; if you tell me afterwards to go, I will, I promise.'

'She just wants her money, like the others.' The bitter whiny voice of Mark's father echoed in the hallway.

'I don't want your money, Mark, you don't even have to pay my expenses. Just give me two minutes, it's all I ask, just two minutes.'

Mark's face was set. Jayne took her foot away, he moved to close the door.

'Just two minutes and we'll never see you again?' It was the hidden father again.

'That's correct.'

'And we won't have to pay your expenses?'

The father was as stingy as ever. What did it matter?

'You won't have to pay my expenses.'

The father appeared at the door beside Mark. 'Well, you'd better come in then, otherwise the neighbours will start talking.'

The old man walked away. Mark opened the door wider without saying a word. Jayne stepped into the dark, dingy hallway. God, how she disliked this house. Mark must have hated growing up here, just him and his father and this.

She walked into the front room. It was as pokey and dingy as before. The smell of stale cigarette smoke infested everything.

The old man pointed at the clock. 'Your time has already started.'

Chapter Seventy-One

Sale, Manchester. April 3, 2016.

'Are you sure this is right?' asked Mark leaning in to look at the picture on her phone.

'It still doesn't prove they were married,' said the father. He had lit another one of his cigarettes. The smoke was drifting lazily up to the ceiling.

Mark spread his fingers to make the picture of the hotel register from 1916 larger on the iPhone. In a strong firm hand someone had written the name Toby Russell, with the room number as 23. The checkout date was April 26th.

'It proves he lied to the court and your great grandmother told the truth. He was in Gretna Green the day she married your great grandfather. In his evidence, he stated he was at home.'

'His mother backed him up,' Mark said.

'The toffs, they always back each other up,' snarled the old man, taking another drag on his cigarette.

'Why would he lie?' said Jayne, 'unless he had been the witness to the wedding. Your great grandmother was telling the truth, it wasn't a fantasy.'

Mark's face lit up. 'If he was in Gretna, perhaps he removed the record from the register. But why?'

'Maybe his family didn't approve of the wedding. The mother certainly lied about his presence at home.'

'She was a shopgirl, he was a Lord. Of course they didn't approve of the wedding.'

'But to go to the lengths they did, following Rose to Gretna, ripping out the page from the register.' Mark shook his head. 'And it still doesn't explain why there's no record of the marriage in Edinburgh.'

Jayne stared at her feet.

'We're no closer to proving the marriage than we were before she started on the case.' The old man threw the butt of his cigarette into the open fire.

'But we know he lied and your grandmother told the truth. He was at the wedding.'

'Prove it,' the old man challenged her.

Jayne thought furiously. There must be something they could do. It all can't end here, in a dingy living room in some suburb of Manchester. She had to find the truth, for Rose, for David, for herself.

'Can I see the letter again?' she eventually said, 'David's last letter to Rose.'

'What good's it going to do? You've seen it already.'

'It can't hurt, Father.' Mark reached down and lifted the old case onto his lap. He flicked the latches, searched through the papers inside and gave her the letter.

'Waste of time,' muttered the old man, lighting another cigarette.

'Actually, it's the envelope I want to see.'

Mark rummaged around in the case, finally producing the faded yellow envelope.

Jayne turned to the back. 'It says 'Found on a British officer at Feldlazarett 27'. I googled 'Feldlazarett'. It's the German for field hospital or casualty clearing station.'

'So?'

'So, remember the newspaper article, it said David was alive but wounded when Crawford saw him on July 3rd.'

'You think he was taken to one of these 'Feldlazaretts'?

'More than likely.'

'But how does this help?' Mark asked.

Jayne stood up. 'I'm not certain, but I've a hunch. I need to go to London.'

'London,' said the old man, 'and who's going to pay?'

'If I'm right, you are Mr Russell, and happily I think. But first, I need to make a phone call.'

Chapter Seventy-Two

Sale, Manchester. April 3, 2016.

Jayne opened the door to the hall; she didn't want the Russells to hear what she was going to do, particularly the old man. If he found out the medallion and the photograph had been stolen, she would never hear the last of it. He would be moaning from now until the next millennium.

She dialled the number from memory and it was answered after two rings.

'DI Tanner.' The voice was rough and ready, with the peculiar whine she heard on every Oasis record. Rob said he had gone to the same school as the Gallagher brothers. The joke was nobody knew Borstal was a school.

'It's Jayne Sinclair, Rob…'

'DI Sinclair, what a pleasure to hear your voice. And that reminds me, you still owe me chocolate, haven't paid your debts, yet.'

'Not a DI any more, Rob, just an ordinary member of Joe Public.'

'You'll always be the DI for me, Jayne, but it doesn't mean you can welch on a debt.'

Rob Tanner had just been promoted to detective constable when he joined Jayne's team. He was wet behind the ears but as smart as a tailor's dummy. Under her, he'd soon learnt the ropes. 'Now's the time to double it, Rob.'

'There's an offer I can't refuse. How can I help?'

'You know my place was done over the other night?'

'I heard. Criminals must be getting more stupid these days…'

'Don't I know. Anyway, I've worked out who did it and I need an address.'

'I thought Harris and Meagher were working your case?'

'You mean Tweedledum and Tweedledumber?'

'I must admit they're not the sharpest knives in the tool-box, but at least they're straight.'

'I know, I know. But you know me, Rob.'

'You'd prefer to sort it out yourself.'

'Right first time. The prick who did it stole something from me; I want it back not stuck as evidence for the next 15 years.'

'What's the name?'

'Herbert Small. And I've a number too. It's 0161-823 4454.'

'Give me a sec.'

Jayne heard the sound of keyboard keys being pressed and the whirr of a computer.

'Here it is, Jayne. An address in the Northern Quarter. A bit of a hipster is he?'

'No, he's short, fat and bald. But that was quick, the computer system's been upgraded since I was a copper.'

'Nah, it's still as useless as ever. I used the White Pages, Jayne. You should use it, directory enquiries is quicker than anything we have.'

Jayne smiled. 'Still the same old Rob.'

'Still the same man. I've just messaged you the address. You now owe me two blocks of chocolate. A single estate Valrhona would be nice.'

'I'll make sure it arrives next week. Thanks for the help, Rob.'

'No worries, Jayne. And a word of warning, no rough stuff. I wouldn't like to pull you in.'

'Me? Rough stuff? You must be thinking of another

woman, Rob.'

'I'm thinking of the woman who always told me to get my retaliation in first.'

'Useful advice for a copper.'

'But not for a member of Joe Public.'

'I hear you, Rob.'

'But hearing and doing are two different things.'

'You know me so well. Anyway, I have to go now.'

'Jayne, I…'

She switched off her phone. She knew exactly what Rob was going to say and she didn't want to hear a lecture at the moment.

Chapter Seventy-Three

Sale, Manchester. April 3, 2016.

Jayne returned to the sitting room. Richard and Mark Russell were sitting quietly together, going through the letters one more time.

Mark looked up as she entered. 'My father and I have been talking. We'd both like to come down to London with you.'

'That's not necessary.'

'It's not about necessity; we want to go,' said the old man lighting another cigarette.

'But you'll get in the way, I like to work alone.'

'Did I get in the way in Scotland?'

Jayne didn't answer.

'Listen,' said Mark, 'we have only one day left to discover proof of my great grandparents' marriage. I would have thought you would take any help offered.'

'I haven't been back to London for a long time,' moaned the father.

Jayne knew when she was beaten. 'Fine, fine, you can both come. But don't get in the way, we need to move quickly.'

'We'll be like shit off the end of a shovel,' said the old man, exhaling a long plume of feathery blue smoke. 'You won't even know we're there.'

'The first train to London from Piccadilly is at 5.25 tomorrow morning, don't be late.'

'So early?'

'I'll book the tickets online tonight. Where are we going

in London?' asked Mark.

It was about time they knew. 'To the Imperial War Museum – they hold the records for the Derbyshire Fusiliers. If we are going to find out anything about David Russell, this is our last shot.'

Chapter Seventy-Four

Northern Quarter, Manchester. April 3, 2016.

'I wondered when you would find me, Mrs Sinclair…'

As he opened the door, Jayne pushed the little man backwards, pressing her forearm into his throat. She lifted him up against the wall forcing him to stand on tiptoe.

'I…' was all he managed to say before he felt the pressure of her elbow across his Adam's apple.

Jayne leant in closer. 'It's time for you to listen, Herbert.'

She released the pressure slightly. Herbert Small half choked, gasping for air.

'Are you listening, Herbert?'

He nodded, eyes staring at her face just inches from his.

'You have something of mine. Something you took from my house.'

'Let go of me or I'll tell…'

She pressed her elbow deep into his throat once more. 'You are in no position to threaten, Herbert. Why did you break into my house?'

She eased the pressure on her elbow. Immediately, Herbert Small sucked in air and began to cough.

'I'll repeat the question, Herbert, why did you break into my house?'

'I… had to… see… what you…'

'What I had discovered.'

Herbert Small nodded and began coughing once more.

'Not a good move, Herbert. Did you think I wouldn't find you?'

For the first time, a small smile crossed the man's face.

'I knew you...' he sucked in air, '...would find me. Wanted you... to...'

'You wanted me to find you?'

Herbert Small nodded again.

'Why?'

Another smile, this time broader, the ends of his mouth turning upwards and his eyes glinting. 'Cos if you were looking... for me... not looking for... marriage certificate.'

Jayne let the little man go. He collapsed with his hands on his knees, sucking in vast gulps of air, his face dripping with sweat.

'Do you know where it is?'

'That would be telling, Mrs Sinclair. You have just one day left. After that, whatever money was left by Lord Lappiter will vanish into the sticky fingers of Her Majesty's Treasury.'

Jayne put her hands in her jacket pocket.

The more he recovered, the bolder Herbert Small became. 'I hope you enjoyed the wild goose chase, Mrs Sinclair.'

The little man was standing upright now, adjusting his tie and smoothing down his hair.

'But you did trash my house, stealing the medallion and the photo?'

He chuckled and walked behind his desk, just far enough out of her reach to feel safe. 'I enjoyed smashing your house up. I know now why the Greeks find it cathartic. The medallion and the photo are on top of my filing cabinet, still in their envelopes. The medallion particularly is a fine piece. I'm not surprised the Russells didn't give it to me.'

'How did you get into my house?'

'For an ex-policeman, your security is very lax, Mrs

Sinclair. Over the years I've broken into many houses, it's a particular gift I have. Lets me see what other researchers are up to, shortcut my research.'

'Did you take little keepsakes from them too?'

'The filing cabinet is full of them. Some have a tolerable value, but others are just for memories, little souvenirs.'

A sharp knock on the door. Herbert Small looked up, surprised.

Jayne Sinclair walked slowly to the door and opened it. 'Rob, I thought you'd never get here. Another minute and I would be kicking the living daylights out of the smug bastard.'

'Sorry, Jayne, we had to wait until he convicted himself. Judges these days need you to hit them over the head with the evidence before they pass sentence.'

'But... but... how...?'

Jayne pulled her hand out of her pocket. In it was a mobile phone, the screen shining brightly. 'I hope you recorded everything he said, Rob.'

A constable took hold of Herbert Small's hands and began to handcuff him behind his back.

'Of course, Jayne.'

'She assaulted me... attacked me...' spluttered Herbert Small.

'Did you hear any assault, Rob?'

'Not a dickie bird, Jayne. Just heard this man confessing to a crime.' As Herbert Small was led away past Jayne, she whispered in his ear, 'Next time you go near my house, Mr Small, I'll rip off your head and piss in the hole. Do you understand?'

For a moment, Herbert Small's eyes met hers and then looked away. 'You still won't find the marriage certificate.'

'Wanna bet?'

Chapter Seventy-Five

Piccadilly Station, Manchester. April 4, 2016.

Jayne grabbed a quick coffee from the Starbucks next to the stone concourse. She stood under the announcement board, enjoying the warmth of the coffee in her hand. It was a typical Manchester spring morning; cold, with a hint of drizzle in the air.

Her father always joked about Manchester that if you could see the hills around the city it meant it was going to rain. And if you couldn't see them, it was already raining. It was that sort of morning.

She checked her watch again. Ten minutes to the train leaving. The announcement board said it was on time, for a change. Where were they?

She would give them five more minutes before hurrying to find her seat. She couldn't miss this train, not if she were to get to the Imperial War Museum just as it was opening.

There they were, Mark in the lead with his father following behind. The old man was unshaven, but wearing a long jacket and over-large brothel creepers. Despite his unkempt appearance, his hair was still forward and upwards in a resplendent quiff.

Mark looked his father up and down. 'It's the only suit he has.'

'This was the height of fashion when I bought it.'

'Back in the 60s, I'm sure it was.'

Jayne stepped between them. 'Never mind, we need to get going, shouldn't miss the train.'

They bustled down the platform, finding their seats in a

near-empty compartment.

'I haven't been to London for over 30 years,' explained the old man.

'You still kept your accent.'

'Well, you don't lose what you grew up with, do you? Can't imagine speaking in a Manchester whinge.'

'Why did you move north anyway?' asked Jayne as the conductor blew his whistle and the train edged slowly out of the station.

The old man pointed at Mark. 'His mother was from Manchester. Once my dad had died, there was no point staying in London. The wife hated the place anyway. Probably hated me more though, she did a bunk as soon as we got here, leaving me to bring up Mark on my own.'

Jayne thought of her and Paul. At least there were no children to make the break-up even more difficult than it actually was.

Mark changed the subject. 'What do you think we will find in London?'

'I don't know,' Jayne answered honestly. 'There's not a lot of detail in the catalogue.'

'So this is a long shot?'

'It's our only shot. We've exhausted every other line of enquiry. This is it.'

'And if we don't find something before the end of today, the estate passes to the Treasury.'

'I'm afraid that's true.'

Mark became quiet, staring out of the window as the Cheshire countryside flashed past.

Eventually, it was the old man who broke the silence. 'I'm looking forward to seeing London. The pubs, the shows, the museums.'

'We're coming back this evening on the 9.40 train, Dad.'

'Are we? Oh well, at least I can enjoy a full English when we get there.'

Jayne produced the two envelopes from her bag. 'I thought I should return these to you. Apparently the medallion is quite valuable.' Jayne had put them quietly into her pocket after the arrest of Herbert Small. Sitting in an evidence locker for six months would do nobody any good. Rob had enough to go on with the other stolen items to convict the man.

'Thank you,' said Mark.

'And now we may as well use the time to fill in some forms. If we find anything, we need to go straight to the Government Legal Office to file our claim.'

After completing the forms, all three of them lapsed into silence. Mark flicked through his Guardian reading every article, his father spent hours lingering over page three of the Sun, while Jayne stared out the window, going through every detail of the investigation in her mind. Had she missed anything? Was there anything else she could have done?

As her mind raced over all the events of the past week, she knew she wouldn't have done anything differently. The past is what it is, sometimes just out of reach, at other times, a startling reminder of the present.

Looking at Mark and his dad, she thought of her own father. She hoped he found happiness with Vera. If anyone deserved a better life, it was him; after all, he had put up with her mother for 20 years before she died. An experience deserving of the Victoria Cross in her view.

An announcement came over the tannoy. 'We will shortly be arriving in Euston station, please do not leave anything behind as you depart this train. It has been a pleasure serving you aboard this Virgin service from Manchester to

London, we hope you enjoyed your journey and we will see you again soon.'

The announcer seemed as bored at saying the words as Jayne was of hearing them. Outside the window, the smog of London hid the city's ugliness. The train hurried past the back windows of terraced houses, grimed from years of neglect.

Jayne wondered how people lived so close to the line. Did they look out their window every day and see people going somewhere while they stayed where they were? Or did they simply not notice the trains any more?

Whatever it was, Jayne would hate to live in this city. Its remorseless anonymity would crush her soul.

The train ground to a halt.

'We're here,' announced the old man.

'So we are,' said Jayne.

Chapter Seventy-Six

The Imperial War Museum, London. April 4, 2016.

They had been shown to the research room on the second floor of the East Wing as soon as they arrived. The archivist was friendly and informative, going off to access the requested material as soon as Jayne had shown him her driving licence.

The assistant archivist was apologetic. 'I'm sorry, we can only allow two people in the research room today. We're short of space.'

The old man decided he was hungry and wanted to see the Great War exhibition.

Jayne and Mark sat down, waiting for the documents to arrive. She explained what they were waiting for. 'Remember the man who testified seeing David Russell in a German casualty clearing station on July 3rd?'

'From the trial? Lieutenant Crawford, wasn't it?'

'I checked up on him. He left all his documents, including a diary written during the war, to the Imperial War Museum.'

'We're going to look at his diary?'

Jayne nodded. 'It might be useful or it might not. But it's our last chance to find out what happened to your great grandfather.'

'A Hail Mary, as the Americans say.'

Just then, the archivist returned carrying a box file.

'As these are original documents, I must ask that you both wear gloves when handling them. The sweat on your fingers contains acids which are damaging to the paper.'

Both Jayne and Mark put on the gloves.

'I see you're booked in until five this evening. If you need anything else, just ask, I'll be over there.' The young man smiled and pointed to his desk.

'Thank you.' Jayne stared at the box. 'I guess we should start.'

Neither moved.

Finally, Jayne undid the clasp and lifted the lid. On top was an inventory of the contents. She removed this and saw some old documents that gave off a faint odour of must and damp.

Beneath these sat a small brown diary, the sort a woman would keep in her handbag. On the cover, the date 1916 was stamped in gold leaf.

She lifted it out of the box file and opened the cover. In a simple, almost childish script was written *'Diary of a Soldier, 1916 by Lt. John Crawford, 4th Battalion, Derbyshire Fusiliers.'*

Mark leant in closer. She could feel his breath on her neck as he leant over her shoulder to read the diary with her.

She opened the first page. On it appeared a short entry for the first of January, written in faded pencil. The paper was spotted with rust and water marks as if it had been dunked in a bath full of iron.

'Well, the year begins with a bang, literally. At 6 a.m. this morning, the Germans shelled our trench. Only two men wounded fortunately, but it was a wake-up call we didn't need this morning. I had to arrange their evacuation by the medics despite suffering from a sore head from the night before. Looks like Corporal Henshaw has a Blighty wound. Lucky bugger! What I wouldn't give to be at home

right now with Mother and Father in Shrewsbury rather than here.

Last night, I dreamed of my office and Mr Spencer, the chief accountant of the bank. Strange dream. He was standing at the front of all the clerks wearing no trousers and reciting the poems of Longfellow. Note to self. Do not drink any more of Sergeant Flaherty's whisky. I don't know where he gets the stuff but it can't be good for anybody.'

Here, the first entry ended. Jayne turned the page. This one was dated January 3rd.

'Relieved at last by the Manchesters. Thank God for that. One more day in the bloody trenches and I think I would have killed somebody. And it probably wouldn't have been a German. We've been taken out of the line and sent back to Maumet for rest and recuperation which, for the men, means spending as much time as possible in the village's brothels. I'll stay away this time. After the last little illness, the doctor says I should give myself a rest. For once, I'm going to take his advice. Rumour is we're going to be pulled even further back for training. With a bit of luck, I might be able to wangle a pass for Paris. I'll have to get into the CO's good books. When it's needed I can brown nose with the best of them.'

They continued reading Lieutenant Crawford's diary. It soon became obvious he was a chatty, indiscreet soul, trying to survive as best he could. He wrote of the daily tribulations of the men, his relations with his fellow officers and his ongoing battle to do as little as possible, as safely as possible.

It wasn't until June 10th that they first read about David

Russell in the diary.

'The new Captain for B Company arrived today. He's a regular officer, formerly with the first battalion and has been in France since the early days of the war. It'll be good to have someone with experience leading the men and leading me. I've never been in battle and I'm not sure how I'll behave. Will I run away at the first shell or stick with it to the end? I hope it's the latter. I would hate to explain to Father why I'm being accused of cowardice.

Anyway, the new company commander, Captain Russell, seems a good enough sort. Tall and handsome in a rugged way, he's quite diffident, simply telling his subalterns he's been sent to help the battalion in any way possible.

I haven't had time to talk with him yet. I'll try to get him alone for a chat. Don't know if I'll tell him how I feel. You can never tell with the regular army chaps. Some of them can be sticklers for form and duty.'

'It's your great grandfather, Mark, I'm sure of it. The right time and the right regiment.'

'But nothing about him or Rose.'

'Not so far, let's read on.'

They carried on reading. There were a few other mentions of David in passing, until they read the entry for June 26th.

'Captain Russell seemed unsettled today, bothered by some news from home I think. After we had been round to check on the men, we walked back to our billet in the farmhouse. On our left a howitzer battery were sending over their steel presents wishing Fritz a long, hot summer. I asked him if he was okay. He just shrugged his shoulders

and said, 'My wife's pregnant.' Congratulations was my reply but he seemed worried. Everything is going fine, isn't it? I asked him. 'She's a nurse, working too hard, but everything should be good with the baby,' he replied. And then he blurted out, 'It's just I don't know what will happen to her if anything happens to me.' Of course, I pretended he shouldn't be silly, nothing was going to happen to him. But actually I was thanking my lucky stars I wasn't married. I'd hate to worry about a wife too.'

Mark spoke first. 'The man has just confirmed the marriage and the baby. It must be Rose.'

'True, Mark, but unfortunately this document isn't valid in the eyes of the Bona Vacantia authorities. We need something more concrete. Let's read on.'

They turned the next few pages. Lieutenant Crawford was preoccupied with the organisation of supplies for the attack on July 1st — ladders to order, hot food for the men, entrenching tools, spools of barbed wire, gallons of rum, sandbags full of chalk, Brodie helmets, clean puttees, new bayonets, ammo for the Lee-Enfields — the list seemed endless. It wasn't until the day before the attack that he mentioned David again.

'I'm lying here on my bunk in the dugout and it's about as comfortable as a wet Wednesday in Llandudno. Captain Russell is sitting opposite me, writing letters about who knows what to God knows whom. He's been quiet the last few days. I think the thought of the big push tomorrow is getting to him. Not that he's scared, he just seems preoccupied as if the weight of the world were on his shoulders rather than the fate of 100 or so men of the New Army. At one point, he asked me to take care of his marriage certifi-

cate. Then, I pointed out I was just as likely to be killed as he was. Probably more likely as at least he had some experience of war and I was a virgin in battle if not in life. He laughed when I told him this. I like it when he laughs. Just for a moment, I could see the real person behind the mask of office. A nice person, a good person, somebody I could be friends with back in England. Not here though. To him, I'm just the commander of No.5 platoon and he must ensure I do my job to the best of my ability. And I think that's what I will do tomorrow. Whatever happens, I mustn't let myself or the men down.'

'David mentions his wife. It must be Rose. But why didn't he tell the army he was married, Jayne?'

'He probably did. You have to understand all their resources were concentrating on the Battle of the Somme. It would have been easy for something like this to slip through the bureaucratic cracks.'

Jayne turned the page. It was empty. Quickly, she flicked through the rest of the diary, her gloves slipping across the pages. There were no more entries.

'That's it. He obviously survived the war if he testified at the trial.'

'Why didn't he tell them about David's worries?'

'Nobody asked him. Or if they did, it wasn't reported in the papers. It would have been hearsay evidence anyway. He never met Rose.'

Mark shook his head. 'She didn't have a cat in hell's chance, did she?'

Jayne didn't answer. One more sheet of paper lay at the bottom of the box file, its blue ink faded to the colour of a summer's day. She picked it up and began to read. The language was formal and efficient, so different from the chatty voice of the diary.

TO: Lt. Col. Anthony Flumbsborne, O/C 4th Derbyshire Fusiliers.

Report of Lt John Crawford, 4th Battalion, Derbyshire Fusiliers, into the events of July 1-2, 1916.

At exactly 07.35 hours on the morning of July 1st, Captain Russell blew his whistle for the second wave attack to begin. The men assembled calmly in front of the line. The attack walked forward as instructed, keeping a steady pace of four miles an hour. Captain Russell led the way and I was with my platoon on the left. As we neared the first German line, we were targeted in enfilading fire by enemy machine guns on the ridge. The wire was uncut in front of us and the men funnelled into a gap. The machine guns proceeded to decimate the attack. I saw Captain Russell rush forward with Sergeant Flaherty and three other men. I followed them with the two remaining men of my platoon. We took cover in a shell hole. There was a flash of light and I was knocked off my feet. When I came to, a German soldier was standing over me, gesturing for me to go towards his lines. He prodded me with his bayonet so I had no choice but to accede to his demands.

When we reached a junction between two trenches, I saw Captain Russell and two other men from my platoon lying on the ground. One was already dead, Pte Longworth. The other, Pte O'Malley, had a badly smashed leg. Captain Russell was bleeding profusely from the head and the hip region.

The German officer ordered me to place both of the wounded men on an ammunition cart and wheel them to the German casualty clearing station in the rear. This I pro-

ceeded to do, reaching the field hospital at 11.45 in the morning of July 1st.

The wounded men were placed in the area in front of the clearing station and I was told to sit with the other prisoners.

We stayed there for the rest of the day and into the next without food or water. The Germans seemed not to know what to do with us. Occasionally our own batteries shelled our position and we were forced to seek shelter even closer to the hospital.

On the morning of July 3rd, I saw both Pte O'Malley and Captain Russell being taken inside the hut that served as a holding area for the clearing station. Both were still alive at that time.

I was approached by one of the surgeons at noon and given 37 army paybooks and 14 officer notebooks. The surgeon, Hauptmann Redel, explained these men had been captured and were being treated by him. I'm sorry to say he told me which men had survived and which had died, but I was in such a state, I forgot who they were. He then released me and ordered me to return to the British lines. I was escorted to the front line that evening and directed where to find my comrades.

I deposited the paybooks and notebooks with the adjutant of the regiment who immediately ordered my arrest.

Sir, this is a true and fair account of the events of July 1-2, 1916. I hope they will be accepted as such by yourself and the other officers attending my court martial.

I remain, sir, your faithful and obedient servant.

Signed,

John Crawford (Lt)

'What was the charge?' asked Mark.

Jayne rubbed her eyes. 'I don't know. I suppose it will be in the records somewhere. Perhaps they found him not guilty. There certainly seemed no stigma attached to him after the war.'

She looked in the box file.

Nothing.

On the clock facing her, the time was 12.45. 'Let's take a break for a coffee and find your father.'

'What do we do now, Jayne?'

'Honestly, Mark, I don't know.'

Mark raised his voice. 'But we only have four more hours before the Bona Vacantia office closes. If we don't find it by then…'

Another researcher stared at them and hissed loudly.

Jayne pulled him to her. 'Let's have a coffee and work it out,' she whispered.

'What's to work out? We're finished. There's nothing left for us.'

Again, the researcher hissed at them. The young archivist came from behind his desk. 'I'm afraid you have to be quiet, there are people working here.'

'I am sorry, we just need a break.' Jayne stood up and pulled Mark out of the research room. 'Come on, let's find your father.'

Chapter Seventy-Seven

The Imperial War Museum, London. April 4, 2016.

The atmosphere in the cafe was quiet and restrained. Mark was hunched over his coffee, head resting in his hands. Jayne was reading through her notes, desperately looking for a clue, any clue, what to do next. Even Richard Russell was silent, staring into the murky depths of his cup of tea.

Finally, he spoke. 'At least we definitely know he was married to Rose, from what you told me, it all adds up.'

'But we have no proof, Dad. Nothing that will stand up in court.'

The old man reached out and placed his hand on his son's arm. 'Look, it doesn't matter. Remember, we wanted to investigate to find out if my grandmother was telling the truth about her marriage. Well, she was and that's enough for me.' He thought for a moment before adding, 'The money would be nice, but...'

Mark sat up straight in his chair. 'You're right, Dad. Rose Clarke married David Russell on the 25th April, 1916. End of story.'

'Not quite,' said Jayne, 'she had a child, your grandther. Even though David Russell's name was on the b certificate, without proof of a marriage, he was illegitin in the eyes of the law. My bet is the marriage certifi was lost by the army during the war.'

Again, silence descended on the three people. where in the cafe, people chatted, children played, cro rattled and steam hissed from a coffee machine.

'Well, I had a lovely morning. Had my full English. Nothing beats eggs, bacon, sausage, fried bread, black pudding and beans in the morning. Never eat the tomato though, don't know why they even put it there. I mean, who eats the tomato?'

'I do,' said Jayne.

'That explains everything.'

'What did you do after exploring the culinary boundaries of breakfast, Dad?'

'I visited the museum, never been here before. They're showing an exhibition from the Somme. You know, they made a movie about it all, taken by a cameraman who was actually there. He may even have filmed my grandfather.'

'I guess we'll never know, Dad.'

'And there are some wonderful exhibits. Shells and bullets, bits of kit from the time. I spent a long time reading an officer's notebook. It had all the details of what they were supposed to do and when. Problem is some of them never even reached the German front line…'

'That's it!' Jayne suddenly shouted.

'What? What's happening?' Richard Russell asked.

Jayne stared into mid-air, her eyes betraying the rapidity of her thoughts. 'It's a long shot, but we have nothing else,' she said to herself.

'What? What's going on?'

Jayne stood up, draining the last dregs of her coffee. 'Come on, Mark, we've some research to do. And we only have three hours to find the answer.'

She began to run toward the door. Mark left the table and ran after her. Only Richard Russell was left in the cafe. He flicked back his quiff with his right hand. 'What's going on?' he asked.

Nobody answered.

Chapter Seventy-Eight

The Imperial War Museum, London. April 4, 2016.

As they were running up the stairs to the second floor, Mark caught up with Jayne. 'What are we looking for?'

'The paybooks and officer notebooks. Remember Crawford said he was given them by the German doctor before he was sent back through the lines?'

Jayne strode into the research room. 'Well, it's a long shot but David Russell was in the hospital. Perhaps his notebook was one of those given to Crawford.'

'But what if it was? It's just his army stuff.'

Jayne stopped and faced Mark. 'But it's where they kept everything; instructions, notes, personal effects...'

'He might have kept the marriage certificate there?'

'It's a long shot, but we have nothing else.'

They saw the archivist behind his desk.

'In the diary of Lieutenant Crawford...'

'The one you were researching this morning?'

'That's correct. In it he says he was captured on the first day of the Battle of the Somme, but released by a German doctor.'

The archivist smiled. 'It's quite a celebrated case. He was court-martialled by his General, Rawlinson, but found not guilty. Killed his career in the army though. We still have the paybooks and notebooks he brought back that day. One of them is on display in the exhibition.'

Jayne let out a long sigh. 'Thank God. Could we look at them?'

'You're supposed to give three days' notice, but as you're

here...' The archivist checked his watch, '...Our people are at lunch at the moment, but just fill in the form and I'll get them to dig it out for you.'

'Thanks a bundle, Peter,' said Jayne reading the man's name tag. 'I don't want to be a bother but when do you think they'll get it?'

'Just as soon as they can, Ms Sinclair.'

Jayne realised it was futile and rude to push any harder. 'Thanks, Peter.'

They returned to their desk and notes. Jayne sighed, 'Now, we just sit and wait.'

'It might not be there anyway. And even if it is, there's little chance he put the marriage certificate in the notebook.'

'We just have to hope, Mark.'

'Hope is not a plan.'

'But without it we have nothing, do we Mark?'

The minutes passed remorselessly. Jayne couldn't help herself, she glanced at the clock on the wall every five minutes.

'2.30 and it's still not here,' whispered Mark. 'Let's go.'

'Just a few minutes more, Mark, be patient.'

There was movement behind the archivist's desk. He came out carrying a large box and walked to another table, placing it down in front of a young researcher.

As he walked back, he glanced in their direction and shrugged his shoulders. He mimed making a telephone call. Jayne nodded back to him.

Again, she looked at the clock. Only a minute had passed since she last inspected it. The second hand seemed to be moving more slowly now, taking years to sweep around the dial. Jayne checked her own watch to confirm the time. The clock on the wall was two minutes slow.

'It's 3 p.m., Jayne, even if it comes now, by the time we've done the research it will be past five o'clock and the government office will be closed.'

Just as Jayne was about to give up hope, the archivist came running from the back room with a large box. 'Here it is, they're busy today. These are the documents brought by Lieutenant Crawford from the German field hospital. There's one missing, it's on display in the exhibition.' He placed the box on the table in front of them. 'Gloves please.'

Jayne and Mark put their gloves back on. Jayne opened the lid of the box. Inside were a stack of small brown books in plastic bags. She removed the top one from its wrapping. On the cover in block capitals were the words:

ARMY BOOK 64

And beneath it:

SOLDIER'S PAYBOOK FOR USE ON
ACTIVE SERVICE

Inside was a flap and a long section, detailing in bullet form the instructions to a soldier. She turned the page. At the top, written in pencil were the words: 4th Battalion, Derbyshire Fusiliers. And further down, the soldier's army number, his rank and finally his name. In this case, Michael Kelly.

'He must have been in your great grandfather's regiment.'

'One of the men who survived or one who died?' asked Mark.

'We'll never know.'

Jayne closed the book. Mark reached in and took the next one on the pile.

'We don't want these. They are AB 64s, enlisted men's paybooks.' She began to remove each of the plastic bags from the box, placing them carefully on the table.

Eventually, she saw one that looked different. It was blue and on the cover was the title:

OFFICER'S RECORD OF SERVICES
ARMY BOOK 439

Jayne opened it carefully. Inside a few yellowed pages marked Army Courses and Languages Spoken were loosely attached to the top. In the centre was the name Robert Higgins with his rank as second lieutenant and the places he had served.

She showed it to Mark. 'Not our man, but at least he's an officer.' She dug deeper into the box. There were three more blue service books and then she saw it, a brown leather notebook, hinged at the top and bound with an old rubber band. On the cover the initials D.R. were embossed in gold letters.

Gingerly, she reached in and took it out of its plastic bag. 'I think this is it, Mark.'

She showed the book to him. He stopped what he was doing and looked up. For a second, she saw a look of fear in his eyes, as if he had waited for this moment for so long and now it was here, he couldn't bear to find out the truth. 'Do you want to open it?'

He shook his head.

Jayne removed the rubber band, placing it in the plastic bag. She opened the leather cover. On the inside page in faded brown ink, the words Capt. David Russell and a date of 12th February, 1916 were written in a beautiful cursive script. This wasn't an army issue notebook, but something far more personal.

'It's his.'

Mark breathed out. 'My great grandfather's book. He must have held it, written in it. So long ago...' His voice trailed off.

Jayne turned the page. Inside, written in a variety of inks and pencil were pages of dates and training instructions, notes to himself, addresses including Rose's in Wibbersley Hospital and a printed list of army instructions for officers. Halfway through, after the date July 1st 1916, the pages were blank. Jayne quickly flicked through the rest of the book.

All blank.

Nothing.

'No mention of Rose or a marriage?'

Jayne shook her head. 'Nothing.'

As she lifted up the book, a sheet of paper folded into a small square drifted down onto the table. It was a page torn from the notebook.

Jayne picked it up and stared at the words written in pencil on the yellowed paper, before finally reading them out.

In the event of my death, I, David Russell, leave all my property, effects and belongings to my wife, Rose Russell nee Clarke, Ward 5, Wibbersley Hospital, Flixton, Manchester.

Signed, David Russell, Capt.

Jayne's whole body collapsed and she sighed. 'Finally, he acknowledges he's married to her. The signature matches the one on the letters and the hotel register.'

'But it's not proof, it's not official.'

'But don't you realise, it's better than that.'

Mark frowned. 'I don't understand.'

'It's a will, Mark.'

'I still don't get it.'

'He's leaving everything he owns to his wife, Rose.'

'But it's written in pencil on a bit of paper. There's no lawyers or witnesses.'

Jayne laughed. 'It doesn't matter. It's a soldier's will. They were recognised as legally binding after the war. The men had to write them before going in to battle, David must have written this one too. And even better, he's signed it.' She stood up. 'Come on, we need to get this photo-copied. It's four o'clock now. We need to get to the Bona Vacantia offices on Kemble Street before they close.'

Chapter Seventy-Nine

Government Legal Department, London.
April 4, 2016.

The archivist moved quickly when he saw the urgency in Jayne's face. Mark texted his father to meet them outside.

Within ten minutes they were in a taxi and heading across London.

'Kemble Street? Nah, I could take Westminster Bridge and then you would see the Houses of Parliament and Westminster Abbey, but this time of day, it's going to be full of tour buses. Those buggers haven't got a clue how to drive. Or I could go by Waterloo…'

'That sounds nice, see the sights,' said Mark's father.

'Go whichever way is quickest, we're in a rush.'

'Aren't we all. It's the modern life. Rush here, rush there, missing the beauty of the world.'

Just what Jayne needed, a taxi philosopher. 'We need to be at Kemble Street before five.'

'Nah worries, I'll take Waterloo, should be clear at this time. You going to the Government Legal Department?'

Jane saw a pair of eyes staring at her in the rear view mirror and nodded.

'You'd better get a move on. Them lot close up shop on the dot at five. Civil servants don't work a minute past then. Nah, you take me, for instance, I start at 3.30 and work until…'

Jayne switched off as the cab driver went into excruciating detail of his working life. The modern, functional buildings of South London slipped past in a blur of mediocrity. Red, open-topped tour buses waited to pick up their sightseers outside Waterloo Station. The traffic thickened as they approached the river, pedestrians being jostled by cyclists as they dodged and weaved in between the stationary traffic. Jayne remembered one of those arcane facts that occasionally stuck in her mind; traffic in London now moved at exactly the same pace as it had back in the 1900s, back when Rose and David were living and loving.

She looked down at her watch. 4.30.

'Will we make it in time?' Mark asked.

'Nah worries, mate, we'll have you across the river in two shakes of Tommy Cooper's fez.'

The brutal slab of concrete known as the National Theatre zoomed by on the right and they were over the river, the boats drifting downstream beneath them as they had for centuries.

'Won't be long now, we'll take the underpass to avoid all the buses along the Strand. I was stuck there for 30 minutes last week, hell of a jam.'

The taxi suddenly accelerated through the traffic. Jayne was thrown against Mark and Richard Russell. It headed downhill into a dark, concrete tunnel beneath one of London's busiest thoroughfares.

Jayne checked her watch again. She could have been taking life easy, enjoying a carefree weekend with Paul, seeing a show, doing some shopping along Regent Street, enjoying the sights. Instead she was stuck in a taxi with an old man and his son and she wouldn't have swapped it for the world.

The taxi accelerated to a stop, the driver beeping his horn loudly. 'Bleedin' Arabs, should be driving a camel not a Bentley.'

The taxi swung left past the slow-moving vehicle as they both began to emerge from the dark, turning sharp left and then left again.

'Here you are squires, Kemble Street, Government offices on the left.'

Jayne reached into her bag to pay the cabbie but the old man had beaten her to it, giving him a 20-pound note saying, 'Keep the change.'

'Fanks very much, guv.'

The old man beamed. The last of the big spenders.

Jayne and Mark stood in front of the tall, round tower. 'Come on,' she said, 'no time to lose.' She hustled Mark and his father through the revolving doors into the lobby. It was a classic 70s building inside; all marble and chandeliers, but strangely dowdy, as if none of it had ever been cleaned properly.

A pair of security guards stood watch behind a desk. 'Where are you going?'

'The Bona Vacantia Division of the Government Legal Department.'

'Do you have an appointment?'

Jane shook her head.

'I'll have to ring up to see if they are available.' The man slowly began to enter the number. He reminded Jayne of a sloth the way his movements were so slow and deliberate. Behind his head, a clock on the wall ticked over to 4.40.

'The phone is ringing,' the guard said.

He held it away from his ear so she could hear the ring.

No answer.

He was just about to put it down when Jayne heard a faint voice at the other end. The guard put the handset to his ear, slowly, and began nodding his head.

Finally, he replaced the phone. 'You can go up now. ID

please.'

Jayne fished in her bag, looking for her driving licence. Eventually she found it next to the wrapping of a bar of Valrhona. She handed it to the man and waited patiently for a visitor pass.

Mark and his father shuffled impatiently next to her as the man spent a lifetime sorting through the box on his desk. Taking three visitor passes he handed them to Jayne and pointed to a bank of lifts on the left. A stream of people were already flowing out of the door, leaving work early.

Jayne rushed to catch a departing lift. She bundled Mark and his father into it and pressed the number for the floor.

The lift doors closed, slowly. It ascended creaking like an arthritic pensioner. Jayne checked her watch again. Mark was also looking at his. The old man was staring at the numbers above the lift door.

'There's no number thirteen. You wouldn't think a government office full of lawyers would be superstitious, would you?'

Jayne checked her watch again. Just twelve minutes before five. The lift doors opened and they rushed out to meet the receptionist.

'Can I help you?'

'We'd like to file a claim against one of the estates on the list.'

The receptionist answered in a slightly bored voice. 'Please put your documents into the tray, somebody will look at them as soon as they are available.'

Jayne leant forward, getting as close as she could, and immediately attracting the attention of the woman. 'You don't understand, the claim becomes forfeit at 5 p.m. this evening. We need somebody to look at it straight away.'

The woman seemed to think. 'This is unusual, most claims come by courier.' And then her eyes widened, 'Tom's still around, I'll get him to look at it.'

She vanished into the office. Jayne, Mark and his father were left standing in the reception area, a steady stream of people filing past them on their way home. Jayne looked at her watch again. Why was the second hand moving so fast? They were running out of time.

A large, chubby man with a red face came out of the door and stood behind the desk. 'How can I help you?'

'It's Tom, is it?' Jayne turned on the charm she had never really learned in the Police.

The man nodded.

'We have a claim against an estate. Unfortunately, it runs out in ten minutes.'

'You've left it a bit late. We keep the files open for 30 years and you only come forward now?'

'Sorry, we've just found the documents.'

The man sighed but held out his hand. Jayne handed over the folder with all the signed and completed documents. 'We only found the proof this afternoon at the Imperial War Museum.' Jayne indicated the photocopy of David's will.

The man pored over the family tree and the supporting documents of the Russells. 'And you are?'

'Richard Russell.' Mark's father pointed to his name on the family tree.

The man returned to reading the documents, finally shuffling them into a neat pile, inserting them back in the folder.

'Well, it's most unusual, but as you are in time, I will forward these to our senior for review.'

Jayne and Mark smiled, patting each other on the back.

The old man let out a whoop of triumph.

'Thank you, you don't know how pleased we are that we managed to make it,' said Jayne.

The man held up his hand. 'Unfortunately though, your claim will probably fail.'

Everybody went quiet. Jayne noticed a clock behind the man's head tick jerkily to ten minutes to five. Why were there so many clocks? It was the first time she had noticed how many clocks existed in offices. As if people had to be constantly reminded of the time they were wasting.

'You see, the document from the War Museum, the soldier's will, has not been officially notarised. There's no proof of provenance. It could have come from anywhere.'

'But there was no time to get it notarised…'

The man shrugged his shoulders. 'I would have thought 30 years is long enough. The rules are clear. The claim must be submitted before 30 years have expired, otherwise it is forfeited and the estate passes to the Treasury.

'But… but…' For once Jayne was at a loss for words. Mark and his father stood there, open-mouthed.

'There is one other document missing. A proof of marriage between Rose Clarke and David Russell, Lord Lappiter.'

'But David's will states that Rose Clarke was his wife.'

'Ah,' the man held up his finger and spoke with the certainty of a solicitor, 'we don't know which Rose Clarke he means, do we?'

Chapter Eighty

'So that's it?' Mark's shoulders slumped forward.

They were standing outside One Kemble Street. A stream of besuited civil servants flowed past them, paying no attention to the forlorn group standing on the pavement, intent on catching the 5.13 from Waterloo to the leafy suburbs of Maidenhead.

'I'm afraid that's it, Mark, nothing else we can do.'

The group fell silent. Jayne checked her watch one last time, seven minutes to five. So near, yet so far.

The old man smiled. 'Why are we so unhappy? Look, with Jayne's help we managed to prove my grandmother wasn't a liar, she told the truth. She married David Russell, Lord Lappiter. They had a child, my father, and you are their living descendant.' He prodded Mark in the chest.

'But we failed, Dad, we didn't get the evidence in time. There'll be no inheritance, no money.'

'Money, schmoney. Who needs it?' The old man seemed to think for a moment before answering his own question, 'Well, we do. But money isn't everything.' He put his arm around Mark's shoulder, having to reach up on tip toes. 'We've got each other, Mark, and that's more important to me than anything else.'

Mark resisted for a moment before smiling and lifting his dad up into the air. 'And you've still got your Elvis quiff.'

'Never lose it, Mark, he was king, you know? And besides, the girls could never resist the quiff. Pulled more totty in my time than you've had hot dinners.'

'Too much information, Dad.'

Jayne's phone rang in her bag. She was tempted to ignore it, thinking it could only be Paul and she didn't want to speak to him right now.

'Let's go for a good Italian and splash out on a bottle of Prosecco to celebrate,' said Mark.

The phone continued to ring.

'The best idea you've had since this morning,' said his father.

The phone carried on ringing. Jayne searched in her bag, eventually finding it. She didn't recognise the number. Who the hell was it?

She pressed the answer button.

'Jayne Sinclair?' a voice asked tentatively from the other end of the line.

Jayne hoped it wasn't somebody trying to sell her double glazing. She would rip their throat out if it was. 'Speaking,' she replied curtly.

'I have the results of your request, Mrs Sinclair.'

The voice was vaguely Scottish. 'What results? What request?'

The voice on the other end giggled. 'I'm sorry, I'll start again from the beginning. Earlier this week, you made a request at the Scottish People's Research Centre in Edinburgh to see the original returns from Gretna Green for the period of April 1916.'

Jayne remembered now. It was the Scottish Chinese archivist. What was her name? 'Is this Julia speaking?'

'It is, Mrs Sinclair, anyway I just thought I'd ring to tell you the returns are now available for you to look at. Would you like me to book a time in the Reid Room for you?'

Jayne looked at Mark and his father. They were both waiting patiently for her to finish her phone conversation so they could go and eat. Mark indicated with a nod of his head that it was time to go.

'I don't think...' Jayne began to say before she was interrupted.

'And I must apologise to you, Mrs Sinclair, we found an error at the centre.'

Jayne stopped speaking. For a moment, there was a rushing noise in her earpiece, like a wave crashing against a shore. Then she heard the woman's voice as clearly as if she were standing next to her.

'We made a mistake. For some reason, the returns for April 25th, 1916 were filed under Glasgow and not Dumfries and Galloway. We've found the marriage record you were looking for between...' here the sound stopped as the woman searched for the names,'...a Captain David Russell and a Miss Rose Alexandria Clarke.'

Jayne didn't hear the rest of the woman's explanation. Something about wartime and the lack of experienced staff. She turned to Mark and his father. 'They've found the record.'

The next few minutes passed in a blur. Rushing back into the building, persuading the same security guard they wanted to revisit the same department. More phone calls, more waiting, more silent journeys in a lift.

Meeting Tom again, this time he was wearing a jacket and obviously ready to go home. Begging him to check his fax machine, the proof of marriage would be arriving from the Scottish People's Research Centre. Jayne checking her watch. Mark glancing nervously at her. The old man stroking his white Elvis quiff again and again. Watching the clock in the foyer tick over to one minute to five.

Finally, Tom came round from behind the desk, holding a limp fax sheet in his hand. 'I have received this paper. It seems to be confirmation of the marriage of David Russell and a Rose Alexandria Clarke, and it's signed by the archivist.' He checked the time. The clock ticked over so the hour hand was pointing straight upwards at the twelve.

Five o'clock exactly.

'It's very tight timing after 30 years, but I will place this confirmation with the rest of the documents in your file. It will be up to my senior to adjudicate on the validity of the claim in due course. Meanwhile, I would get them notarised if I were you.'

Jayne reached over and gave him a big kiss on the side of the face. He went red with embarrassment.

'There's no need, I'm simply doing my job.'

'There's always a need for a hug, Tom, don't you agree, Mr Russell?'

The old man walked up to Tom, Elvis quiff quivering on top of his head, and placed another big kiss on the solicitor's cheek. 'Don't reason the need, Tom, just enjoy.'

Chapter Eighty-One

The Eagle Pub, Didsbury, Manchester.
April 24, 2016.

'I've never had champagne in a pub before.' Mark's father held up his glass to the light, watching the little bubbles fight their way to the surface. 'I didn't even know pubs sold champagne.'

'Well they do, Dad, so cheers.' Mark raised his glass to Jayne and his father.

'Can we afford this?' asked the old man after swallowing a large mouthful. His quiff looked even more extravagant now, teased into a large curl of hair that was folded back on itself and stroked with Brylcreem.

'Not really, but it's my treat.'

'You've finally been told of the value of the estate?' asked Jayne.

'2,468 pounds and 68 pence. The Bona Vacantia people even informed me they paid interest on the sum for the first 12 years but not after that.'

'I thought it would be worth a lot more.'

'The last Lord Lappiter lived life to the full and then some. What with taxes, death duties, debts and the rest, there's not much left.'

'What about Holton Hall?'

Mark shrugged his shoulders. 'Mortgaged to the hilt, and then mortgaged again. Something had to fund his lifestyle. The land sale has been halted though. Our claim has thrown the whole process into disarray. The developer won't be building 'executive residences and country maisonettes', whatever they are, for a very long time.

'I went to Holton Hall, it's a falling apart. Aren't you just a bit sad?'

'Not at all, the place only held bad memories for myself and my father. Good riddance to bad rubbish is what I say. And remember we started this quest to vindicate my great grandmother and discover the truth. We've done that, the money doesn't matter.' He raised his glass once more, 'Cheers.'

They toasted each other once more. This time the old man finished his glass and held it out for a refill. 'Quite nice this champagne stuff, bit like lemonade.'

'But one amazing result has come from our investigations. The College of Heralds is looking into whether my father has the right to call himself Lord Lappiter,' Mark said.

Jayne bowed in the direction of Mark's father.

'Even funnier, if they find in his favour, he will have the right to sit in the House of Lords. The first Elvis impersonator to take a seat.'

The old man rubbed his hands. 'I'm looking forward to the money; 300 quid a day for signing my name in a book.' He rubbed his hands in glee. 'Money for old rope or old dopes. That's what I call a job.'

Mark filled all their glasses. 'Jayne, you called us here. What was the news you were so excited about?'

Jayne put her glass down on the table and pulled out a folder from her bag. 'I don't know if excited is the right word. After we came back from London, something was troubling me.'

'Could be fleas. London's full of them, that's what the Daily Mail says.' The old man had a slightly glassy look to his eyes. The champagne was definitely going to his head.

'It was the court case. Lieutenant Crawford reported seeing David Russell alive on the 3rd July, but he was reported as killed on the 1st July. Then, there was the letter from the Feldlazarett. It all made me wonder: What if David Russell didn't die at the Somme? What if he survived?'

Chapter Eighty-Two

Queen Mary's Hospital, Sidcup, Kent.
August 12, 1919.

'I can assure you, Lord Lappiter, that here in Queen Mary's we are at the cutting edge of the latest medical developments.' The doctor waved his hand to take in all the buildings of the hospital. Two nurses walking past caught his eye and smiled.

Toby stifled a yawn. This earnest young doctor bored him to distraction. He would much prefer to be in London, indulging in the delights of Fanny Ross, a delicate little actress at the Haymarket.

His mother nudged him to pay attention. 'I thought Mr Gillies was going to meet us?' asked the Dowager Lady Lappiter.

'I'm afraid he's unavailable at the moment, pressure of work, you know.'

Lady Lappiter stared at the young doctor. 'How disappointing.'

The man coughed nervously. 'Facial reconstruction or plastic surgery as he calls it, is in its infancy. He's writing a book on it at the moment, based on his experience and medical practice during the war.'

'I'm sure he would have had many opportunities to practise,' she said.

The young doctor coughed again. 'I'm sure he did. Over 5000 men have passed through this hospital. But let's be moving on. The patient is waiting in the recreation room.'

He held out his arm to guide them towards the left.

'My son was reported killed on the Somme, Mr...?'

'It's Doctor Moore, actually.'

Lady Lappiter stared at him again. 'So young for a medical doctor. Because of the war, no doubt,' she sniffed. 'Anyway, Doctor Moore, my son was reported killed on the Somme in 1916, so you can imagine my surprise when I received Doctor Gillies' letter saying he was here in the hospital.'

They pushed through the swing doors guarding the entrance to the wards. A patient was coming through in the opposite direction, propelling his wheelchair. Lady Lappiter stared at the heavily bandaged face as the man passed by. A shiver of disgust ran down her spine.

The young doctor frowned. 'I thought Mr Gillies made it clear in his letter. We're not actually sure this is your son. The patient has suffered extensive damage to the left side of the face and head. There seems to be brain damage, because even though the voice box and throat remain intact, the man has no power of speech or memory of who he is.'

They pushed through another set of swing doors into a bright, cool area. On their right a small group of men were weaving baskets, their hands moving quickly as they threaded the lengths of willow through upright spokes. All had bandaged faces with only the mouth or nose visible. All except one. This man had an open space where his nose should have been, and a hole the size of an orange in his left cheek.

Lady Lappiter could see the teeth sticking out from raw, red gums through the hole. She shuddered again, and quickly marched on.

'If he can't speak and can't remember who he is, how do you know he's my brother?' asked Toby.

'We don't. That is, we're not certain. In the Prisoner of

War Hospital in Germany he was identified by one of his fellow officers.'

'Why weren't we notified straight away? We published his obituary in the Times, for God's sake.'

The doctor shrugged. 'The answer is I don't now. There wasn't much communication with the POWs, and he only came to us last week from Germany. We wrote to you as soon as we could.'

The doctor approached one patient sitting all on his own, concentrating on weaving a small basket.

'Captain Russell?'

No response. The man carried on weaving his basket.

The doctor reached forward and touched him on the shoulder. 'Captain Russell?'

He looked up. The left side of his face was enfolded in a fresh white bandage, covering the top of the head and ending below the jaw line. The only visible eye was glazed and watery, the eyelid hanging over it like wet washing. The tongue lolled from the corner of the mouth, saliva dripping from its end.

'Captain Russell, I've brought some guests to see you.' The doctor placed two chairs in front of the Captain.

The man stared at Toby and Lady Lappiter for a long while before finally returning to weaving his basket.

'As you can see, he's not communicative at the moment. But we feel, given time, and once the surgical procedures have been completed, he will at least be able to interact with people.'

The man stopped what he was doing and stared at them both through his one functioning eye.

Lady Lappiter looked away. She could see an anger there, a bitter betrayal.

'Anyway, I'll leave you alone together for a few minutes. We often find talking with relatives helps the patient recover lost memories.'

The young doctor marched back out through the swing doors.

Lady Lappiter and Toby sat down on the chairs, facing the patient.

'David.' Lady Lappiter reached forward and touched her son's hand. He recoiled immediately and stared at her once again.

She knew it was her son the moment he looked at her. She knew David's face, even though only half of it was visible. It was him, her son was alive.

She reached forward again. 'David.'

The man jerked his hand back before she could even come close to touching him. He started to cry and a muffled grunt, like a piglet calling for its mother, came from his lips.

'Don't touch him mother. You'll only set him off.'

Lady Lappiter sat back in her chair. What was she going to do with her son?

As if hearing her thoughts, Toby said, 'This puts the cat amongst the pigeons, doesn't it? Now we have two Lord Lappiters. How will the College of Heralds answer this conundrum?'

He took out a Turkish cigarette from his silver case, tapped it twice to loosen the tobacco and then lit it with a gold Dunhill lighter.

'Toby, I do wish you wouldn't practise that awful habit in front of me.' She waved the smoke away from her nose. 'I think the answer is very obvious, don't you?'

The two of them talked together while David continued weaving his basket until the doctor returned.

'Well, any progress?' He rubbed his hands together like

a contented seal.

Lady Lappiter stood up, slowly putting on her black leather gloves. 'I'm afraid there has been a terrible mistake. This man is not my son.'

The doctor was confused for a moment. 'Are you sure, Lady Lappiter, he was…'

'I am positive, Dr Moore. A mother knows her own son when she sees him.' She pointed to David Russell, still intent on weaving his basket. 'And this man is not my son. He died on the Somme in 1916, a war hero.'

The man in front of them began to open his mouth like a fish out of water. His body rocked back and forth, until the chair toppled on the floor and he lay sprawled on the ground.

The doctor rushed over, and was joined by a nurse from the end of the ward.

Lady Lappiter and Toby Russell decided that now was the perfect time to leave the hospital.

Neither of them took a last look at their son and brother lying prostrate on the floor, banging his head on the black and white tiles.

Chapter Eighty-Three

Queen Mary's Hospital, Sidcup, Kent.
August 12, 1919.

The noises inside his head stopped for a moment. If he concentrated on the work with his hands, they went away. Must concentrate on weaving the willow.

In.

Out.

In.

Out.

Building up the walls of the basket, shoring up the ruins, making them stronger.

Somebody spoke to him. He heard his name, but far away, distant.

Nobody spoke to him any more. Unless it was that doctor, asking him how he felt today. Or the nurse with the soft hands and softer smile who bandaged his head. She looked like Rose when she did it, the way her tongue kissed her teeth as she wove the white bandages around and around.

It made him cry, thinking of Rose, tears filmed his one good eye. The nurse always got it wrong. 'I'm sorry it's so painful, Captain Russell, I'll be finished in a tick.'

He tried to speak, to tell the nurse not to worry. But the words wouldn't come out. He tried and tried and tried, but it was like there was something missing between his mouth and his throat; a key to unlock the words buried deep.

There was no pain. He felt nothing any more. Except the terrible loss of Rose. Why had she never visited him? What had happened to his child?

The doctor called his name again and he felt a touch on his shoulder.

Who were these people standing in front of him? They looked familiar, as if he had seen them before in a movie or at the theatre. He concentrated on their clothes, nice clothes, modern clothes.

The doctor left and the woman sat down in front of him. She called him by a name, 'David.' Was that his name? It seemed familiar. Was he David? He shook his head. Why couldn't he remember?

The man began to smoke. He remembered the smell, Turkish tobacco. Lieutenant Crawford had smoked cigarettes like these.

Who was Lieutenant Crawford?

An image flashed across his mind. Running across a field. Barbed wire. A sergeant falling backwards. The noise of shells and bullets and screaming.

Was this what had happened to him?

The man and woman were speaking together now. He concentrated on his weaving.

In.

Out.

In.

Out.

He picked up a new length of willow from the table.

Stop.

Concentrate on them.

What are they saying?

'You are Lord Lappiter now, Toby. This thing in front of us is no more my son that a jugged hare. Just look at him.'

Were they talking about him? He wanted to join in, to say something, but the words hid in his throat, so he could never find them.

The man was speaking in between swallowing mouthfuls of smoke. 'But what can we do, Mother? He's been identified as David Russell.'

The woman snorted. 'Leave it to me, Toby. You're just like your father, he avoided dealing with life's difficulties too. Why break the habit of a lifetime?'

'But Mother...'

The woman banged the table. David jumped back holding his basket in front of him.

'See, you've scared him, Toby,' the woman said but she wasn't smiling or warm or comforting. 'Best to leave him here, where the doctors and nurses can rebuild his face and care for him.'

'But what happens if he ever remembers?'

'It's our word against his. And you should remember he has been declared dead by the War Ministry. They won't like one of their soldiers coming back to life, especially not a Lord.'

'I suppose you're right, Mother.'

'I am, Toby. I always am.'

They were standing up now, the doctor had returned. The woman was putting on a pair of black leather gloves.

Soft gloves, soft leather.

He remembered those gloves. He bought them for his mother from Rose's shop. He gave them to his mother for Christmas.

He tried to speak, to say something to this woman, his mother, but the words wouldn't come.

And she was pointing at him, saying something with a stern, unhappy face.

'And this man is not my son. He died on the Somme in 1916, a war hero.'

David Russell knew then that he was dead.

He started to scream but no noise came from his throat. His body rocked from side to side on the chair, until he fell over and sprawled on the floor. He banged his head on the tiles, trying to get rid of the noise and the pain and the nightmares, trying to bring Rose back into his mind.

His Rose.

Beautiful Rose.

His wife.

The man and woman were gone when he woke up the next morning tied to his bed.

Where was Rose?

Chapter Eighty-Four

Buxton, near Manchester. May 18, 2016.

Jayne had just pushed through the fire doors and was walking to her father's usual place in the corner, facing the picture window with its view of the oak tree and the garden, when she felt a light tap on her shoulder.

A man leaned in and kissed her on the cheek. 'Good morning, lass, good to see you here.'

'Dad, I'm so…'

'Surprised? Shocked?'

'I was going to say, I'm so pleased to see you.'

Jayne's father was standing in front of her, wearing a dapper waistcoat, freshly ironed shirt and trousers, and brightly polished shoes. His hair had been cut short with a sharp parting on the left. Even more, the moustache had been removed and the rest of his face was clean shaven.

He stroked his chin. 'Smooth as a baby's bum, but it does feel strange without the tash. I got used to tasting my soup twice.'

'You look great, Dad. I suppose this is Vera's influence? Where is she anyway?'

'Out for the day with her daughter.'

'So those two have buried the hatchet?'

'Aye, and not in each other's head. Now, lass, come and sit down, I've got some news for you.'

He led her by the hand to his usual corner.

'Is it good news or bad news, Dad?'

'Oh, definitely good.'

He sat her down in his usual sofa and pulled up a chair

facing her. 'Now, lass, might as well tell you straight. Me and Vera, well, we're going to be married.'

Instinctively, Jayne's hand covered her face. Her dad married again after all this time?

'First time I've ever seen you stumped for words, Jayne.'

Then, she leant forward and hugged his thin body. 'I'm so happy for you, Dad. When did you decide?'

'I asked her this morning, after the boiled eggs but before the second serving of tea. Didn't get down on one knee though, wasn't certain I could get up again.'

'Oh Dad, that's wonderful news.' She reached forward and hugged him again. 'I've talked with Matron and we can stay here still. They've got rooms for married couples.'

Jayne stopped smiling for a moment. 'You are sure, Dad?'

'As sure as I'll ever be. Vera is a lovely lass, any man would be proud to call her his wife. And she can do the crossword better than me, too.'

'When's the day?'

'Three weeks on Wednesday. I wanted to have it quicker, but Vera wants to do it properly. New dresses and all that.'

'Where's it going to be held?'

Her father spread his arms wide. 'Why here, lass, where else? I've spoken to Matron and she's all for it. Said it will be good to have a proper knees-up.' His face went serious again. 'I want you to be my best woman, Jayne, to give me away on the day.'

'I'd love to, Dad. I'll get a new frock too.'

'Aye, it'll be good to see you in a dress for once. You've got lovely knees, I remember. And what about you? What have you been doing?'

She let go of his hands. 'Not much recently. Mark has

decided he wants to research for himself if his great grand-father survived the Somme.'

'You're not upset?'

'Not at all. I pointed him in the right direction; the POW records held by the ICRC, and the Gillies Archive for Medical Records at the Royal College of Surgeons. He has to find out for himself, Dad, it's his journey, not mine any more.'

'And Paul? Are you two getting divorced?'

Jayne nodded.

'It's for the best, lass. Might not seem so right now, but it is. You two need to get on with life separate from each other.'

Jayne nodded again. 'I know, Dad, just it's never easy going through the process.'

It was her father's turn to take her hands in his. 'Vera and I will always be here for you, lass. Vera loves you as a daughter.'

Jayne wiped a tear from her eye, quickly sitting up straight. 'I have one piece of good news. It's from some-body in the American embassy, an email came this morn-ing. They want me to go down to London for a meeting.'

'What's it about, lass?'

Jayne shrugged her shoulders. 'They wouldn't say. But I guess it's some sort of genealogical investigation they want me to undertake.'

'You're going?'

'A thousand revving BMWs couldn't stop me.'

'Well done. But wait until after the wedding, please. I need help choosing a new suit.'

Jayne leaned forward and gave her father a long, long hug.

She knew it was time to forget about the past and move

on with her life.

Except she wouldn't. The past was always there.

Somewhere.

Hidden deep, but still there, waiting to be discovered.

She reached forward and gave her father another squeeze.

'Hey, lass, are you going soft on me after all these years?'

'No, Dad. But it's time to get a few hugs in before Vera bans them completely.'

'No, Jayne, she'll never do that. You'll just have to hug both of us, instead of one scrawny old man.'

And Jayne hugged her scrawny old man even tighter, not wanting to let go.

If you have enjoyed this book by M J Lee, please leave a review on Amazon. It's always great to hear feedback.

If you would like to hear more about M J Lee and his books, go to his website at www.writermjlee.com, his Facebook page at writermjlee or his twitter feed at, you guessed it, writermjlee.

Made in the USA
Lexington, KY
08 June 2019